"Why don't you ask him if you can go see Jasper now?"

When they all stepped inside the barn and approached the horse's stall, Gavin's son's eyes went wide.

"Whoa," he said in amazement, drawing chuckles from both Maya and Gavin.

"Would you like to pet him?" Gavin asked.

Max nodded, but he hesitated when Gavin lowered himself and offered his arms to give Max a lift. A glance at Jasper, however, had the desire to pet a horse winning out over any lingering fear of this man he didn't remember.

When Gavin took Max into his arms and lifted him, Maya had to bite her lower lip and look away for a moment so she wouldn't cry. The look on Gavin's face, a mixture of heartbreak dispelled and the purest happiness she'd ever witnessed, was powerful.

And though it was the wrong time to have such a thought, Gavin suddenly seemed a hundred times more attractive even though she would have sworn only a minute ago that wasn't possible.

Dear Reader,

Welcome back to Jade Valley, Wyoming, where the crisp, sunny days of fall that we saw at the end of *The Rancher's Unexpected Twins* have given way to the cold, snowy depths of winter. But in the midst of the cold is the warmth of a mountain cabin, cups of hot cocoa and a totally unexpected blossoming romance between chipper newspaper editor Maya Pine and reclusive rancher Gavin Olsen.

While I personally don't like wintry weather (I moved to Florida to escape it), it's undeniable that it can be beautiful and romantic. That's what Maya and Gavin find out, despite obstacles that stand tall between the moment they meet and the moment they realize they've fallen in love with each other. I hope you enjoy the sometimes bumpy, snowy road they travel to happily-ever-after.

I love to hear from readers. You can contact me through my website at trishmilburn.com.

Trish Milburn

HEARTWARMING

Reclaiming the Rancher's Son

—

Trish Milburn

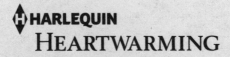

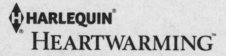

HARLEQUIN®
HEARTWARMING™

ISBN-13: 978-1-335-42670-3

Reclaiming the Rancher's Son

Copyright © 2022 by Trish Milburn

Recycling programs for this product may not exist in your area.

For questions and comments about the quality of this book, please contact us at CustomerService@Harlequin.com.

Harlequin Enterprises ULC
22 Adelaide St. West, 41st Floor
Toronto, Ontario M5H 4E3, Canada
www.Harlequin.com

Printed in U.S.A.

Trish Milburn is the author of more than fifty novels and novellas, romances set everywhere from quaint small towns in the American West to the bustling city of Seoul, South Korea. When she's not writing or brainstorming new stories, she enjoys reading, listening to K-pop, watching K-dramas, spending probably way too much time on Twitter and, since she lives in Florida, yes, walks on the beach.

Books by Trish Milburn

Harlequin Heartwarming

Jade Valley, Wyoming

The Rancher's Unexpected Twins

Harlequin Western Romance

Blue Falls, Texas

Her Perfect Cowboy
Having the Cowboy's Baby
Marrying the Cowboy
The Doctor's Cowboy
Her Cowboy Groom
The Heart of a Cowboy
Home on the Ranch
A Rancher to Love
The Cowboy Takes a Wife
In the Rancher's Arms

Visit the Author Profile page
at Harlequin.com for more titles.

To all my fellow journalists out there still fighting the good fight of fact-based truth telling, no matter the obstacles. You are doing important work. Thank you.

CHAPTER ONE

MAYA PINE ALREADY had a newspaper dead-line, a demanding boss and an approaching snowstorm on her plate, so the last thing she needed to add was a matchmaking mama. But she was getting it anyway.

As she listened to her mom encourage her to go out with Rory Tillman, Maya grabbed her camera, purse and car keys. She should be on her way to conduct an interview before the predicted snowstorm moved into Jade Valley, but here she stood in the tiny office of the *Valley Post*, cell phone to ear, listening to the hopeful tone in her mom's voice.

"Nope, not happening," Maya said as soon as her mother took a breath.

"Why not?"

"One, I don't have time to date. And, two, do you not remember that Rory was the mastermind behind my car ending up parked in the middle of Mr. Eagle's front lawn? And with the radio blaring 'Loser' by 3 Doors

Down as the cherry on top." Maya had thought the little dirt-brown compact with one yellow door had been stolen, but Rory and his buddies had temporarily relocated it to the principal's yard, much to Maya's and Mr. Eagle's mutual displeasure.

"Really?"

"Yes, Mom, really. So you can stop searching high and low for a man for me as if my expiration date is nigh." Maya was pretty sure her mom had been looking under rocks on the Wind River Reservation for a potential son-in-law.

"I hate to see you alone."

"If it doesn't bother me, it shouldn't bother you. But if this is about your sisters outpacing you with grandchildren, you're just going to have to enjoy being a great-auntie."

"Well, I feel called out."

Maya laughed. "I know how you think, woman."

"They're just so annoying with their grand-baby stories."

"You love those kids every bit as much as they do. I've seen you slipping them sweet treats when their moms weren't looking."

This time it was her mom who sighed, causing Maya to laugh again.

"Listen, if a hot man crosses my path, I'm not going to look the other way. But I'd say the likelihood of that is on the slim side. I mean, Sunny snatched up one of the few decent-looking eligible bachelors in the valley."

Not that Maya had been interested in Dean Wheeler. They'd known each other too long. And despite him being attractive, Maya had never been attracted to him. Which was good since her best friend and he were currently sappy newlyweds.

Most of the rest of the unattached men in the area fell into one of three categories: too young, too old or not in a million years.

A gust of wind rattled the front door, reminding Maya that she'd best get on the road.

"Mom, I've got to go. The paper doesn't write itself."

Before her mom asked any further questions that might lead to Maya fibbing about what was next on her schedule, she hung up the phone. Her mom didn't need to know that Maya was heading up the mountain when a snowstorm was supposed to move into the area in a few hours. She locked the door behind her since Janie Oberlin, the only other employee of the *Post*, was at the high school interviewing the basketball coach about the boys' season so far and the plans for the upcoming tournament.

As Maya headed to her car, the cold, humid air already smelled like snow. She was going to have to conduct this interview with as much speed as possible to maximize her time with elusive mystery author Benjamin St. Michaels while allowing enough to get back to town before the mountain road became dangerous.

But she couldn't miss this opportunity. St. Michaels hadn't given an interview in years, and for her to score one with him was a big deal. His legions of fans would likely give the paper at least a one-week bump in sales. Every little bit helped when the Clarkes, the family who owned newspapers and radio stations all over Wyoming and Montana, were constantly on her case to increase the paper's revenue. That was difficult when the population of Jade Valley was five hundred and some of those were too young to read.

She'd even gotten the wild idea to possibly ask St. Michaels if he might become a regular contributor to the paper, maybe write some short fiction. It all depended on how this interview went.

As she rolled through the small downtown area, which was free of any traffic lights, she waved to half a dozen familiar faces. One of those belonged to Sherriff Angie Lee, so Maya made sure not to go over the speed limit until she was a mile outside of town. Even though she and Angie were friends and had gone to school together, Maya knew Angie wouldn't give her a free pass to break the law. Angie had a fairness streak a mile wide, so that was how she policed and what she also expected from the deputies who worked for her.

By the time Maya was ascending the mountain road and halfway to her destination, the sun had disappeared behind the gunmetal-gray clouds. Why couldn't this interview have taken place yesterday when the sky had been a beautiful blue and the temperature several degrees warmer?

Oh well, it wouldn't be the first time she'd done her job in unpleasant conditions. Also wouldn't be the last.

When she reached the turn onto the gravel road that led back to St. Michaels's vacation cabin, she mentally went through her list of questions for him again. She'd read all of his books about a Wyoming-based FBI agent, so she hadn't had any trouble coming up with questions many of his fans might have. Such as, was the protagonist's brother a good or bad guy? With each book, Maya's opinion on that changed.

She had to laugh when she saw the "cabin" because the house she rented could probably fit inside it twice. Some of those sweet, sweet bestseller dollars had obviously gone into the vacation home. She would bet it had expansive windows on the eastern side, affording stunning views of the valley and the stretch of mountains that lay on the other side.

Maya didn't see a vehicle, but it was probably tucked away in the garage. She glanced up at the tops of the surrounding lodgepole pines, noting the way they were swaying in the breeze. Nothing to be concerned about yet, but she didn't have time to dawdle either.

She grabbed what she needed and stepped out of the car. It was noticeably colder thanks to the gain in elevation. This spot would be beautiful with a white powdery coating of snow, but she didn't plan to be here when it started falling. Pulling her coat's collar up around her neck, she hurried toward the front door. Before knocking, she noted how the small pane of glass at the top of the wooden door was etched with a feather quill. How appropriate for the home of a writer. She wondered if some of the Hank Gulliver series had been written mere feet from where she stood.

She lifted her hand and knocked, then waited for St. Michaels to appear. But not only did he not open the door, she also didn't hear any approaching footsteps. Wondering if he was in a part of the house that made it difficult for him to hear her, she knocked louder the second time. Still no answer. Was it possible the man was asleep or listening to music through headphones? Occupied in the bathroom? Was he the absentminded sort who'd already forgotten their appointment?

After glancing to the side and seeing there wasn't a doorbell, she knocked even louder. Still facing a closed door, she retrieved her phone from her purse and called the number St. Michaels had given her. When the call also went unanswered, her frustration grew.

Okay, she'd tried the professional, front-door approach. Time to do some exploring. She left the porch and rounded the house to find an expansive deck and, yes, a wall of floor-to-ceiling windows that afforded an incredible view of the valley, the river winding through it, and the snowcapped mountain range in the distance.

Maya climbed the steps to the deck and repeated her knocking at a side door just around the corner from the picture windows. By this point she wasn't surprised when she received no response, especially because it looked as if the visible interior was unoccupied and perhaps had been for a while.

She paced the deck as she called again and left a message, hoping that perhaps the man was on his way. While she waited, she pulled out her camera and took some photos of the incredible view. It didn't matter that she called the valley below home and had probably covered every inch of it since starting first as a reporter for the *Valley Post* and then becoming the editor two months later when the previous one decided to retire early. Despite her familiarity with Jade Valley, it still managed to take her breath away when she looked at it from this type of vantage point.

After she'd taken several photos, she lowered the camera in time to see a few snowflakes fly past on a sudden gust of wind. She lifted her gaze to the sky, which had grown darker.

No, no, no. Why was this storm moving

in faster than had been forecast? Even if St. Michaels had opened the door after her first knock, they would barely be getting started with the interview. Resisting the idea that this opportunity was a bust, she knocked one more time, placed another unanswered call and paced the deck for a couple of minutes.

But she wasn't a fool. You didn't live in Wyoming your entire life and not respect the weather's mercurial nature. If you didn't respect it, you could end up dead. So she hurried down the steps and back around the house to her little blue hatchback, which already had a few flakes sticking to the windshield. This storm was impatient.

By the time she'd traveled the short distance to the end of the gravel drive, the pace of the snowfall had picked up. Yeah, not good. She wanted to race down the mountain, but that also wasn't smart considering the temperature at this elevation already had some white flakes sticking to the road. And while her car did fine in the valley, snowy, mountainous roads were another story entirely.

Biting her lip, she tried to balance her driving between the urgency to get to a lower elevation, and thus hopefully out of the snow, and her desire to not slide off the road. After about five minutes, she eased around a curve, thankful her car seemed to be handling the conditions well so far.

"Way to go, Blueberry."

She'd give the dash an affectionate pat if she didn't need to keep both hands on the steering wheel. But the tension in her shoulders actually eased a bit, and she exhaled a deep breath.

In the next moment a flash of brown jumped in front of her car, and she instinctually hit the brakes. She knew immediately it was a mistake when she started to slide, but it was too late to correct it. She gasped when the front wheels left the roadway, pointing her downhill into a thick stand of trees.

THE FIRST THOUGHT to surface after Maya woke was that her head throbbed. She slowly blinked to focus her eyes, which led to her second realization—that she'd been knocked out long enough for the world around her to be coated in white. Considering the pace at which the snowflakes had been increasing when she'd swerved to avoid what she now realized had been a deer, she might have only been unconscious for a few minutes.

Moving slowly, she reached for her purse

in the passenger seat, only to realize it was on the floor with the contents spilled everywhere. She pressed her hand to her forehead and unbuckled her seat belt. Again moving slowly, she leaned over and scooped up all her belongings. She needed to call for help and hope that the road conditions were such that someone could reach her.

But when she grabbed her phone, it wouldn't turn on. Either the battery had died or the phone had been damaged internally in the crash.

This was not good. Really, really not good.

Though her head continued to throb, she knew she couldn't stay where she was. To do so would almost certainly mean she'd freeze to death. She might be used to Wyoming winters, but that was not the way she wanted to go.

Even though she felt addled and must have hit her head on the window, she was careful to make sure she was fully covered in her coat, gloves and the hat her mom had knitted for her last Christmas. Then she crawled over to the passenger door since the driver's side was wedged against a tree. But she was thankful for that tree or she might have tumbled even farther down the mountain and not woken up at all.

By the time she was standing outside in the snow, she was already ridiculously tired.

"Come on, Pine. You're not going to end up a skeleton in the woods."

She shivered, though whether it was because of that mental image or the cold she wasn't sure. Her feet slipped some on the fresh snow, but she managed not to fall as she climbed up the incline toward the roadway. She was fairly certain she'd aged a year by the time she stepped onto the pavement, which was now totally white. Trying not to panic that it was unlikely a vehicle would come along, she set off down the road. She had to keep moving if she hoped to survive the day. Even if no cars passed, she'd eventually come to someone's house. Now, if she could just remember where the nearest house was to where she'd gone off the road.

As she hurried down the side of the road, she did her best to focus on anything other than how much her head hurt or how cold air seemed to be seeping straight through her coat. She thought about how Benjamin St. Michaels had stood her up, and how that had led to her being at exactly the wrong spot when that deer had decided he absolutely must be on the other side of the road despite the oncoming car.

Of course, with the weather turning bad quicker than expected, she probably would have left before being able to complete the interview. That or not have been able to leave. She laughed. Being trapped at the home of someone you didn't know didn't sound like the most awesome time ever. More like awkward at best.

When she thought she heard a vehicle, she turned quickly to look behind her. But not only was there no approaching help, she also managed to send a fresh wave of throbbing pain through her head.

She picked up her pace, hoping her blood would pump hard enough that her feet would warm up. If she thought she wouldn't fall or it wouldn't cause further pain in her head, she'd start running. Better to keep a decent walking pace than risk further injury.

She had no idea how much time had passed when she realized she was shivering and that taking a nap on the side of the road had started to sound appealing. She fought that thought, somehow grasping that if she didn't find shelter soon she was going to be in danger of becoming hypothermic. At that realization, panic started to set in. She had to find shelter before she lost her ability to reason.

Smoke winding its way up through the treetops caught her attention. Whether she was imagining it or not, she didn't know, but she had to hope it was real as she stepped off the road and started in that direction.

Despite it hurting worse and making her sick to her stomach, she shook her head to clear it as she wove her way through the trees. She was not going to give in to Mother Nature this close to potential salvation.

Please help me make it.

Right as she was beginning to doubt what she'd seen, Maya broke free of the trees and spotted a modest log home. The thought that she recognized the house managed to surface through the thick fog in her head. The old… Black…thorn place. Even her thoughts were shivering. She shook her head again, but it felt as if she were moving in water this time— sluggish, with the surrounding sound muted.

Her steps were slower too, her feet…what was the word? Started with an *H*. She blinked but almost couldn't lift her eyelids. The house was right…th-th-there. The next time she blinked, her lids refused to open and her legs seemed to freeze in place like mechanical gears seizing up in the cold.

In the next moment she was falling, but she didn't feel the impact with the ground.

AFTER SEEING TO his horse's needs, Gavin Olsen headed out of the barn. He'd check on his small herd of cattle again after the snowstorm passed, but for now he wanted a warm meal and hot coffee while surrounded by four thick, solid walls. Even though he was used to wintry weather, he also appreciated being able to retreat inside when his work was done.

As long as he didn't lose power, he planned to kick back and watch some TV after a long day that had started before dawn. When you worked outside, you structured your days based on the weather forecast as best you could.

A gust of wind had him tightening his grip on the barn door as he pushed it closed and secured it. Thankfully, he'd managed to complete the most important repairs to the structure before winter set in, so he was confident that Jasper would stay comfortable inside. Now it was his turn to move to warmer quarters.

He turned toward the house, but movement

out of the corner of his eye drew his attention. Had he been living out here alone with his thoughts and sorrow so long that he was now seeing things? Because it sure looked as if a woman was walking toward the house from the direction of the tree line. Actually, *walking* might not be the best description of what she was doing, because she was obviously struggling even though the snow wasn't deep yet.

Who was she? What was she doing here? Was she a hiker who'd somehow gotten lost and bewildered in the storm? How long had she been out in the cold? His pulse jumped when she stumbled. She appeared to try to right herself, but in the next moment she crumpled to the ground.

Gavin stood for a moment, battling the instinctual frustration that someone had invaded his private space, even if accidentally. But he wasn't so bitter that he would let her freeze to death. So he ran toward her, knowing he had to get this unknown woman out of the cold. There was no telling how long she'd been wandering around in this weather, and despite her winter attire she might be close to hypothermic.

Don't let her die on my front lawn.

He dropped to his knees next to her.

"Hey, can you hear me?"

No response, but thankfully she was still breathing. Not wasting any time because the storm was only getting worse, he placed his arms behind her back and knees and lifted her off the cold ground. He winced a bit when his boot slid on the snow, but he kept on his feet and quickly moved toward the house.

Once he managed to open the door and get her inside, he set her on the couch before hurriedly closing the front door. Facing her again, he sighed and knelt in front of her.

"Hey, can you wake up?" He knew he sounded curt, but that was how he felt most days. When she again offered no response, he shook her arm a bit. Even if he didn't want her here, he still possessed some basic human decency. "You need to get out of this coat and your shoes. They're wet."

She grunted a bit as if in response to pain. Had she injured her arm?

With another sigh, he realized he was going to have to help her out of her wet winter outerwear. He hoped she didn't wake up in the middle and totally freak out that she was being undressed by a man she didn't know.

As he got her out of her coat, gloves, shoes

and socks, he noticed her wince. When he removed her knitted hat, he spotted a trickle of dried blood. It wasn't fresh enough to be a result of her tumble in his yard, so she'd already been injured somehow.

He hurried to get a wet cloth and washed away the blood, glad to see the injury was only a small cut. Still, it was concerning that she was still unconscious. What was worse than some strange woman freezing to death in his yard? Her dying on his couch.

Hoping once again that she didn't misunderstand if she woke up, he set about checking her limbs for serious damage that would require him trying to get her to the little local hospital despite the fact that it might be more dangerous trying to get down the mountain now than staying put. And with the rate at which the snow was falling, he doubted an ambulance could make it up here. He was just going to have to make do, no matter how much he disliked the situation.

Thankfully, nothing seemed to be broken, but he noticed a knot that was bruising at the edge of her hair on the left side of her forehead close to the cut.

After stretching her out on the couch and propping her head with a pillow, he covered her with two quilts. That accomplished, he crossed to the freezer and put together an ice pack. When he eased it against the bump on her head, she winced more visibly before settling. He really hoped she didn't have a concussion, because if she did wasn't he supposed to wake her up?

He'd just keep an eye on her because going out in the storm could end up doing more harm than good to his unexpected guest. Deciding hot food when she woke up would increase her chances of surviving, he strode back across the room to the kitchen area. It was probably a good idea to put distance between them anyway. He wanted it to be abundantly clear when she woke up that he wasn't a physical threat to her, even if he wasn't likely to be the friendliest of hosts.

If she had some sort of identification with her, he'd try to contact a relative. But he hadn't seen any purse or backpack, and there'd been nothing in the pockets of her coat.

He opened some cans of hearty chicken noodle soup because that seemed to be the accepted cure-all and dumped them into a pot on the stove. A great cook, he was not, but he got by. He doubted his guest would be too picky if what she was offered helped to warm her up.

He glanced over his shoulder, saw that the woman hadn't moved at all, then redirected his attention out the window above the kitchen sink. The snow was coming down so fast now that he could barely identify the trees. Seeing into the valley where his cattle were was impossible.

Why did this woman have to stumble onto his property of all places?

The quiet that filled his house now was exactly the opposite of what he wanted. Since moving back to Wyoming a broken man and buying a ranch in need of a substantial amount of work, he'd done his best to keep his hands and mind occupied with his to-do list. But his plan to turn on the TV to whatever would keep his thoughts off why he'd left Denver was put on hold. And thus his memories waltzed in and assaulted him. An unexpected—and admittedly unfair—wave of anger at the woman on his couch hit him. Her presence made the difficult task of forgetting even harder, though she'd had nothing to do with his loss.

He turned and stared at her prone form. He needed her to wake up and the storm to clear so he could get her out of his space. At least chances were she'd be totally on board with that. Then he could go back to the only marginally successful job of staying so busy that he didn't have time to curl in on himself and give up entirely.

CHAPTER TWO

WHO HAD HIT her in the head with a baseball bat? that was Maya's first question as she
began to emerge into consciousness. Even before she opened her eyes, she lifted her hand
and pressed it against her forehead, hoping to
alleviate the pain. But this wasn't a sinus or
tension headache where activating pressure
points would work. The reason for the pain
slowly came back to her. And—good news—
if she had the queen of all headaches, she was
pretty sure she wasn't dead.

As she opened her eyes to unfamiliar surroundings, she tried to remember where she'd
been right before she'd evidently blacked out.
She'd been meeting with someone for a story.
No, that hadn't worked out, and that had led
to her accident. She remembered crawling out
of the car, walking through the snow, and…
Oh, she'd turned toward the sight of smoke
curling up from a chimney.

The mental images of weaving through

trees and deepening snow were fuzzier. Even more so was the one of a cabin, almost as if she'd seen it through fog or water. She scanned the wooden ceiling above her, then realized she was lying on a blue couch, and finally that shc was blessedly warm even if her head did feel as if it might explode at any moment.

"I take it you have a headache."

Maya startled so violently that pain pierced her skull like a flaming arrow, making the headache of moments before seem like bumping a feather in comparison.

"Don't move too fast. It'll make it worse." The unknown man was saying the right words, but if he was a doctor his bedside manner needed some work.

"Duh," she replied without thinking while she tried to not throw up.

"Would you like some Tylenol?" Did he really sound begrudging, or was she just in a foul mood because she felt terrible?

Doing her best to not sound so rude to the man who'd evidently saved her from freezing to death in the snow, no matter how annoyed he sounded, she said, "Please."

In truth, she felt as if an entire bottle of acetaminophen didn't stand a chance against the throbbing in her head. Even blinking seemed to add to the ache. Thus, Maya didn't look up when the man returned from another room with a big bottle of "please, give me some relief" and a glass of water. She did notice he stayed on the opposite side of the sturdy coffee table, perhaps sensing that it was a good idea to have some sort of barrier between himself and the woman who'd found herself lying on a stranger's couch. Maybe that was why he didn't sound overly friendly. He didn't want her to get any wrong ideas.

"Thank you." She moved carefully as she sat up, swallowed two pills and drank almost the entire glass of water. "Sorry for being rude before."

He grunted acknowledgment from several feet away, making Maya realize that he'd created even more distance between them. "You've apparently had a not-so-great day." The way he sounded, the same was true for him.

Hey, buddy, I'm not thrilled to be here either.

"That is, quite literally, the biggest understatement I've heard in my entire adult life." She winced at a fresh throb of pain, and she reached up to gingerly touch what she knew had to be a substantial goose egg on the left side of her head. "I ran off the road thanks to a deer that was really impatient to see the scenery on the other side."

"That explains the cut and knot on your head and why you were wandering around in a snowstorm."

Whoever her savior was, he had a nice, deep voice with a rich tone that would be great at lulling you to sleep with a bedtime story. At least when he didn't sound irritated. Wondering what kind of face went with the voice, she eased her gaze up until she spotted him standing, arms crossed, where the living area flowed into the kitchen on the other side of the main room.

She blinked a few times to focus and was rewarded with a view of the handsomest man she'd seen in Jade Valley in...maybe ever. Nice build, a healthy tan, sandy brown hair, probably a bit over six feet tall.

"It's possible you have a concussion," he said, making her wonder if his words had been prompted by her staring at him too long.

Maya lowered her gaze to the coffee table and downed the rest of the water before replying.

"Maybe, but I woke up, so that's a good

sign. Thanks for not letting me turn into human tundra in your front yard."

"Trust me, I didn't want that either." He sounded very much like he thought an ice brick of a body in front of his house would be incredibly annoying.

He seemed to be a matter-of-fact man of few words. Of course, he probably hadn't expected to have to carry a half-frozen woman into his house either. Her face heated at the thought of him carrying her, and she unconsciously pulled a quilt up and around her shoulders.

"Cold?"

"No, I'm fine." What a dumb answer. If she wasn't cold, why would she be wrapping herself up? The knock on the head had evidently relieved her of any common sense she'd once possessed.

"I warmed up some chicken noodle soup."

"That sounds really good." She'd skipped lunch to make the interview that hadn't happened, and the granola bar she'd had for breakfast was long gone. Hopefully having something in her stomach would prevent the queasy feeling every time she moved her head too quickly. "What time is it, anyway?"

"Just after six."

She slowly turned and looked outside to see it had grown dark.

"I would have called your family, but you didn't have any ID with you."

"I—" She looked around for her purse but didn't see it. "I must have lost my bag along the way."

"You were pretty out of it, close to hypothermia, so that's not surprising." His tone made it sound like she'd willingly done something idiotic.

She bit down on a snappy comeback, reminding herself that maintaining a friendly attitude had served her better in the past than snark or rudeness.

"Maya," she said. "Maya Pine, that's my name."

"Okay. Do you want to call your family?"

"If I could make a couple of calls, I would appreciate it."

The man, who hadn't offered up his name, grabbed a cell phone from the kitchen counter and crossed the room to offer it to her. She was careful not to make contact with his hand as she took it. He might have saved her and was providing her with the things she needed, but she still didn't know him. And it was obvious he wasn't thrilled to have her as a houseguest.

"Where can I tell them I am?"

Instead of revealing his name, he offered up the address.

"But I don't think anyone is making it up the mountain tonight. The snow hasn't stopped yet." He did not sound happy about this state of affairs.

So she was going to have to spend the night under the same roof as a man who had yet to identify himself. She was fairly certain she wasn't going to sleep a wink.

As her host went back to the kitchen and started scooping soup into a bowl, she called Trina Gray, her next-door neighbor, to have her check on and feed Blossom, her cat. After they hung up, she took a deep breath and called her mother.

"Hey, Mom. Just wanted to let you know that my phone went kaput in case you tried to call or text me, and I obviously won't be able to get a new one until this storm is over."

"Whose phone are you using? I don't recognize this number."

"Someone I met at work. Listen, just wanted to let you know. I gotta go."

"You're not getting out in this storm, are you?"

"Don't worry. My car isn't moving an inch." Her mom didn't need to know about the current location and condition of Maya's car, however.

When she ended the call and placed the phone on the coffee table, Maya felt as if she'd expended way more energy than she had. In the next moment, a steaming bowl of soup and a refilled glass of water were placed in front of her.

"Thank you." She attacked the soup as if she hadn't eaten in days instead of hours. Despite that she could tell immediately it was canned soup, in her current situation it was in the running for the best-tasting food that had ever passed her lips. The soup warmed her from the inside while the fire in the wood-burning stove and the quilts did the same on the outside. The hot food finally pushed away the last of the chill that had invaded her body during her wintry search for safety.

"I'm sorry I'm imposing on you like this," she said once she was about halfway through with the bowl of soup.

The man nodded once and uttered a simple, "Um."

So he didn't like having his space invaded, but he wasn't cruel enough to leave her to the elements. She was just glad she hadn't wound up in the home of someone creepy and dangerous.

"Do you mind if I ask your name?"

He hesitated in answering for several seconds, long enough that she wondered if he actually would answer.

"Gavin Olsen."

"It's nice to meet you, even if the circumstances are not ideal."

Again with the simple nod as a response. She was getting the distinct impression that this guy lived here alone and liked it that way.

"Would you like some more soup?" he asked.

"No, thanks. I'm not finished with this bowl yet." She noticed how he was standing next to the stove but not serving himself any of the soup he'd prepared. "You should have some too. I'm sure saving people from their own stupidity works up an appetite."

Maya saw not even a hint of a smile. She half expected him to decline for some reason, but in the next moment he served up a bowl of soup and seated himself at one end of the wooden kitchen table. Still keeping his distance.

She took her time finishing her soup, then slowly started to push to her feet, careful not to jostle her head too much.

"You can leave the bowl on the coffee table," he said.

"Actually, I need to use your bathroom."

"Oh," he said, looking more embarrassed than annoyed this time. "Door at the end."

He directed her down a short hallway. As she went down it, she noticed a door on either side. She caught a quick glimpse of a bed in one, and the other appeared to be used for storage. Before she returned to the main room, she took a few moments to straighten her hair and wash her face. The bump at the hairline of her forehead made it look as if she was on the verge of growing a horn.

As she was about to emerge from the hallway into the brightly lit kitchen, a wave of dizziness hit her and she reached out a hand and pressed it against the wall to steady herself.

Gavin was suddenly in front of her, seemingly ready to catch her if she passed out again.

She managed a smile as the spinning in her head receded. "I'm okay. Just a little woozy."

"You should sit."

"I think you're right." But instead of heading for the couch again, she pointed herself toward the kitchen table and claimed the chair opposite where Gavin had been sitting. When she glanced up, he appeared to be surprised by her choice.

"Don't you think you should lie down?" She couldn't tell if there was any true concern in his question or if he simply wanted to keep the original distance between them.

"I need to move around so I don't get any stiffer than I already am. For some reason, the human body doesn't like crashing into trees. Who knew?"

He didn't laugh at her attempt at humor.

Instead of sitting again, Gavin moved to the refrigerator and refilled the bag-type ice pack she realized he'd been holding. Even when he placed it near her on the table, she noticed that he fully extended his arm so he didn't come any closer than necessary. Was he shy? Was that why he lived alone and wasn't happy about suddenly having to share his space? Or was he only trying to make sure she knew he wasn't a threat?

She pointed toward his half-full bowl as she placed the fresh ice pack gently against her head.

"You should finish your soup before it gets cold."

After a moment of standing behind his chair, he pulled it out and sat. Instead of saying anything, he focused all of his attention on his soup. Maya barely suppressed a smile by pressing her lips together.

"I was glad to hear someone finally bought this place," she said, hoping to generate some more conversation to fill the silence and keep awkwardness at bay. "How do you like it so far?"

Gavin looked up from his soup and stared at her as if he couldn't identify her species.

"What?" she asked at the confusion on his face.

"You're awfully at ease considering you woke up in a stranger's house."

She tried to ignore the curt tone of his observation, like he thought she might actually be stupid.

"But you're not exactly a stranger anymore. I know your name, that you saved this place from falling into complete disrepair, and you rescue frozen wanderers." She pointed at his bowl. "And you warm up a mean can of soup."

He glanced down at the bowl before meeting her gaze again. "I wasn't expecting company."

Honestly, she doubted he ever had any. She tried to understand what it must be like for him, if he was used to being alone, to suddenly have a talkative guest.

"I sincerely don't mind. I think it counts as the most welcome bowl of soup I've ever consumed." She paused for a moment. "And I figure that if you intended me harm, you would have perpetrated it already. You wouldn't be making sure I stay warm, fed and supplied with ice for my goose egg. And you wouldn't be obviously keeping your distance."

"I didn't want to scare you or give you any reason to suspect me."

"Unless you start acting drastically different, you're safe from my suspicion. And thank you, again, for saving my life. If you hadn't found me when you did, I don't think I'd be alive right now."

"You wouldn't be."

The reality of that caused a shiver to run down her spine.

"You cold?" he asked her for the second time since she'd awoken on his couch.

She slowly shook her head. "No, it's nice and toasty in here. I was just thinking of all the stories I've heard of people dying of exposure due to hypothermia, and how close I came to becoming one of those statistics."

Gavin looked toward the front window, and quiet settled between them for several seconds.

"How long were you out in that weather?" His tone suggested that his desire to not engage with her had lost out to his curiosity, and he wasn't happy about it.

"I'm not sure. What time did you find me?"

"Shortly after noon."

"It must have been about an hour, then, but part of that I was knocked out in my car."

"Are you injured anywhere else? I only checked to see if there were any obvious broken bones."

"There doesn't seem to be anything other than what I'm sure is going to be a collection of colorful bruises. I got lucky."

Despite his kindness, albeit given reluctantly, Maya was pretty sure Gavin Olsen did not share the same view about how his day had turned out.

GAVIN WOKE THE next morning hoping the previous day had been nothing more than a vivid dream. But when he heard the commode flush in the bathroom, he realized the memory that he had an unexpected houseguest was all too real. He had the urge to pull his covers up over his head as if he could hide from her, the same trick he'd tried to use to get out of going to school when he was a kid. It wasn't going to work now any more than it did back then.

Why was this happening to him? He just wanted to be left alone. He was no longer fit for human interaction.

When he finally forced himself out of bed and walked over to the window, he couldn't believe his eyes. It was still snowing. The weather people had gotten the forecast for this storm all kinds of wrong—the timing of its arrival, the amount of snowfall, how long it would last. He growled inwardly and ran a hand over his face. Looked as if his unwanted guest wasn't going to be able to leave today either. Thank goodness he had work he could do outside, because the idea of being trapped in the house with her all day made him want to take up residence in the barn.

Despite what she'd gone through the day

before, she seemed to be one of those look-on-the-bright-side kind of people. He had no energy to deal with that, not to mention he thought those people were lying to themselves. Life was not all sunshine and rainbows. It was dark clouds and cold, pelting rain more often than not.

Putting off having to face her for a few more minutes, he retreated to his blessedly private bathroom to take a shower and shave. By the time he was finished and dressed, he figured if he waited any longer it would be obvious he was avoiding her. And though that was exactly what he'd like to do, he did realize that she'd not chosen to invade his solitude. He wanted to be able to blame her for being out in the storm in the first place, but she'd likely been surprised by the timing of its arrival the way he had. He hadn't talked to her long, but she didn't seem like the type of person to make stupid decisions, her bright personality notwithstanding. In fact, she came across as someone who thought things through and arrived at common-sense decisions.

If only *he'd* always possessed those qualities.

He reminded himself that Maya Pine

wasn't a permanent fixture in his home. As soon as the road was clear enough for travel, she'd thankfully be gone—whether someone came to pick her up or he drove her into town. He'd prefer the former but would do the latter if it allowed him to reclaim his solitude sooner.

When he opened his bedroom door, he was hit with the smell of bacon. Unless he had unknowingly started cooking while sleepwalking, Maya had gotten hungry and taken it upon herself to raid a stranger's fridge. He bit down on instant annoyance until he reminded himself that he couldn't exactly starve her. And at least by her taking the initiative, he didn't have to cook for her again.

Despite his desire to flee the house, his stomach growled in response to the delicious scent. When he stepped into the kitchen, he was surprised to see that Maya either had a huge appetite or she'd cooked enough for him as well.

"Oh, good morning," she said with a wide smile that belied the fact that she'd wrecked her car and nearly frozen to death the day before.

"You cooked breakfast?" Obviously.

"Yes. I hope you don't mind." She gestured

toward the spread gracing the table. "Call it a thank-you."

"This wasn't necessary." How messed up was he that her kind gesture made him uncomfortable? And suspicious.

"I'd say this isn't much considering what you've done for me."

His stomach growled again, louder this time. Maya laughed at his audible hunger.

"Looks as if I finished up just in time."

Even though he didn't typically make so much for breakfast, it looked and smelled great. He felt edgy and out of sorts, but maybe filling his stomach wasn't a terrible idea before venturing out into the cold. After all, food shouldn't go to waste. And no matter how hungry Maya might be, he didn't think she could eat everything she'd made.

When he took his first bite of scrambled eggs, it was all he could do not to moan in appreciation. Did she have some magical way of making eggs? Because his efforts never produced such stellar results. Not that he tried to do more than simply fill his belly when the need arose. As with most things, he hadn't taken much pleasure in food in a long time.

"I hope scrambled eggs are okay," Maya

said. "I didn't know how you liked them, and I'll admit to not being the world's best cook."

"They're good," he said.

She didn't fish for more compliments, something else he appreciated. Compliments invited people to become friendlier and more talkative, and that wasn't what he wanted. He got the distinct feeling she'd deduced that he'd rather be alone and was doing her best to be helpful rather than a burden. Oddly, that softened him the smallest fraction toward her.

"How does your head feel?"

"About as well as can be expected." She lifted her hand and pushed her hair away from the knot. "It's all kinds of pretty colors today. I'm thinking of changing my name to Rainbow."

He was unexpectedly tempted to smile at that, but it never made it past a slight tug at the corner of his mouth. He honestly couldn't remember the last time he'd smiled. Of course, he hadn't had anything to smile about since he'd lost his son.

No, he couldn't think about Max now. He didn't want to risk his pain showing on his face and Maya asking questions.

They ate in silence for a bit before Maya spoke again.

"I'm sorry to report that the snow hasn't seen fit to stop falling."

"I saw." Because none of this was her fault and he sounded like a jerk with his short, clipped replies, he added, "Feel free to watch TV. I'll be out of the house working most of the day. And there's a landline phone if you need to make more calls." He pointed toward the phone on the wall.

"Is that a *rotary* phone?"

"Yes. The previous occupant hadn't updated in quite some time."

"I'll say. But that's not surprising. If Ansel Blackthorn had told me he'd been living here before Wyoming gained statehood, I would have believed him. He was quite a character and averse to change, as you've gathered by his blast-from-the-past phone."

Gavin wondered if this place attracted hermits, because he'd sure been living up to that label since moving here.

"When he passed, no one in town could quite believe it. He seemed eternal somehow."

He gave a "hmm" and a nod in reply, and she seemed to take the hint and fell into silence as she ate. He wondered how difficult it was for her to stay quiet, because she seemed like a cheery, chatty person—the complete opposite of him. All the more reason to get her out of his home as soon as possible. But as much as he wanted her gone, he wasn't about to shove her out the door before it was safe to do so. Maybe if she lived nearby her departure could be sooner rather than later though.

"Do you live up the mountain?"

"No, in town. I was up here to meet someone to do an interview, but he didn't show up."

"A job interview?"

She shook her head as she ripped a piece of bacon in half. "An interview for the paper. I'm the editor of the *Valley Post*."

His breakfast threatened to sour in his stomach. Of all the damsels in distress to collapse on his property, it had to be a reporter.

He stood quickly, almost knocking over his chair in the process. "Work to do."

He retrieved his coat and hat and strode out of the house. When the door was closed safely behind him, he took a moment on the front porch to inhale a deep breath. The air was visible when he exhaled. He had the strangest thought that he wished he was a dragon so he could burn away the snow, making a clear path for Maya Pine to leave and occupy space anywhere else but his home.

CHAPTER THREE

MAYA STARED AT the front door for probably a full thirty seconds after Gavin walked out. She needed that long to process his sudden departure and the most likely reason for it— the revelation that she was a reporter.

She sighed. To some extent she could understand why people had a negative opinion of her profession. There were definitely journalists out there who wouldn't know truth and journalistic ethics if they slapped them upside the head. But they were the ones who were after big national audiences, and often weren't real journalists anyway. They weren't running little local papers on a shoestring budget like her. Some people didn't distinguish between the two, however. If you asked people questions for a living, some thought you were evil incarnate.

She bit into a slice of bacon more aggressively than was required, disappointed that there would likely be no chance of increasing the friendliness of the conversations with her host now.

After finishing her food, putting away leftovers and washing the dishes, she took some medicine for the dull headache that was still lingering. She wished her laptop was handy, but even if she'd had it with her, it would likely be buried in the snow somewhere alongside her purse.

Despite being stranded, she had to work every bit as much as Gavin did. So she used the ancient phone to call Janie, her one and only staffer at the paper, to let her know what was going on.

"You're where?"

"The old Blackthorn place. The new owner, quite literally, saved my life."

"That should be the article you write to replace the one that fell through."

"Yeah, not happening. He's not a fan of reporters."

"So…are you in a bad situation?"

"No, nothing like that. He's just the quiet sort." And grumpy. "But he's not even here now. I'm sure he's out doing rancher things. Ranching waits for no one and nothing, not even a snowstorm."

Out feeding cows and probably wishing she'd fallen face-first in someone else's yard.

"So, what are the road conditions like?" Maya asked. If she and her car could be retrieved soon, that would probably be best for both her and her not-so-happy host.

"Terrible and getting worse. The crews are having a hard time keeping even the main roads somewhat passable."

So much for giving Gavin his privacy back.

Janie assured Maya that she'd get the weather story done for the front page and make sure the paper got sent to press on time if Maya could come up with something to fill the spot she'd been saving for the St. Michaels feature.

"I've got an idea, but I'll have to call you back later to dictate it to you."

"Okay, I'll get everything else wrapped up in the meantime."

"Thanks. You're the best."

"I know. Employee of the Month every month."

Maya laughed before hanging up and seeking some paper and a pen. When was the last time she'd written a story longhand? Probably three years before when they'd had a storm knock out the power and her laptop battery ran out.

As she sat at the kitchen table and got to work on a piece about the state's new infrastructure plans for the county, something she'd slotted for next week's issue, she mentally chewed out Benjamin St. Michaels again. She doubted a story about funding for roads and bridges was going to draw lots of extra purchases of this week's issue.

By the time she'd filled the first page of the small notebook, she had to stretch her hand. She looked down at the words scrawled across the page and shook her head. Her handwriting got worse with each passing year.

When she was satisfied with the article, she called Janie back and read it to her so she could type it in.

"You sure you're okay there?" Janie asked once they were finished. "I could ask Angie if there's a way to come get you."

"No, I'm fine. You said the road conditions were rotten. I'm not putting anyone else at risk simply because I find myself in an awkward situation. Besides, maybe I can convince him that all reporters aren't bad."

Though she wasn't going to bet her savings on that.

"Oh yeah?" Janie asked. "What exactly does this guy look like?"

"Janie! That's not what I meant."

"You didn't answer the question."

"Go do your work or you're fired."

Janie was still laughing at the absurdity of Maya firing her one and only staff member when Maya hung up the phone.

Maya scanned her surroundings, but it looked the same as it had when she'd taken it all in while waiting for Gavin to emerge from his room earlier. Simple furnishings, a few books on a shelf, a good-size TV, but no personalization such as family photos or mementos.

To be honest, it seemed somewhat odd that a man who looked like Gavin Olsen was living out here alone. A litany of possible reasons why ran through her head: he wasn't a people person (evidence pointed toward this), he was a workaholic with no time for relationships (maybe, but that didn't ring particularly true), he was unlucky in love (hey, it happened to people of all attractiveness levels), he was a serial killer (nope), or he simply hadn't found the right person (dude, you're not alone).

She could empathize with the last possibility. Dating in a small town was a challenge if it was even feasible once you discounted all the people you were either related to or who you knew way too much about. The fact that she'd never even seen Gavin in town added to the unlikelihood of him dating anyone local.

As much as she'd nixed her mother's matchmaking efforts and swatted away her best friend Sunny's teasing about her dating, it wasn't as if Maya wanted to spend the rest of her life alone. But her hectic work schedule combined with limited eligible bachelors made happily-ever-after more difficult.

Sunny had gotten lucky—the man who'd been head over heels for her since they were both teenagers was sitting right there on her family's ranch when she made the decision to come back to Jade Valley after years away. The only guys to cause a flicker of interest for Maya seemed to always be attractive tourists stopping at one of the two sit-down restaurants in town on their way through.

She shook her head, trying to clear away her wandering thoughts of romance. Even if Gavin Olsen was an attractive man, she didn't know enough about him to determine whether she could like him as more than her literal savior. For that she'd always be grateful, despite his curt manner. And judging by his reaction to the news that she was a reporter, she'd venture a solid guess that she was way, way down his list of potential romantic partners. The best she could hope for was to convince him that not all reporters were the same. There were plenty who simply did their jobs reporting the actual news and shining a spotlight on worthy stories in their communities instead of capitalizing on people's fears for ratings and sales.

That gave her an idea for an article. She flipped to a fresh page in the notebook and started a bulleted list of points to cover. By the time she looked up from the pages she'd filled, she realized three things. One, this was more material than could fit into a single article. Two, this had the potential to be a series picked up nationally. And three, two hours had elapsed without her realizing how stiff she'd become while sitting on the hard kitchen chair.

She stood and stretched her aching muscles, some of the soreness caused by her accident. What she could really use was a massage, but that was nowhere on her horizon. But maybe a hot shower would suffice, and while Gavin was away from the house was the best time to take one. He hadn't given her any reason to be afraid of him, but it would still feel weird to take a shower in the home of a man she didn't really know.

She planned it to be a quick shower, but the moment she stepped under the stream of hot water she didn't want it to end. The warmth soaked into her aching muscles, giving her relief she hadn't fully been aware she needed. Gavin's shampoo didn't smell feminine, but it felt great to wash her hair, even if she had to be gentle with the area she'd injured.

Not wanting to use all the hot water, she reluctantly stepped out of the shower and made quick work of drying off and putting her clothes back on. Thankful Gavin actually owned a hair dryer, she dried her hair and pulled it up into a knot.

Speaking of knots, she wiped the steam off the mirror and checked out her colorful goose egg.

"You sure don't do anything halfway, do you?" she asked her reflection.

With a gentle shake of her head, she left the bathroom. Judging by how quiet the house was, Gavin had still not returned. Since he'd obviously skipped lunch, possibly to avoid her, he was going to be starving when he finally came back for the night. Still conscious that he'd saved her and that he was stuck with an obviously unwanted houseguest, she went to the kitchen to see what she could make for dinner. She had to eat too, after all. And maybe her making something warm and hearty could begin to chip away at his preconceptions about the type of person she was based on her profession.

It would probably help if she was as good a cook as her mom, but you worked with what you had.

After examining the contents of the fridge, freezer and pantry, she decided on beef stew. It seemed perfect for the kind of cold, snowy weather they were experiencing, especially after Gavin had been out in the elements all day.

What had he been doing during all those hours he'd been absent?

The ancient telephone had a long enough cord that she was able to call and talk to Sunny while she was assembling the stew.

"Um, let me get this straight," Sunny said after Maya explained her current situation. "You are making dinner for a man you don't know, who resents you being there, while being trapped in his house?"

"Don't make it sound so sinister," Maya said. "He's been a perfect gentleman, if not super friendly, and I have to eat as well. It's not as if I'm an invalid who can't fend for herself."

"What do you know about him? Have you called Angie to see what she knows?"

Maya rolled her eyes. "Have you been watching true crime shows or something? If he was planning to off me, do you think he would have let me use the phone? Or left me alone all day?"

Sunny hesitated before responding. "I suppose those are valid points."

"Thank you. I'm kind of known for having a good sense about people, remember?"

Sunny grunted her reluctant agreement in a way that made Maya laugh.

"So, how old is this Gavin Olsen? Where did he come from?"

"I'd say late twenties, but maybe early thirties. And I don't know where he moved from, but my gut instinct says he has ranching experience, because he didn't act like a hobby rancher."

She glanced around the room, noticing again that it wasn't fancy but rather comfortable in its simplicity.

"And this isn't the kind of place that someone who is playing at ranching would buy."

"You truly believe you're safe?"

"Yes, I have no concerns about that at all." It was honestly amazing how quickly she'd come to that conclusion about Gavin. "I get the distinct feeling that he'll actually be relieved when I leave."

"So he's a loner."

"Seems so, but there are lots of valid reasons for liking to be in only your own company. I mean, you and I are obviously not like that, but I realize that not everyone is a social butterfly."

She didn't divulge the information about Gavin evidently not liking reporters, and she wasn't sure why. Maybe she just wanted time to figure out on her own why he held that view and try to change it. At least help him understand that reporters weren't a monolith. Their views on how to convey the news varied widely.

A cry from the other end of the call brought Maya out of her wandering thoughts.

"Sounds like one of your wee people isn't happy."

"Liam hasn't been feeling well, and we're keeping him separated from his sister so Lily doesn't get sick too. Let's say neither of the twins is happy with this new arrangement. I better go and check on him before he goes into full meltdown."

"Kisses to the kiddos from Auntie Maya to your adorable niece and nephew."

"Call me immediately if anything changes and you need help. I'll send out a snowmobile brigade or organize an airlift or something."

"Seriously, stop worrying about me. You've got enough on your plate, woman." With raising her brother's two orphaned toddlers, a husband who was one part rancher and one part entrepreneur, and her own consulting business, Sunny Breckinridge Wheeler was one busy woman. But that was exactly how she liked it. Sunny was always so full of new ideas on how to diversify the ranch, expand her business's offerings, improve the community of Jade Valley or the twins' early education opportunities that Maya didn't know when she slept.

Sunny laughed. "You're not wrong there. I'll talk to you later."

After she hung up, the house around her seemed extra quiet. Of course, when it was snowy like this, it seemed to put a hush on the world. If this were her home and she didn't always have work to do, she could imagine finding the weather relaxing—well, now that she wasn't in danger of dying out in it. But the thought of kicking back in a pair of soft pajamas, with an equally soft blanket, a good book and a cup of hot cocoa with plenty of marshmallows sounded fabulous.

But she rarely got that kind of time to relax. Not that she was complaining, not much anyway. She loved her job, but it wasn't one she could leave at five in the afternoon and not have to think about until the next morning. The news never stopped, even in a little town like Jade Valley. There were always accidents to cover, sports events at the schools, local government decisions, feel-good features about someone's cat that had come home after wandering for six months, or a blue ribbon won at the state fair.

Even while stuck in a stranger's house with no access to her computer and with an ugly, painful knot on her head, she'd been working. A little voice at the back of her mind kept whispering that if she stopped, everything she'd worked for would disappear. She wanted to make the *Valley Post* successful enough that she'd stop getting messages from the owners pressuring her to do more, sell more. But to reach that goal, she had to be innovative.

Once she had the stew on the stove, she visited the pantry again and found some little boxes of cornbread mix. That sounded as if it would go well with the stew, so she set about preparing that while she let her mind wander through ideas for the paper.

She was pouring the prepared mix into a pan when she realized her thoughts had drifted away from work and toward when Gavin might reappear. Sunny's questions about him had gotten Maya's own curiosity to spinning. Was he a Wyoming native? Did he know anyone in Jade Valley? And if not, why move here? Or was not knowing anyone the reason he'd relocated here? Had he always been an introvert?

She reined in her runaway questions, reminding herself that he was not someone she was interviewing. He was the person who'd saved her life and was allowing her to stay in his home until she could safely leave. She needed to respect his privacy as much as sharing the same space would allow. Even so, she thought casual conversation would help to alleviate any awkwardness between them. She just had to find the right balance between encouraging conversation and not letting her inclination to find out about people go too far. There was definitely a line between interested and nosy, and Gavin wouldn't appreciate her crossing it. Or perhaps even getting within spitting distance of it.

With the stew on the stove and the bread in the oven, she returned to her notes and jotted down the names of other small-town journalists she planned to consult. If this series turned out how she hoped, she'd actually have Gavin to thank for the idea. Somehow she doubted he'd want any part of it though.

Unless she could change his mind. What an awesome twist ending to the series that would be.

When the door suddenly opened, revealing the man she'd just been thinking about, an uncharacteristic wave of embarrassment caused her face to flush. Why, she wasn't sure. It wasn't as if she was thinking about him in an inappropriate way.

He took off his hat and hung it on the peg next to the door, revealing his face was red too but from the cold.

"I take it that it hasn't suddenly turned spring outside," she said.

He looked at her with an expression that

almost seemed as if he'd forgotten she was there, though she doubted very much that was the case.

"Unless spring looks and feels like Hoth, then no."

He sounded incredibly exasperated, but she couldn't help but laugh at the *Star Wars* reference. When she did, he looked surprised yet again.

"What? I've seen all the movies, the animated series, and even read some of the books. And my brother's room is filled with model ships, droids, stations, you name it. I half expect to hear 'The Imperial March' when I step into his room."

If she wasn't mistaken Gavin almost smiled. Or maybe that was wishful thinking on her part. Whatever the expression had been, it disappeared when he glanced at her, but in its place was an unasked question.

"What?"

He shook his head.

"If you're curious about something, you can ask."

He seemed to weigh his curiosity against the likelihood that she'd ask something in return. Or possibly against the moral implications of tossing her out into the snow after he'd saved her from it.

"Don't worry, I won't launch into a thousand questions about you," she said, adding a smile to hopefully put him at ease. Not to mention herself. The impression that he didn't seem to like her very much bothered her, though she was trying to not let that show. She was the one who'd invaded his home, so she didn't have the right to expect him to be cheery about it.

"I didn't say you would," he said, his tone chilly but not completely frozen.

"You didn't have to. I picked up pretty easily on the fact you're not fond of my profession, but I won't ask why. Everyone is entitled to their opinions."

Did she hope by giving him an out that he might feel more comfortable sharing something about himself? Yes. She'd be lying if she claimed otherwise. But would she be offended if he didn't? No. Sure, she liked to dig until she found good stories, and the stories behind the stories, but she didn't drag them out against people's wills. Unless, of course, they were politicians or criminals (or both), and then all bets were off.

Gavin took his time hanging his coat on

the peg next to his hat and slipping off his boots. Even when he was finished, he didn't immediately face her and she could almost feel the tenseness in his body, the tumult of his thoughts. Finally he slowly turned and hesitated a moment before exhaling an audible breath then asking, "So you have a brother who is a lot younger than you?"

He wasn't winning any awards for being warm and friendly, but at least this was progress.

She nodded. "Though Ethan's not a kid anymore, if that's what you're thinking. He's in college in Laramie. But he's still a big sci-fi nerd. I tease him about it, but I like it too. I'm a big believer in finding what you like and embracing it, no matter what anyone else thinks."

"Healthy attitude." He said the words, so why did it sound like he didn't quite believe them?

"Yes, but it's not always popular with the older or stick-in-the-mud crowd."

"Few things are."

There was a note of bitterness in his voice, but she pretended not to notice and laughed instead.

Gavin seemed to catch the scent of the stew. "You didn't have to cook again."

"Something else about me, I get bored easily. I have to have things to do or I go stir-crazy. Plus, again, there's that little fact of you saving my life. I'm pretty sure I could cook meals for you for the next decade and it wouldn't be enough."

As those words left her mouth, a strange wave of awkwardness hit her. She hadn't considered how…intimate they could be interpreted, and she hoped that Gavin didn't take them that way.

Thank heaven that possibility seemed to fly past him as he moved toward the kitchen.

"It smells good." His stomach growled, quite audibly, which must be common for him.

"Well, evidently your stomach agrees."

While Gavin wordlessly excused himself to take a shower, she pulled the bread from the oven and tried not to think about there being a naked man who she barely knew not that far away. She wasn't prudish by any means, but it still felt strange. So much so that she exhaled in relief when the shower shut off and he'd had enough time to properly clothe himself. Still, when he stepped out with damp hair, wearing a T-shirt instead of the usual long-sleeve work shirts, she wondered if the short amount of time she'd been stuck in Gavin's house was enough to make her lose her common sense. Because the thought that she didn't mind being snowbound with a surly man she'd just met flitted through her mind, laughing as it went.

She turned to spoon stew into bowls, glad to be able to have a few moments to compose herself before facing him again. Had she let her mother's matchmaking latch on to some part of her brain? She shuddered at the thought, then spoke before Gavin could ask her if she was cold yet again.

"I brought in some more wood earlier from the pile outside," she said, using the ladle in her hand to deliberately point his attention toward the woodbin behind the stove.

"You di—"

"If you say I didn't have to do that, I'm going to toss it back outside into the snow." She turned and placed the filled bowls on the table.

He stared at her for a long moment, seemingly confused by her response, before nodding once. "Point taken. Thank you." He hesitated again before continuing. "If you feel bad or dizzy, don't push yourself. Don't cause problems we can't fix."

"Deal. Trust me, I don't want to face plant off your porch and smother in a snowdrift while you're out feeding cattle, causing you to come back to a human popsicle. That just seems rude after you saved me once already. Twice seems to be pushing it."

"You joke about that a lot."

"What?"

"How close you came to dying," he said, not mincing words. He looked at her as if he couldn't wrap his mind around her way of thinking.

She shrugged. "Maybe it's a coping mechanism, or maybe just my personality, but I've always been that way. I figure dwelling on negatives and what-might-have-beens doesn't do me or anyone else any good, so why bother? Be thankful or deal with it, as the case may be, and move on."

"It's not always that easy." Gavin pulled out his chair, seating himself in front of his steaming bowl of stew.

His comment made her wonder about his past, if there was something that he couldn't move beyond. Maybe it was why he was so distant and bordering on ill-tempered. But, true to her word, she didn't pry.

"That's true. Some things that happen are more difficult to navigate or get over than others." She placed the plate of cornbread muffins on the table along with a tub of butter and a knife before taking her own seat. "I'm just thankful that I survived, and I don't want to dwell on the fact that I almost didn't."

Maya hesitated as the full weight of what she'd gone through suddenly slammed into her, as if it had been waiting nearby for the slightest invitation. She stared at her stew as another shiver ran through her, for a very different reason this time.

"I won't lie. I was scared, especially when I started having thoughts some part of my brain was telling me I shouldn't."

"Hypothermia," he said, having still not touched his food.

She nodded, then took a deep breath and met Gavin's gaze. "Seriously, thank you for saving me. I don't think I would have lasted out there much longer."

He stared at her for several seconds before responding with a solitary nod. "You're welcome."

His response surprised her, but she was thankful for it all the same.

They both dug into their stew as if ravenous. How she was so hungry after not doing much all day, she didn't have a clue. But winter was like that. The short, cold days made you want to eat and sleep.

She swallowed a bit of her cornbread then stared at the muffin in her hand.

"You ever wonder if humans are part bear?"

"Um, no." His response sounded very much as if he wondered if she'd taken leave of her senses.

"Hear me out. Days like today," she said, gesturing toward the window, "make me want to eat all the calories, then burrow under about ten blankets and sleep like I'm hibernating."

"It's just the body's instinct for self-preservation. Staying warm and being well-fed are at the top of that list."

She didn't allow her next thought to attach itself to her voice, that it was easier to stay warm when sharing body heat. Yeah, her mom's attempts to find her dates and Sunny's newly wedded bliss were messing with her brain. Or her body chemistry. When was the last time she went on a date? And that disaster of an evening with the delivery guy who brought orders to both Trudy's Café and Alma's Diner each week one hundred and ten percent did not count.

She needed to stop thinking about dates and bodies and eat her dinner instead.

And find a safe topic of conversation.

"So, was everything okay when you went out today?"

He nodded again. "Yes."

Maya sighed inwardly. He was back to single-word answers.

"That's good. My best friend's family has a ranch in the valley. I know it's a ton of work in all kinds of weather. You have to love it to put up with being frozen to the bone in the winter and burning up in the summer." She tore off another piece of muffin and crumbled it up in her stew. "But I guess there are good and bad points to every career."

Even though she loved her job, it wasn't perfect. She could live without the pressure from the paper's owners and the requests for feature articles that were not-at-all-veiled attempts to get free advertising, and a vacation every now and then would be nice. More than once, she'd envied Sunny's posts from around the world before Sunny had moved back from Los Angeles. Maya had wondered what it would be like to explore places such as Singapore or Brazil or Ireland. The amount of stories Sunny could write about her adventures would fill volumes.

Maya noticed that Gavin didn't say anything in response. Her instincts told her that he had zero interest in hearing about her chosen field. Curiosity nibbled away at her, but she held it in check.

"Sometimes you just do what you know," he finally said, surprising her.

"You've ranched before?"

Again, a nod. "Grew up on a ranch."

Had she managed to create a small crack in his icy exterior?

Questions came to her quickly, one right after another. Did his parents still operate a ranch? If so, why didn't he work with them? Or had they passed? Maybe the ranch was gone instead. Why had he chosen Jade Valley?

Once again, she pulled the brakes on her mental query train.

The phone rang, startling them both. She'd bet her meager savings that Gavin didn't get a lot of phone calls. When he answered, Maya had to press her lips together to keep from laughing at how he looked as if the phone might actually bite him.

"She's right here." He extended the receiver, surprising her further.

Had Janie run into an issue with the paper? She realized the more likely caller as she answered. "Yes, I'm still alive."

She smiled when Gavin turned toward her with his eyes wider than normal, probably without thinking.

"Maya! He'll hear you," Sunny said.

"Definitely. He's about five feet from me."

Gavin Olsen looked as if he'd give any amount of money to have her stop talking and then get immediately out of his house.

Maya would swear she could hear Sunny's eye roll.

"Well, now that I've reassured myself you're still among the living, I'm going to go spend time with my incredibly handsome husband."

"This has to be the record for the shortest phone call we've ever had."

"Hey, you need to take that off," Sunny said, obviously talking to Dean.

"TMI! Goodbye!" Maya hung up the

phone in dramatic fashion, then shivered in an equally excessive way. "Ugh, newlyweds."

During the remarkably short phone call, Gavin had evidently inhaled the rest of his stew since he was now rinsing his bowl at the sink.

"Sorry about that," she said. "My best friend is a little…overprotective."

"Oh," he replied without looking at her.

"I already told her earlier today that I was pretty sure you aren't an ax murderer."

"Well, that's good to know."

Maya laughed. "Be careful. That sounded almost like humor."

He glanced at her, his forehead knitted in question. She walked over and leaned back against the kitchen counter a couple of arm's lengths away from him.

"Listen, I know you'd rather I not be here. I'd a million times rather not have totaled my car and nearly frozen to death, but here we are, stuck for the time being. I figure the best way to get through situations we don't plan for is to make the most of them. In case you haven't figured that part out about me yet, I tend to do that with humor."

"How do you know I'm not an ax murderer?"

She barely resisted laughing because he looked so serious.

"Well, for one, I woke up this morning. And two, the ax has stayed outside. So, two points in your favor."

He looked out the window above the sink into the darkness. "Why is it always an ax?"

"Huh?"

He looked back at her. "Why is it always an ax murderer? I don't think there are that many Lizzie Bordens walking around."

Maya stared at Gavin for a couple of seconds before she busted out laughing. There was no holding it in this time. "I have no idea. Maybe baseball bat murderer is too long."

Why she found it so funny that he knew who Lizzie Borden was, she wasn't sure. Maybe because the historical tidbit seemed so random. Did he like to read about history? True crime? She glanced toward the books on the shelf. She hadn't examined the titles yet. She'd do that the next time he left the house. Perhaps it would give her a little more information about Gavin. Tonight she'd already discovered that he did have a sense of humor, even if he was hesitant to show it or it was rusty for lack of use.

She finished the last few bites of her own

meal then brought her dishes to the sink. Gavin extended his hand for the bowl and spoon.

"I can wash them."

"No. You cooked, twice. I'll do the dishes." She couldn't tell if he was thankful or simply didn't want to be indebted to her, as if her cooking a few meals could ever repay him for saving her life. He nodded toward the living room. "Watch some TV if you want."

When she clicked on the television, she found it already tuned to the Casper news. Unsurprisingly, the weather was the top story. She watched as the meteorologist talked about snowfall amounts, additional accumulation and the frigid temperatures expected in the days ahead.

"I don't know whether to believe him or not," she said as Gavin surprised her by settling into the recliner opposite from where she sat on the couch. "The weather people don't have a good track record with this storm."

Gavin only grunted, a sound that seemed to communicate he agreed. Did he group weather people on TV in with all other reporters? That would be a tad extreme, but she still wasn't going to ask any questions tonight. They'd actually had a bit of a conversation.

He had loosened up the tiniest fraction. If she was going to be stuck here for the foreseeable future, she didn't want to risk making him retreat again. Her instincts told her that she had to toe a fine line to have him talk to her at all.

As soon as the weather coverage was over, Gavin leaned forward and grabbed the remote control. He looked over at her as if silently asking if she minded him changing the channel.

Maya motioned toward the television. "It's your TV."

Gavin flipped a few channels until she spotted a distinctive opening text scroll.

"Wait," she said, then laughed when she realized they'd landed on the opening credits of the original 1977 *Star Wars* after talking about the franchise earlier. "What are the odds?"

They settled in to watch the movie, even though she'd seen it so many times that she couldn't remember an exact count.

"Too bad we don't have any popcorn," she said.

He didn't respond, and she didn't push him to. Being willing to watch a movie with her seemed like enough of a step toward him thawing toward her for the time being.

When the first movie ended, the second in the original trilogy started immediately.

"This one is my favorite," she said.

Gavin got up from his chair, and she thought he must be going to bed in preparation for another early day tomorrow. But he simply shoved a couple of pieces of wood in the stove before returning to his chair.

It was oddly comfortable watching a *Star Wars* marathon with Gavin. Though she was the chatty sort, she didn't like people to talk during movies. In this way, Gavin proved to be the perfect movie buddy.

When *The Empire Strikes Back* ended and *Return of the Jedi* started, she turned to ask Gavin if he wanted something to drink. But she discovered that the reason he'd been so quiet wasn't because he was engrossed in the movie. Because he wasn't snoring like her dad and brother did, she hadn't realized he'd fallen asleep.

She found herself staring at him the way she couldn't when he was awake. He appeared more relaxed than he'd been at any point in their short acquaintance. If she was being honest, he wasn't hard to look at. She almost giggled remembering how she'd told her mom that she wouldn't look the other way if a hot man crossed her path. She hadn't imagined collapsing in front of his house and him having to save her from freezing to death, but life was strange sometimes.

But, like any other good-looking man she'd encountered, there was a substantial obstacle standing in the way of it developing into anything more than a brief meeting. Tourists went home, and her savior would probably throw a one-person party when she departed.

Even so, she found herself grabbing one of the quilts she'd used the night before and easing over to drape it across him. She held her breath, hoping he didn't wake up and see her standing above him.

Or maybe she hoped he would.

She shook her head at the strange thought. What was wrong with her? Why was she so interested in this man who was less than interested in her? Wondering if she'd knocked something vital to proper reasoning loose in her head in the wreck, she retreated to the relative safety of the couch. She turned off the lamp, covered herself in the remaining quilt, and stretched out with her back toward Gavin.

Gavin's obvious desire for her to go home as soon as possible suddenly seemed like the smartest idea any human had ever had.

CHAPTER FOUR

GAVIN WOKE THE next morning with pain in his chest. As he came awake, he was already rubbing at an ache that couldn't be alleviated, a hole that couldn't be filled. The dream and its emotional effects still lingered like a thick morning fog. He missed his son every day. Knowing that he was only a state away but he couldn't see him…he wouldn't wish that on any parent.

As he blinked away more of the lingering sleep, he noticed things were not normal. For one, it was later than he typically slept. He also wasn't in his bed.

Realizing he must have fallen asleep while watching TV, he glanced toward the screen to see it had been turned off. And a quilt had been draped over him. He looked to his right and noticed Maya curled up on the couch with her back toward him. She looked cold, and although she was only a temporary guest that he didn't want, he nevertheless didn't like the idea of her not being warm enough, especially after what she'd gone through.

Even after he'd been cold toward her, she persisted in friendly and kind gestures. Either she wasn't very bright or she was a good-hearted person. Evidence pointed toward the latter, so she didn't deserve to be the target of his foul attitude. He didn't have it in him to be cheery, but maybe he could try to be less gruff.

As quietly as he could, he lowered the footrest of his recliner and returned the quilt to its proper place. Maya rolled over as he settled the quilt atop her, and he froze. The last thing a woman needed to wake up to was a man she barely knew standing above her, even if she had decided he wasn't an ax murderer.

He smiled a fraction, surprising himself. Despite his not liking the media as a whole, Maya Pine seemed like a decent person. And despite her being a reporter, she hadn't grilled him for answers about his past or anything else. He was one for giving credit where credit was due, and her restraint though she was probably curious deserved acknowledgment, even if it was only to himself.

When it seemed Maya had settled back into sleep, he eased away from her and headed for the bathroom. Afterward, to keep from waking her, he exited the house via the door off the laundry room. He was greeted with a gust of frigid air that had him turning up the collar of his insulated jacket.

Unbidden, his thoughts returned to the arguably more comfortable life he'd been living prior to returning to Wyoming. There had been no early mornings making his way through deep snow to feed animals and make sure his livelihood was safe. Keeping warm was a certainty as long as the electricity stayed on. Instead of living like a recluse, he'd had a family, friends, had been following his dream.

But now that family, those friends and that dream were all part of the past, no matter how much he'd tried to keep them all.

He trudged toward the barn, hoping the freezing weather would take over all his thoughts because thinking about the past couldn't change it. He knew that from lots of experience.

"Good morning," he said to Jasper as he entered the barn. He walked over to the stall and scratched between the horse's ears. "Sorry, buddy, but we need to go for a ride."

A few minutes later, as he rode among the

snow-laden trees down toward his pasture, he enjoyed the momentary sunshine even though he felt no warmth from it. And he wasn't fooled that it would last for long, because already the wind was blowing in heavy gray clouds that promised more snow. At this rate, he was going to be stuck with a roommate until spring.

It struck him as odd that he didn't hate that idea as much as he had a couple of days ago. Had he been that starved for human interaction and fooled himself into thinking he didn't need it? Because if he had been home alone, he was certain he wouldn't have stayed up late watching a sci-fi movie marathon.

His stomach grumbled, reminding him that he had slipped out without eating breakfast. But he'd had no idea how late Maya had been awake watching TV and he didn't want to wake her.

He shook his head. How quickly he'd adjusted the way he did things because of a virtual stranger.

She wouldn't be a stranger if you talked to her.

Cattle. He needed to focus his thoughts on cattle, not the woman with shoulder-length black hair, pretty dark eyes and a smile that broadcasted her fun-loving personality. He actually laughed a little at the memory of her short conversation with her friend the night before, at her response to her friend's obvious and understandable concern for her safety.

Cows, cows, cows.

He lost count how many times he had to tell himself to refocus on his work and that the very last thing he needed in his life was a woman. The last time he'd been romantically involved had ended in a spectacularly bad fashion. He was not venturing down that road again. He'd be a fool to.

When he was satisfied the herd was safe and had everything necessary, he was in need of both food and warmth so he headed back uphill toward the barn and house. By the time he led Jasper into the barn and tended to the horse's needs, he'd almost convinced himself that there was no reason to be anxious about seeing Maya again. It wasn't as if they'd kissed or something. They'd simply watched movies together, fallen asleep in the same room, and she'd shown enough compassion to place a quilt over him so he wouldn't get cold. That was just basic human courtesy, something that he was out of practice offering.

He headed toward the house but halfway there stopped in his literal tracks.

"What in the world?"

He moved closer to the object that had not been in his front yard that morning, stopped to stare at it, and then couldn't help laughing though the sound was foreign from disuse. Staring back at him was a snowman wearing one of his older hats, a smile made from wood bark and a flannel shirt held wide open by the stick arms that made it look as if it was a flasher.

He couldn't remember the last time that something had made him laugh so much. In a way, it felt wrong. But he couldn't deny it also felt good.

Maya smiled at the sound of male laughter. Glancing out the window, she noticed that laughter looked good on Gavin Olsen. He was a handsome man to begin with, but a smile made him even more so.

She might not know what existed in his past that may have made him quiet and withdrawn, but her gut instincts had been telling her that he hadn't always been that way and that he needed reasons to smile again. It wasn't her job to make him smile, but she was glad her little joke had done the trick.

When he headed up the front steps, she spun back around and stared at the notes spread out in front of her on the coffee table. She'd spent the day outlining every possible article she could think of that would make sense to run in the paper and then worked on writing part of the small-town press series by hand. She couldn't recall the last time she'd written so much that way, and she'd had to stop several times to massage the muscles and joints in her hand and wrist as a result.

She glanced up when Gavin walked through the front door and went through the already familiar pattern of hanging up his hat and coat and slipping off his wet boots.

"Sounded as if you found your new lawn decoration amusing," she said.

"If the sheriff could get up here, I think that snowman would be arrested for indecent exposure."

She laughed. "Angie would just laugh and save her citations for living, breathing criminals."

"Angie? That the sheriff?"

"Yeah. She's a friend."

"You friends with everyone in town?" Why

did he sound a bit suspicious? Did he think that she only pretended to be friends with people so she could pump them for information when her job called for it? She couldn't deny that thought stung.

"Not everyone. And I know how to separate personal from professional." This time, she was the one whose reply was clipped.

Gavin stopped and stared at her for a long moment, as if he didn't know how to respond, before walking away toward the bathroom.

Perhaps she'd been too direct, but she was a straight-to-the-point kind of person. Surely he'd picked up on that by now.

That said, she also knew when to push forward and when to hold back, so when he returned to the living room she changed the topic of conversation.

"So, I hate to ask this, but do you happen to have anything I could wear while I wash my clothes? If I wear these much longer, you're going to kick me out into the jaws of winter."

"I'll see what I can find after I eat."

She started to stand, but he waved her back down.

"I can fend for myself."

But when he placed food on the table a few minutes later, there were two plates filled with ham, turkey and cheese sandwiches and plain potato chips.

"Come eat," he said without looking in her direction.

Maya pressed her lips together to keep from smiling at his standoffish tone because he was using it after having fixed her lunch. She joined him and noticed he'd cut her sandwich in half while his remained whole.

"It's nothing fancy, but it's food," he said.

"Thanks. I didn't know if you'd be back for lunch."

"It's not your job to cook for me." He glanced toward the living room. "You appear to have been busy doing your actual job."

"As much as I can without a computer anyway. I'll be lucky if I can read my own dreadful handwriting."

"You should run a terrible snowman contest and use yours as an example."

"Hey!" Before she thought about what she was doing, she swatted him on the arm. "I'll have you know I put substantial thought and effort into Snowy."

Gavin choked on the food he'd just swallowed and took a drink of his orange soda to wash it down.

"Snowy? Really? Why not just call him Flasher?"

"Oh, that gives me a great idea! The cousins of Santa's reindeer." She held up a new finger each time she called out the name that rhymed with those of the original reindeer. "Flasher, Stupid, Honor, Necromancer."

"I doubt the locals are ready for a snow reindeer that raises the dead."

She sighed. "You're probably right. I doubt that would fly even for Halloween."

Maya caught Gavin staring at her as if trying to figure out a complex puzzle. Or perhaps trying to understand why he'd just allowed himself to converse with her in more than grunts and single-word replies.

"What?"

"You're unexpected."

"Because I'm a journalist with a sense of humor or because I don't seem like I live in a small town?"

He tilted his head a fraction. "Both."

"News flash, not everyone who lives in small towns fits the stereotype, although some around here no doubt find me odd. But I make friends easily despite that."

"I guess that helps with your job." He returned his attention to his food, shoving chips into his mouth.

"It does, but I don't use friendships to get stories. Well, except when I roped Sunny into doing travel pieces because she's been all around the world and I thought at least a handful of readers would find the articles interesting."

Gavin made a sound of acknowledgment that he'd heard her but one that telegraphed he had his doubts. She wanted so much to ask him what his beef with journalists was, but she held herself back. Those instincts of hers were communicating that doing so was not the right tactic in getting him to change his mind. Best to let him sit with what she'd said and continue to show him that she was a decent person.

Why do you even care what he thinks?

She pondered that question as she ate the rest of her lunch. Partly, she didn't like being lumped together with people whom she didn't agree with on how reporting should be done. She admired a lot of big-time journalists, but others who wore that mantle were little more than propaganda artists or were more concerned with their own advancement than with giving the public the unvarnished truth they deserved. Not all journalists were alike, just as not all practitioners of any profession were the same. There were good and bad elements in every field, even Gavin's. But she didn't voice those thoughts. She kept them stored away for potential later use.

She glanced across the room toward the window and saw fat snowflakes falling again.

"You've got to be kidding me," she said.

"Saw that coming."

"You don't happen to have skis or a snow-mobile, do you?" She was only half kidding.

"Afraid not." He glanced at her before returning his attention to the fresh supply of chips he'd poured onto his plate. "Why did you schedule an interview when a snowstorm was due to move in?"

"Because I was afraid if I didn't do it then, I'd miss the opportunity. I was supposed to meet with the mystery author Benjamin St. Michaels. He has a vacation place near here. But he wasn't there and never showed up. Combined with the storm moving in earlier than expected and an unfortunate run-in with wildlife, it just wasn't my day."

"I'll say." Gavin paused for a moment before asking, "Did you reschedule for after the storm is over?"

Wait, what was that? Was Gavin asking her work-related questions without any disdain in his voice? Maybe she'd made a bit of progress changing his mind already.

"No. He didn't return any of my calls or texts when I was standing outside his house, nor as I was driving away. And I don't remember his number. It's stored in the phone I lost. He hasn't called the paper either or Janie, my one staffer, would have told me."

"He seems rude."

Though she could legitimately level that accusation at Gavin as well, it wasn't the same. She hadn't had an invitation into his home as she'd had with St. Michaels. While some people were rude by nature, others had situational reasons for being so.

"There's always the possibility that something happened that prevented him from being there or responding." After she'd gotten over being upset, that thought had occurred to her.

"There's the possibility it didn't too."

"Oh well, that's just how it goes sometimes. Only most of the time I don't crash my car and nearly freeze to death as a result." She shrugged, again making light of what had happened because thinking about how close she really had come to dying made her want to throw up. She kept reminding herself that she wasn't someone who dwelled on the past, because it was a useless endeavor.

After lunch, Gavin disappeared into his room. A couple of minutes later, he emerged and extended some items of clothing to her.

"These will be huge on you, but it's the best I can do."

"Thank you. Your olfactory receptors will thank you too."

A hint of amusement appeared in Gavin's eyes. Even though it paled when compared with the wide smile he'd worn earlier when he'd encountered the snowman, she was glad to see it. He might still prefer she be gone from his home, but at least he seemed to be thawing around the edges a little.

WHEN GAVIN RETURNED to work, Maya did more of her own. But feeling guilty that the continual snow accumulation would make it more difficult for her to vacate the premises, she didn't only wash her own clothing. She hoped Gavin didn't see it as overstepping, but she washed his accumulated laundry too. And then she found herself cleaning house, which would make her mom hurt herself laughing if she wasn't freaking out about her only daughter cohabitating with a male stranger.

As if thinking about her mother prompted the universe to nudge her mom, the phone rang. Somehow Maya knew who it was before she answered, that her mother had obviously gotten the landline number from either Janie or Sunny. Maya took a moment to prepare before answering.

"Hello," she said, trying to sound cheerful but not overly so.

"Don't hello me. Where are you?"

Her mom wouldn't have driven from her home on the reservation into Jade Valley in this weather, so something else had led to her tracking down Gavin's number and the current tone she was using.

"At a friend's."

Friend was stretching it, but the truth would make this conversation go downhill fast. Her mom was likely to try calling out military air rescue.

"What friend? And don't tell me it's Sunny or Janie, because I've talked to both of them and know you're not at either of their houses. Obviously, since I called this mysterious friend's number."

"Mom, why do you sound as if you're freaking out? I told you my phone died."

"The one at the paper didn't, and yet Janie is always the only one there when I call."

Maya sighed. She was going to be forced to give her mom at least a slice of the truth. This should be fun.

"Listen, I'm perfectly okay, but I was up the mountain to do an interview and the storm came in faster than expected. I slid off the road but one of the residents has been nice enough to give me a place to stay until the road is cleared."

"What resident?"

"You don't know them."

"Them? So it's a family?"

Maya closed her eyes and asked the universe for patience.

"No, Mom, his name is Gavin Olsen and he's been a perfect gentleman the entire time I've been here."

A bit grumpy, but a gentleman nonetheless.

"You're staying with a man you don't know?" Her mom's voice held a hint of a screech that was begging to be released.

"He's not a total stranger now."

"What does that mean?"

"Mom, how old am I?"

"Twenty-nine, and before you say you're old enough to make responsible decisions, you will never be old enough for me to not worry about you."

"Like I told Sunny, if he had nefarious intentions, he would have acted on them already."

"You don't know that. He could be lulling you into a false sense of security."

Maya barely restrained herself from mentioning how she'd been totally vulnerable and at his mercy when she collapsed in his yard. That would only add gasoline to the fire of her mother's worry.

"Hey, weren't you the one who has been hoping I'd meet a good-looking man, get married and start giving you grandchildren you can use for grandma clout?"

Whatever her mother said in response, Maya didn't hear it. Because when she turned around, Gavin was standing there. How had he come inside without her noticing him or the accompanying cold air when he opened the door? What she did know was that she was mortified. So much so that she nearly crushed the phone receiver in her hand.

She made a gesture, waving off what she'd just said, as she grimaced. In response, Gavin extended his hand for the phone. Maya shook her head, but he didn't retract his hand.

"Did you hear me?" her mom said in her ear.

"Hang on a moment."

"Maya Jane Pine!"

She lowered the receiver but didn't give it to Gavin. "You don't want to do this," she whispered.

In response, he reached forward and extricated the phone from her hand.

"Hello, this is Gavin Olsen. Am I speaking to Maya's mother?"

Maya really did feel as if she might throw up at any moment as she listened to one side of the conversation. Even that much told her that her mom was giving Gavin a grilling he didn't deserve. And as the conversation progressed, she began to think that her mom also should have been a reporter or possibly an FBI agent because she was getting Gavin to answer questions that Maya hadn't yet asked.

For instance, she now knew his parents ran a ranch near Sheridan but he wanted to make his own path. And that he was a year older than her.

After several minutes of him listening and answering as if he had been dragged in for police interrogation, he finally returned the phone to her.

"I am somewhat more comfortable with your situation," her mom said without prompting.

"So you believe a man you've never met over your own daughter, nice."

Her mom sighed. "I may have overreacted."

"You think?"

"Remember this conversation when you're a mother yourself."

"After this, I'm considering being single and childless my entire life. I'll adopt twenty cats instead. You can show your sisters pictures of them."

When she finally hung up the phone, she stayed facing the laundry room off the kitchen, not wanting to turn around.

"You don't have to be embarrassed," he said, as if he'd read her mind. Though, admittedly, it was probably glaringly obvious how she was feeling.

After blowing out a breath she faced him.

"I'm really, really sorry for all of that, and for what you heard me say before I saw you had come into the house."

"I was pretty sure it was said in jest. I'm not exactly a catch."

But he could be.

She mentally swatted that idea away. That he was handsome and had been kind to her was indisputable, but so was the fact that he'd shown zero interest in her and didn't like what she did for a living, something that was so much of her identity. Plus, she was aware that any positive feelings she might be having toward him were likely rooted in his having rescued her from death's doorstep. Once she was back home in her real world, around other people and able to move about freely, the temptation toward attraction would go away. That would be helped by her suspicion that she'd rarely, if ever, see him in town.

"You'll live longer if you have a healthy self-image," she said, trying to inject a bit of humor into the conversation while also letting him know in a roundabout way that he shouldn't have that kind of negative view of himself. Sure, he might be on the quiet and reclusive side, but perhaps he had valid reasons. As she'd been cleaning earlier, she'd been struck again by the complete absence of family photos, or photos of any kind. His walls were bare except for the hooks where he hung his jacket and hat and one utilitarian clock that was available at any low-cost retailer. The books had revealed themselves to be a dictionary, a couple of novels and, most notably, biographies of painters Frederic Remington and Frida Kahlo.

"I don't think that's a real statistic," he said.

"Maybe they just haven't done the research on the tie between longevity and self-esteem yet. I think I'm onto something."

"Don't reporters claim to base their reporting on facts?"

The way he said it left no doubt that he thought otherwise. "I'm not going to say some don't stretch the truth, and others flat out lie. The latter, in my opinion, shouldn't be able to call themselves journalists."

She hadn't meant there to be any heat in her words, but they came out that way nevertheless. Not wanting to potentially get into an argument with the person with whom she was being forced to share lodging, she turned and walked into the laundry room. After quickly folding the dry clothes, she took hers and exited the room.

To her surprise, Gavin was still standing in the kitchen staring into the fridge. After his last comment, she really didn't feel like fixing him a meal. He was obviously able to feed himself before she arrived, so he could do it again.

"Your clean laundry is on top of the dryer," she said as she headed toward the bathroom to change. Not in the mood to face him and wondering about how quickly her feelings had shifted, she stayed in the bathroom longer than was necessary. After changing, she sat on the edge of the tub and tried to dissect why his question had gotten under her skin when the same type of attitude hadn't bothered her overmuch whenever she'd faced it from other people. Normally she either allowed it to bounce off her and roll away or she was able to charm a change in attitude in the other person, an acknowledgment—if sometimes begrudging—that maybe every reporter in the country wasn't cut from the same cloth.

But it seemed as if despite them getting along fairly well for virtual strangers, Gavin's attitude about people in her profession hadn't changed. That made her one part angry, one part sad and one part intensely curious what had caused him to have that type of entrenched attitude. Had something happened to him because of reporting, or had he simply adopted beliefs held by his parents? She was well aware of how prejudices were handed down from one generation to the next, and not only those against her career choice.

But knowing that didn't make them any easier to swallow.

CHAPTER FIVE

AFTER GAVIN TOOK his clean and folded clothes into his room, he looked around his obviously cleaner house and felt like a complete jerk. Maya had been doing her best not to impose even though it was no doubt obvious that he was used to, and preferred, being alone. But what did he do? He didn't miss an opportunity to trash her career choice. Granted, he had legitimate reasons for not liking the media. They'd played a part in preventing him from seeing his son, after all. But she didn't know that.

Despite how he detested the power the media could hold over people's lives, sometimes ruining them, Maya didn't seem like that type of person. Sure, he didn't know her well, but she hadn't been pummeling him with intrusive questions. And he didn't think she had the money and power to destroy those around her. The one time he'd heard her on the phone talking to her coworker, the conversation had centered on an article about funding for bridge and road improvements. Not exactly yellow or vindictive journalism.

She deserved at least the benefit of the doubt. And he deserved a kick in the rear for taking his hatred out on someone who'd done him not a single wrong.

He noticed she was still in the bathroom, and he'd bet hard-earned money it was to avoid him in the only place she could. He wondered if it would be best to make a quick sandwich and leave the house, or wait until she came out so he could properly apologize.

He chose to split the difference.

Despite the cold and the fact that his grill was covered in snow, he grabbed a couple of steaks he'd pulled from the freezer the night before and wrapped two pre-baked potatoes in foil. Then he bundled up, grabbed the charcoal, lighter and matches, and headed out to the small back deck.

Though the sky was still lead gray with clouds, it had at least stopped snowing for the time being and the wind was calm. After firing up the grill and placing the food on it, he rounded the house and began splitting wood and carrying it to the front porch where it could better dry out before being transferred to the woodbin inside.

He ran gas heat too but supplemented with wood. Having two sources of heat in this part of the country was more than a good idea. And after what Maya had gone through, she shouldn't have to be cold again.

He'd still rather she not be stuck here, but what was the use of making himself even more miserable by staying upset about it?

Gavin stopped after several minutes of splitting wood and looked toward the forest through which Maya had trudged in a nearly frozen state. He wondered if her car had been totally covered by the snowfall as had the purse she'd evidently dropped between here and there. He also wondered when the road would be cleared. Well, first, it had to stop snowing. And despite the reprieve he was currently enjoying, more snowfall was predicted for later in the evening and overnight. Add that to the fact that the road that passed his place, winding up the mountain, was one of the lesser traveled and it could be days still.

If he didn't want those days to be uncomfortable and awkward, he needed to set aside his negative views and apologize.

After a flip of the steaks, he retreated to

the barn to…what? Talk to his horse? Clean the tack that didn't need cleaning? If he had a dog, he could have a one-sided conversation with it. But he'd not gotten one because it reminded him of how Max brightened whenever he was around dogs, cats or literally any animal within view.

There were still some further repairs to be made around the place, but those would have to wait until the weather improved and at least some of the snow melted.

Acknowledging to himself that he was in full-on avoidance mode, he passed the next few minutes doing odds and ends that he couldn't even really remember once he'd done them. Bracing his hands against one of the stalls, he heaved a deep sigh. Why was he out here like a scared chicken when he could be warm and comfortable in his house?

Just apologize and get it over with.

Tired of being so tense and edgy, he returned to the back deck and scooped the steaks and potatoes onto a platter. After beating the snow off his boots, he stepped into the house.

As he entered the kitchen, he noticed Maya had resumed her spot on the couch and appeared to be hard at work judging by the scattered paper in front of her on the coffee table. She didn't even glance up at his entry.

"I made some steaks and potatoes," he said as he placed the platter in the middle of the kitchen table.

She looked up and seemed to be debating whether to decline his peace offering when her hunger evidently won out. As Gavin turned to retrieve plates from the cabinet, he found himself unexpectedly smiling. He didn't think Maya Pine was the type of person who could avoid food or talking for long.

He glanced at her a few times after she seated herself, noticing that she liked a lot of butter and pepper on her potato. Before taking a bite, however, she glanced toward the refrigerator.

"If there's something else you want, feel free." Being somewhat friendlier felt like stretching muscles that hadn't been used in months.

Needing no further prompting, she retrieved a bag of shredded cheddar cheese and covered the top of her buttery potato with it.

"Dairy fan?"

"Someday butter and cheese will catch up to me, but today is not that day."

He smiled at that though she was too busy

diving into her food to notice. That was probably for the best.

After they'd been quietly eating for a few minutes, he paused before looking toward the opposite end of the table.

"I'm sorry."

Maya looked up, a bite of steak on her fork.

"For being a jerk earlier," he said.

Maya nodded. "Apology accepted." And then she shoved the piece of steak into her mouth.

"That's it?"

She finished chewing and swallowed. "You do remember what I said about not holding on to things in the past, right? You apologized, I accepted the apology, the end."

He leaned against the back of his chair. "I've never met anyone like you."

"That's because I'm one of a kind," she replied, then offered up a mischievous grin.

He couldn't hide the smile that felt oddly natural in response to her comment. Maya didn't seem to pay it much mind though as she went right back to cutting her next bite of steak. He found himself watching her, envious of her ability to let the past go so easily. He wondered if she'd been that way her entire life or if she'd cultivated that mindset in response to something in her own past that had hurt her. He hoped it was the former because, from what he'd seen, she didn't deserve to be hurt by anyone. That included him, so for the duration of her stay he was going to do his best to be more than a grudging host. Who knew? Maybe if he engaged a bit more he'd learn how to cultivate his own ability to live in the moment, to only concern himself with things he could change.

To not feel so hollow all the time.

MAYA AWOKE IN the middle of the night, jerked to consciousness by a loud noise. Her heart thumped hard in her chest, and it took her a few moments to realize it was because she'd been dreaming. But already the dream was fading and she wasn't sure if the bang she'd heard had been part of the dream or what had yanked her from it.

In the next moment, a howling gust of wind rattled the windows. She sat up and looked out the window. It was still dark, and even if the moon was shining tonight it was hidden well behind the clouds that were dumping more snow on the world outside. Even though she couldn't see far, she was able to make out the fat flakes of snow blowing nearly horizontal at a fast clip. She wondered if the wind had blown something into the side of the house, and that's what had woken her.

The way things looked and sounded outside, it almost felt as if a world beyond the blinding snow didn't exist. That the entirety of the world lay within Gavin's house. She shook her head at the strange thought.

The sound of his door opening drew her attention.

"The storm woke you up too?" he asked. As he walked into the area lit by the small night-light in the kitchen, her breath caught. It might be a blizzard outside, but he was dressed as if it was summer, in loose shorts and a T-shirt that did amazing things for his upper body.

"Uh, yeah," she said, belatedly remembering he'd asked her a question.

He crossed the room and bent slightly to look out the window, then shook his head.

"Makes a person consider moving to Texas or Florida."

She finally shifted her gaze away from him and forced herself to focus on the snow again. Maybe it would cool down her thoughts.

"I wouldn't be the least bit surprised if a yeti showed up on your front porch."

"Well, that would give you a big front-page story."

"If he didn't eat us for a midnight snack."

"I guess you wouldn't have to worry about deadlines, then."

Maya snorted a laugh. "Or the owners constantly pressuring me to increase revenues. It's not as if I can suddenly double the population of Jade Valley."

She noticed that Gavin didn't respond. When she looked up at him, his face had taken on a tense, faraway look.

"Are you okay?"

"Uh, yeah. Would you like some hot cocoa? I don't think I'm going to be able to go back to sleep."

What had just happened? Had he suddenly remembered he didn't like reporters? But if that was the case, he wouldn't be offering to make her hot cocoa in the middle of the night. She decided to let it go, nodding instead.

"That sounds good."

Though he didn't ask for help, she followed him to the kitchen and pulled two mugs from the appropriate cabinet while he retrieved milk and cocoa. When he pulled out miniature marshmallows, she was surprised.

"Those I wasn't expecting," she said.

"I got used to them a few years ago."

Why did she feel as if there was a story behind that simple statement? But she didn't ask about it, not wanting to give him a reason to abandon the hot drinks and her, disappearing back into his room. She didn't know why, but she didn't feel like sitting alone in the quiet of a snow-hushed night. Even though she was used to a lot of human interaction in any given day, thrived on it, she oddly hadn't felt deprived the past few days with only short conversations with Gavin. But maybe she had reached her max of alone time and just wanted to be in the presence of another person, even if he wasn't the most talkative guy ever.

"Good thing because hot cocoa tastes exponentially better when topped by marshmallows."

Although they were both quiet as he made the cocoa and poured it into the mugs she'd set out, it wasn't an uncomfortable silence. Quite the opposite. If she didn't know better, she'd swear they'd known each other long enough to be content to be in each other's presence without the need for conversation.

After Gavin topped both drinks with a generous amount of tiny marshmallows, he took his mug and headed for the living room. To her surprise, he sank onto the couch. He'd not sat there since her arrival in his home, and she was left wondering if she should sit in his recliner or act as if nothing was different and sink onto the opposite end of the couch. She decided on the latter, as much to convince herself that Gavin's very male presence didn't bother her as for any other reason.

"Umm, this hits the spot," she said after taking her first drink.

He made one of those sounds of agreement he tended to use more often than actually speaking. It was interesting to her how quickly she'd grown used to them.

But then he did say, "Seemed like a better idea than coffee at this hour."

"Yeah, though you're probably going to need a lot of coffee in a few hours."

"Yeah."

"What do you think the noise was?"

"The wind's pretty fierce right now, so it probably caught something that wasn't secured well and tossed it against the house."

Maya suddenly remembered the clothing she'd borrowed for the snowman and spun to look out the window as if she could actually see it.

"What little he was wearing is long gone now."

"I'm sorry. I should have brought the shirt and hat back in after you saw it."

"The loss of an old shirt and hat are worth the laugh I got out of your efforts."

"I'm glad." She paused, questioning whether she should voice her next thought. But now, in the quiet, dimly lit middle of the night, might be the only time he'd actually answer. And the more time she spent in Gavin's home, the more curious she became about him. Like why he had biographies of painters on his shelf but no paintings on his walls.

"I hope you don't mind me saying this, but it seems as if you don't laugh often."

She held her breath, hoping her observation didn't anger him or cause him to leave the room.

"Sometimes life doesn't give you a lot to laugh about."

"That's true."

He looked toward her, wearing an expression that said her response hadn't been what he'd expected.

"Don't look so surprised. Despite my delightful personality, I have not lived my twenty-nine years in unending bliss. Everyone's life has its sad or dark times. The death of grandparents, not having enough money, living in non-white skin in a country that doesn't have a good history with people who look like me."

Gavin took a drink of his cocoa and sat quietly for a few seconds afterward.

"Sorry. I must seem really self-absorbed."

She shook her head. "Everyone deals with the stuff life throws at them in different ways. Though I do believe in airing it, whether that's publicly exposing wrongs or talking through problems with friends."

Gavin grinned the slightest bit. "Subtle."

"That is one thing no one has ever accused me of being."

"I'm shocked."

Maya laughed and relaxed. While she hadn't known Gavin long, at the moment she felt as if she was hanging out with a friend. Granted, he would win the title of Best-Looking Friend, but a friend nonetheless. Or at least it felt as if they were on the road to friendship.

"Is that why you became a reporter, exposing wrongs?"

Maya knew she had to tread carefully with this topic because she still heard the doubt and suspicion in his voice. He didn't totally trust her, but he was at least making an effort. She respected that.

"Kind of. It was a mix of reasons. Writing was the part of school that came most naturally to me for one. And I find it easy to talk to people. My mom has always said I could get scarecrows to talk to me."

"That also would be front-page news. That or the plot for a horror movie."

Maya laughed. "My friend Sunny said something very similar once."

"She's the one who called to make sure I wasn't an ax murderer."

"Yeah. And the one whose family runs a ranch." Now that she thought about it, she'd bet that Gavin and Sunny's husband, Dean, could be friends. Dean wasn't a hermit, but he also wasn't a social butterfly. Sunny had pulled him out of his shell some, but he was also fine with his own company despite having been quite popular in high school.

Maya stirred her cocoa and took another drink. She glanced out the window at the frigid night before continuing.

"But, yes, I've used my writing to focus on topics such as injustice and corruption. I mean, I run a small-town paper, so it's not the same as covering national politics or corporate wrongdoing, but I have written about the time the former principal at the high school was caught embezzling and about BIA decisions and how they affect the reservation."

"Did you grow up on Wind River?"

"Yeah, and lots of my friends and family still live there."

"I knew a guy in high school who used to live there. I heard a couple of stories about encounters he'd had with people after he moved to Sheridan, the names he was called and how he was treated as less than." Gavin shook his head. "I don't understand people most of the time."

"I suppose how some of them act is a point in your favor for staying away from them."

He nodded once while staring at his mug. She got the feeling that while his body was seated not far from her, his mind was somewhere else entirely.

"I wasn't always this way," he said, surprising her and quite possibly himself.

Maya quickly tried to determine how to respond that wouldn't cause him to back out of saying anything further.

"We all change over time in response to things that happen around and to us."

"I guess so." He paused before continuing. "I was married before, but it didn't work out."

"I'm sorry." So many questions bombarded her mind. Despite Gavin being incredibly handsome and accommodating to her, she didn't automatically assume his ex-wife was the one at fault for the demise of the relationship. Maybe he hadn't paid her enough attention. Or he'd been grumpy then too, and his wife had grown tired of it. Perhaps they got married too young and grew apart. Marriages ended for a whole host of reasons, from the relatively simple to the spectacularly awful. Offering her condolences over something that obviously had affected him, even if he'd been at fault, seemed enough for her to do.

He glanced at her. "You're not asking questions."

"This isn't an interview. I'll listen if you want to talk, but it's your personal business."

He stared at her as if he'd stumbled upon a species of creature long thought extinct.

"You're staring and I know for a fact that I am not at my most stunning in the middle of the night." She punctuated her words with a little laugh, attempting to hide the sudden fluttering in her middle.

"I don't know. Don't they give models deliberate bedhead looks for fashion shoots?"

"Maybe if they're advertising lingerie." Did she really just mention lingerie while sitting in half darkness with an incredibly attractive man who had an equally attractive voice? Thank goodness the dim light would hide the unusual heat that had rushed up her neck into her cheeks. Maybe a hot beverage wasn't the best thing for her to be consuming at the moment.

He looked away, perhaps feeling awkward at the direction the conversation had taken. She resisted the urge to apologize, to bring more attention to what she'd said.

"Turns out my parents were right that she and I were too different." She recognized what the tone in his voice meant.

"Annoying when our parents are actually right, isn't it?"

The laugh that burst from him seemed at odds with the quiet of their surroundings, but it made her smile. Laughter helped get one through tough times and difficult conversations.

"You have no idea."

She mentally held her breath as she asked the next question, not sure how far she could go before he shut down or grew cold again. He was harder to read in some ways than many people she'd come across. Maybe that was one of the reasons he intrigued her.

That and, oh yeah, the hotness.

Stop thinking about how hot he is!

"Is that why you don't live near your parents?"

He nodded. "I know I made mistakes, but I really don't need to hear them saying 'We told you so' all the time."

"Yeah, salt in wound and all that."

"Bingo."

"Do you mind me asking how long you were married?"

"Three years. Been divorced for a little over a year now." Gavin shifted in his seat, and she thought he was about to stand and end the conversation. She noticed him wince as if he was in physical pain. But he stayed on the couch, and she wasn't sure if she should keep going forward with the conversation or change the topic altogether.

"I'm going to admit that I don't know what the correct response is to that," she said, hoping he appreciated her honesty.

"Better to say that than a lot of what I've heard from people."

"Things of the platitude variety?"

"So many platitudes."

"I personally think they should be out-lawed."

"I'd vote for that."

She drank the last of her cocoa and set the empty cup on the coffee table.

"Do your parents know why you decided to live this far away from them?"

"I've never come right out and said it, but they have to. Not that I talk to them that much. They've made their disappointment abundantly clear on more than one occasion."

Though he was the kind of strong, hard-working man she was used to seeing toiling on ranches all over the valley, she also heard a vulnerability in his voice that she'd bet a substantial sum he didn't know was there. She hesitated only a moment before she gave in to the impulse to reach over and place her hand over his where it was splayed atop his leg.

"I'm sorry," she said, echoing herself from before.

When Gavin looked up at her, there was something new reflected in his eyes. Some emotion she wasn't sure if she should ignore or be afraid of.

Or perhaps lean into.

CHAPTER SIX

As MUCH TIME as Gavin had spent working outdoors, in all kinds of weather, he had never been struck by lightning. But he wondered if it was anything like the sudden shock that jolted through his body as his gaze connected with Maya's in the middle of their dimly lit conversation. He barely restrained the urge to pull her into his arms and kiss her, which made zero sense considering he'd just been telling her about how his last relationship had ended. Plus, he barely knew her. Not to mention that he'd spent most of his time since meeting her wishing she wasn't there.

From somewhere among his scattered thoughts he remembered he should respond to what she'd said.

"Thanks." Then he shifted his gaze away, purposefully looking at the clock on the wall. "Well, I think we should both try to get some more rest. Hopefully the warm drink will do the trick."

His speaking seemed to remind her that her hand was atop his, and thank goodness she removed it before he had to awkwardly extricate himself. Her hand had barely ceased contact with his when he shot to his feet, too quickly. To try to cover up how quickly, he extended his hand.

"I'll take your cup if you're finished."

"Oh, thanks, yeah." She lifted the cup, which still had a few sips of cocoa in the bottom, no doubt cold now.

Was he imagining that she sounded every bit as awkward as he felt? Best not to think about it. Pretending that moment between them hadn't happened was definitely the wisest course of action, especially considering they were basically trapped together for at least a while longer.

He made sure not to walk toward the kitchen quickly enough to further give away how startled he felt. Instead, he tried to affect a sense of normality as he made for the sink and then as he dumped the remains of Maya's cocoa down the drain and rinsed the cups, leaving them in the sink to wash later.

Before he turned back around, he planned to say a simple good-night on the way to his bedroom. But Maya had already stretched out on the couch, covered herself with a quilt, and presented her back to him.

Had she seen his thoughts in his eyes? Had it freaked her out, especially after all the claims that she was perfectly safe under his roof? He shook his head. Hadn't temporarily losing any semblance of common sense once before taught him anything? Starting now, he needed to keep himself better in check. Maya Pine was not a permanent fixture in his life, so giving in to a momentary desire was a giant no-no. As the saying went…been there, done that.

He retreated to his room, but instead of lying down like Maya had, he sat on the edge of his bed thinking about how he'd spilled more details about his past to her than he'd meant to. But for some reason, she was easy to talk to. And he was beginning to acknowledge that she was not a heartless journalist digging into his life to satisfy some belief in her investigative skills.

The fact was he knew that all journalists were not the same, not even the ones associated with his ex-wife's family. No doubt their own livelihoods had been in danger if they hadn't done as they were told.

He lifted the framed photo of Max laughing while on the toddler swing at the play-ground. The hole inside Gavin's heart gaped wider. How he missed that smile, the sound of his little boy's laughter. He'd never forgive those who'd taken his son away from him.

After placing the photo back on his night-stand, he stretched out under his covers. The last thing he needed to think about if he hoped to get any sleep before dawn was Rinna, her family or what he'd lost. He was only beginning to reconstruct some sort of life for himself. Not exactly a happy life, but one that at least was his own and free from the influence of others.

The memory of the few times he'd laughed since Maya's arrival tempted him to believe he could actually live again instead of simply exist, that maybe he could find a new happi-ness. But he needed to brutally cull that idea from his thoughts. People were never what they first appeared. Maya might seem harm-less, friendly and fun-loving, but there had to be something lurking below the surface that would eventually ruin their tentative pseudo friendship.

Did you tell a not-quite-friend about your sad past? Granted, he hadn't told her the worst parts. After all, it was far from uncommon to meet someone who'd gotten a divorce.

Gavin rubbed his hands down over his face, wishing he could take back everything he'd divulged—the revelations about his marriage, his estrangement from his parents and especially that moment of attraction that had almost gotten the better of him. Maya hadn't even had to drag it out of him. He'd volunteered everything under the influence of hot cocoa, dim lighting and the novelty of having someone to talk to during a long winter night.

The only positive was that none of what he'd said was fodder for a news article. Not that he thought Maya would use anything he'd said to her advantage, but he was grateful none of the information he'd shared would be a temptation. After all, he wasn't famous, unlike the guy she'd been up on the mountain to interview.

If Gavin was Maya, he'd give that author an earful if she ever got to talk to him again. Because the man hadn't lived up to his end of the bargain, Maya had crashed her vehicle, nearly lost her life and ended up stuck in a stranger's house. A stranger who needed her to leave before she presented any more temptation.

He rolled onto his side, punching one of his pillows into submission and reminding himself that he was strong enough to resist temptation. If nothing else, all he'd have to do was think of Rinna and what she'd taken from him. He was never going to allow himself to be in that type of vulnerable position again.

MAYA BARELY SLEPT the rest of the night. Her mind had been too filled with a single question circling her brain like a satellite in orbit—had she really seen interest in Gavin's eyes or had she imagined it? Maybe it had simply been the way the faint light from the kitchen had lit his eyes and face because there was no way he'd be interested in the person who had invaded his home without warning. Right?

She shook her head as she rolled onto her back on the couch and stared at the ceiling that she'd begun to get used to seeing when she woke each day. It was best to pretend she hadn't noticed anything since there had likely been nothing to notice.

Then why had he retreated from the couch, the conversation and the room so quickly?

Ugh, this was one bad part of being an inquisitive person—the tendency to even grill yourself for answers.

No matter if there had been something in Gavin's eyes or not, the best course of action remained the same. So she got to her feet and began Operation Pretend Nothing Has Changed by folding the quilts and placing them at the end of the couch where Gavin had sat the night before when he'd—

Stop it!

She was allowing cabin fever, shared space with a good-looking man, her lack of a dating life and her mother's matchmaking efforts to erode her common sense. Gavin was her host out of necessity, nothing more.

When she wanted to avoid thinking about something, she focused her mind and hands elsewhere. So after setting coffee to brew and whipping up a couple of omelets, she parked herself back on the couch with her work spread out in front of her. By the time Gavin emerged a full half hour later than normal, she had eaten half her breakfast and was hard at work drafting her first piece on small-town journalism.

"This omelet is good," Gavin said a couple of minutes after he entered the kitchen.

"I'm glad you like it," she said, barely looking up from her work.

She noticed Gavin stayed in the kitchen, eating standing up at the counter instead of sitting at the table. He didn't approach the living room, and she couldn't help but wonder if he was in the midst of his own efforts to pretend nothing had shifted between them the night before. Even if she'd imagined the attraction, he might be regretting having shared bits of his past with her. Probably best if she didn't bring up any of the revelations either.

"Did you sleep at all?" Gavin asked after a long silence.

"A little, but my mind started spinning with work stuff so I decided to get an early start."

"You're going to hit a wall later."

"Nah, I'm good. When I get on a roll, I can work for a long time."

Was he buying any of what she was saying?

"Well, I'll leave you to it, then."

Apparently he was.

As soon as she heard his boots crunching in the snow outside, she let out a long exhale and collapsed against the back of the couch. She hadn't realized how tense she'd been until Gavin was no longer under the same roof as her. But the fact that he had acted as if nothing was different between them was a good thing. By the time he returned, she was determined to have all crazy thoughts purged from her mind.

Gavin didn't return for lunch, so she snacked on some cheese, crackers and part of a can of peaches she found in the small pantry. After checking the rest of the contents of the pantry, fridge and freezer, she decided to make spaghetti for dinner. But that could wait awhile. She returned to her work, fighting yawns and heavy eyelids throughout the afternoon.

To wake herself up, she bundled herself into her winter gear and went outside. A gust of cold air whipped around the end of the house, feeling like a slap comprised of ice crystals. How could Gavin stay out in this kind of weather all day? She knew ranchers and other people with outdoor jobs did it all the time, but despite being a Wyoming native she didn't think this weather was fit for man or beast.

She stared toward the barn but didn't see any sign of Gavin. When a twinge of worry tightened in her chest, she told herself to stop being silly. He was a grown man used to working in harsh conditions. And living alone, he likely was conscious of not taking undue risks. Grabbing the shovel she'd seen Gavin use to clear off the front steps and the short path to the woodpile, she got to work following the footprints he'd made earlier. The snow had finally stopped, at least for more than the short breaks they'd had so far, so she was able to see pretty clearly the route he'd taken to the barn that morning. The wind had partially filled in the prints, but they were still visible. By the time she'd shoveled only to the point even with the end of the porch she was already breathing heavily, and her nose was running.

"My nonexistent kingdom for a snow-blower." Evidently Gavin didn't own one or he would have used it by now instead of trudging through snow.

She looked up at the sky and saw more clouds moving to blot out the earlier brightness. It felt very much as if she'd done something to really tick off Mother Nature.

"Tell me what I did and I promise never to do it again," she called out while shaking the shovel at the sky as if that would do any good.

Receiving no answer, she sighed and returned to her task. She'd managed to carve a path halfway to the barn when she ran out of the strength and willpower to go on. Plus, after her near-death experience, the cold held no appeal. While shoveling she'd been thinking how sitting poolside on some tropical island with a fruity drink sounded great right about now. They needed reporters on islands, right?

But Gavin wouldn't be there.

Maya made a sound of frustration as she tossed the shovel down onto the snow in front of her. Why did she keep thinking of Gavin like he was a man?

Well, he is *a man.*

A very appealing man who had actually opened up to her the night before. Of course, he had seemed to regret it, so she needed to not put too much weight on his revelations. Or that might-not-have-actually-been-there look in his eyes as he'd held her gaze for a few moments longer than what occurred during a normal conversation.

New snowflakes started drifting through the air, causing her to shiver at the memory of the day she'd arrived. Was it just the fact that he'd saved her life that had her thinking of him in romantic terms? She didn't think so because her feelings had shifted gradually, at first without her realizing it. Sneaky little things.

And you can sort out your feelings inside the warm confines of Gavin's house instead of standing out in the snow, you fool.

She retrieved the shovel and returned it to its spot on the porch, then carried in enough wood to replenish the supply in the box inside. She felt sweaty after all the activity, so she decided to take a shower while Gavin was still away from the house.

Again she borrowed the clothes Gavin had let her use before while she tossed her dirty ones into a small load of laundry. While she waited for the wash cycle to complete, she returned to the couch to resume her work. She should really call the office to see how things were going, but she couldn't muster the energy to walk to the phone. Despite her outdoor time and the shower, she quickly started getting drowsy again. Maybe all she'd succeeded in doing was making herself even more tired.

She tried concentrating on her notes, deciding which section of her article to work on next, but her eyes kept drifting closed. Maybe if she rested for a few minutes, it would give her a needed boost. But as she leaned against the back of the couch and shut her eyes, she felt sleep pulling her toward its depths.

GAVIN SPENT MORE time away from the house than necessary. He'd made his check on the herd more leisurely than one in their right mind should considering the weather, then he'd ridden the property line just because. When the day began to wane and yet more snow started falling, he began his trek back up to the barn. Once inside, he also didn't rush in taking care of Jasper, who deserved some pampering, or the tack before he put it away.

Yeah, he was full-on avoiding Maya and the unexpected temptation he'd felt the night before. And tonight he planned to use the excuse of not having slept much last night to go to bed early. If he hadn't skipped lunch, he'd bypass dinner in favor of retiring even earlier. But his stomach had been growling audibly for a couple of hours, and there was no way he'd be sleeping without filling it.

Before exiting the barn, he paused in front of Jasper's stall, his hands gripped atop the door.

"You want a roommate for the night, boy?"

Jasper snorted and shook his head as if to say, "You're on your own, buddy."

"Well, you're no help at all."

Unbothered by Gavin's problems, Jasper lowered his head and began to nibble on the fresh supply of hay.

"Guess I'm not the only one who's hungry."

With a sigh and a renewed determination to act as if no suspended moment of staring had happened between Maya and him in those quiet middle-of-the-night hours, he headed out of the barn. Halfway to the house he stopped and stared at the path she'd obviously shoveled. Why in the world had she gone through that effort? Why would she even want to be out in the cold after what she'd gone through?

A twinge of concern had him following the new path the rest of the way to the house. He knocked the snow off his boots on the steps before crossing the porch to the front door.

When he stepped inside, however, he didn't find Maya in the kitchen or even with her head bent over work. She'd evidently hit that wall he'd mentioned that morning because she was out like a light on the couch, though at what looked to be an uncomfortable angle likely to leave a crick in her neck. He eased the front door closed and slipped off his boots beside it.

As he looked at Maya again, he couldn't help smiling. He imagined she'd fought falling asleep because her hand still held a sheet of paper and a couple more lay on her stomach. He wouldn't have been surprised to find them covering her face.

Despite his earlier determination to keep his distance, he found himself moving toward her. She was obviously a grown woman and could take care of herself, but a protective instinct that had been dormant for a while poked at him, even more so than when he'd found her nearly frozen to death in his front yard.

Well, she'd been a complete stranger then. And now…what exactly was she? More than a stranger, more than an unexpected or unwanted guest. An acquaintance bordering on friend? He sat on the sturdy coffee table facing but not touching her. Everyone looked a bit silly when they were sleeping, but if he was being honest she was pretty. Really pretty.

It was her bright personality and the way she looked at the world that made her even more attractive. Maybe that was what he'd been responding to the night before, the way she'd simply listened to him talk about his past without asking too many questions. To be truthful, although he regretted doing so it had felt good to say the words out loud, to let what he'd gone through exist somewhere outside of his head.

He should really move away and let her be, but a part of him he didn't want to examine too closely wanted her to rest in a more comfortable position. Would he be able to help her lie down without waking her? It was no doubt wiser to either leave her be or wake her just enough to tell her to shift to a position less likely to give her a neck ache later. Instead, he found himself standing and removing the papers she held, setting them aside on the coffee table, and then gently nudging her shoulder so that she slid down the back of the couch onto her side, her head against a pillow. Next he carefully lifted her legs by her ankles, aiming to stretch her legs out so he could drape a quilt over her.

Suddenly, she jerked awake and he stepped back so quickly that he tripped over the coffee table. He barely kept himself from tumbling backward onto his rear, but he winced when his calf struck the corner of the table.

"Are you okay?" Maya asked, moving as if to grab him to keep him from falling.

"I'm fine," he said. "I didn't mean to startle you."

Maya dropped back onto the couch and rubbed a hand over her face. "I…" She looked at the clock on the wall. "I didn't mean to sleep so long."

"You obviously needed it, but you were sleeping at an awkward angle when I came in. I was just trying to help you avoid a crick," he said as he pointed toward his neck.

In response, she rubbed her own. "Oh, uh, thanks."

He had stayed away all day to avoid awkwardness between them, so what did he do as soon as he came back? Put them in another awkward position. And if he retreated now as he had the night before, it would be even more obvious in the light of day, waning though it might be. Instead, he pointed toward the front door.

"So between your sleeping position and your sudden need to take up recreational snow shoveling, you must be angling for a trip to the nearest chiropractor."

Maya stopped rubbing her neck and looked up at him. "Hey, I was trying to do a good deed. And, well, I might have been going a little stir-crazy. With a dose of trying to stay awake thrown in."

"Why didn't you just go back to sleep this morning?"

"That doesn't seem particularly fair, does it? You go out into the dreadful weather to work and I lounge around in the warm comfort of your house, snoozing away."

Gavin crossed his arms. "You're not my employee, you know? You are not obligated to do anything here though I'd prefer if you didn't freeze to death in my front yard."

"Trust me, that will not happen. When I can go home again, I'm thinking about packing up a couple of bags and moving to Tahiti."

Gavin laughed. "I might have imagined a sunny beach in Mexico a few times lately."

"Probably a little beach bungalow where you don't have any uninvited guests."

"That's not what I meant." Okay, why had her comment bothered him? Didn't he want her to leave so he could have his solitude back?

"I know. I was just teasing."

Teasing. When had been the last time someone had teased him for fun?

He knew the answer to that, but he didn't want to think about Rinna right now. Or about...

No.

"Are you okay?"

He jerked out of his thoughts to find Maya looking at him with a concerned expression.

"What?"

She made a circular motion toward his face. "You looked as if you suddenly went somewhere else."

"Sorry. Probably hunger and my own lack of sleep catching up to me."

She shifted her gaze toward the kitchen. "I slept right through when I was going to make spaghetti."

"How about I toss a frozen pizza in the oven?"

"Better yet, I'll do that while you go shower."

He grinned a little. "Are you saying I stink?"

"Well, I didn't want to say anything..."

He let his mouth drop open in dramatic fashion, which resulted in Maya laughing. He couldn't say it out loud, probably shouldn't even admit it to himself, but he really liked the sound of her laughter. He didn't want to think about how he was probably going to miss it when she left.

CHAPTER SEVEN

EVIDENTLY ALL IT took to get past their awkwardness was some good-natured teasing and a dinner of cheap frozen pizza, for which Maya was immensely glad.

"I didn't think to check when I was outside earlier," she said in between pizza slices. "Did you figure out what caused the bang last night?"

Gavin shook his head. "Whatever it was has probably blown halfway across the state by now."

"Thank goodness it didn't hit a window."

"Yeah. Maybe I'll figure out what it was if something comes up missing."

The phone rang, startling them both. Only this time it wasn't the house phone but rather Gavin's cell, which was probably the least used cell phone she'd ever been near. Gavin froze when he saw the identity of the caller, his entire body going rigid. Without a word, he got up and stalked to his bedroom and closed the door behind him.

For several seconds, Maya simply stared in that direction. Not once since she'd met Gavin had she seen him that tense or with that kind of tight, stony look on his face. Even after she'd first arrived and he'd barely grunted at her, he hadn't looked as if he was wound so tightly he was on the verge of breaking.

Had it been one of his parents calling him? An unexpected call from an estranged family member might lead to the type of expression that had taken over his face the moment he saw who was calling.

Whatever the caller's identity, it was none of her business. And yet she found herself not only curious but hoping he was okay. Thinking about how alone he seemed to be in the world made her realize how much she took being close to her family for granted. So she ate her last couple of bites of pizza then walked over to the house phone to call her parents, to make sure they were faring okay after the storms.

"I hear you're stuck at Hotel Stranger," her dad said when he answered the phone.

"How much has Mom been driving you crazy with worrying about me?"

"Enough to send me out for more than one walk in this mess."

"Sorry, but I'm really okay."

"I trust you," he said. "You've got a good sense about people, and I figure if he posed a threat you'd simply knock him out with the nearest heavy object."

Maya laughed, then stopped herself. It felt wrong to laugh on one phone while Gavin was very far from laughing on the other.

"I was just calling to see how you all were doing."

"We're fine. Other than worrying, your mom's been cooking as if she thinks the apocalypse is on final approach."

After finding out her mom was next door at Maya's Auntie Fran's house, Maya had a good chat with her dad about the latest goings-on on the reservation, her idea to write about small-town journalism, and the latest good books her dad—a high school English teacher—had read.

"I'm not going to read any more by that St. Michaels guy though after he stood you up."

"Yeah, he's not high on my to-read list anymore either." Though, when it came right down to it, she would probably continue to read the series to hopefully get answers to her pressing questions. She'd just check them out from the library instead of buying them unless he contacted her with a really good explanation. The last time she'd talked to Janie, he hadn't yet called the office.

When she finished her call with her dad, ending with his promise to give her mom the full accounting of their conversation to help alleviate her concerns, Gavin was still shut away in his room. Considering he also hadn't gotten a lot of sleep the night before, it was possible he'd simply gone to bed. With that in mind, she quietly did the dishes and retreated to her usual spot on the couch.

But no matter how much she tried, she couldn't concentrate on work. Her gaze kept wandering to Gavin's closed door, wondering if he was okay. She resisted the urge to move closer, not to hear what he was saying but to simply know if he was still on the phone. Part of her wanted to knock on his bedroom door and ask how he was, but they were not close enough for her to do something like that.

And what if he wasn't okay? It wasn't as if she could comfort him without it seeming awkward at best. Or worse, weird and intrusive.

Unable to stay still, she crossed to the phone again and called Janie to talk about the next issue of the paper. Of course, the big story would be the weather, and she found out that there had been one house fire, a shed collapse from the weight of the snow and half a dozen car accidents, not including her own.

"April has been helping out where she can," Janie said, referring to the editor of the high school's paper who did some interning at the *Post*. "Nothing that puts her in any dangerous situations though."

"Good. The last thing we need is a liability claim."

"One other thing," Janie said, hesitation in her voice.

"What is it?"

"Mr. Clarke called and said he expected the storm coverage to improve our circulation numbers."

Maya sighed. "He realizes this storm won't last forever, right?" Though sometimes it felt as if it might. "No one is going to buy a subscription based on the coverage of one storm. At most we'll get a one-week bump in sales numbers."

"You know how he is. I just listened and 'ummed' in reply at appropriate points."

"I know it's not your job to deal with him.

Does he know I'm out of commission at the moment?"

"I simply said you weren't in the office and you were having some trouble with your cell. Thankfully, he didn't press for further details."

"I'll get back as soon as I can."

"Don't put yourself in danger. April and I have got things covered. I'd tell you to use this as a break, but I know you. I'd bet a substantial sum that you were working on something right before you called me."

"You make me sound like a workaholic."

"You *are* a workaholic. I sometimes worry for poor Blossom, that you'll forget to feed her."

"I would never. I love my kitty." Thankfully Trina had been willing to care for her cat while Maya was stuck away from home.

Janie chuckled. "Perhaps I was exaggerating a bit, but not much. You are always working. I bet you do interviews and write articles in your dreams."

The mention of dreams reminded Maya of something she'd forgotten. During her unintentional nap that afternoon, she'd dreamed about that moment on the couch with Gavin the night before, the one when she'd imagined him looking at her lips and wanting to kiss her. She'd dreamed that he actually had, and the memory of what his kiss had felt like in the dream sent heat rushing through her body.

She gasped a little and brought her fingers to her lips.

"What's wrong?" Janie asked.

"What? Oh nothing. I just…stubbed my toe." She winced at the lie. Not only did she hate lying, but it had been a pitiful one on top of that.

Before Janie could question the truth of her statement, Maya made a quick exit from the phone call. After hanging up, she turned so that her back was to the wall beside the old phone. How had she forgotten that dream? Maybe the way she'd come awake so suddenly to find Gavin next to her had startled the dream right out of her memory. Well, at least for a while, because now it kept replaying in her head.

She had no idea what kind of kisser Gavin was in real life, but in dreamland he was phenomenal.

To avoid having him come out of his room and find her cheeks on fire, she hurried to the bathroom and washed her face with cold water. Maybe she should have gone outside and stuck her head in the nearest snowbank instead. She shivered at that thought, of how she was never going to look at snow and approach winter the same way again. She had a whole new respect for how quickly it could snatch away a person's life.

As she stood looking at herself in the mirror, she realized she didn't hear Gavin's voice. Maybe she'd been right that he'd simply gone to sleep after his call. She hoped her phone conversations hadn't bothered him. Working on the premise that he was asleep, she eased out of the bathroom and back to the couch. But instead of returning to work, she sat looking out the window at the inky blackness of the night and the faint white of the snow under a cloudy, moonless sky.

She thought back over her conversation with Janie, deliberately shoving aside the part about Mr. Clarke. That was nothing new. What had struck her, however, was Janie's comment that Maya was a workaholic. That wasn't exactly news. After all, she didn't have much of a choice if she wanted to keep the paper going on limited resources.

Even knowing that, hearing it now had somehow hit her differently. Was she missing out on a lot of what life had to offer because she was always working?

She shook her head. Why was she thinking this way? She liked her life. Her job was one she enjoyed and believed in. She had good friends, a small and modest home at a decent rental price, and the most adorable kitty to come from the litter born on Sunny's ranch. And she'd survived her brush with death, fortunately rescued by someone who didn't have any ill intentions toward her. Even if her life had its frustrations, like everyone's did from time to time, she was fortunate.

And yet...

She glanced toward Gavin's closed bedroom door. Had she brushed off her mother's matchmaking and Sunny's teasing not because of her busy schedule but rather the fact that she was somehow unaware that maybe part of her life was empty?

And why was it occurring to her now? Here, in this place removed from her normal, everyday life? When she was forced to live each day in close quarters with a man who despite his proximity felt so very far away?

Maya wasn't sure she wanted to know the answers to those questions. She wasn't sure she was ready for those answers.

GAVIN SAT ON THE side of his bed for some unknown amount of time, feeling hollowed out
all over again. He'd at first panicked at seeing
Rinna's number show up on his phone, ter-
rified that something had happened to Max.
But when he heard her say she'd called simply to find out the name of a book his son
had liked being read to him because "he just
won't stop crying about it" and then she refused to let him speak to Max, he'd nearly
crushed his phone into a pile of plastic and
metal molecules.

He missed Max more than he would one of
his own body parts if it suddenly disappeared.
No matter how many times he went over and
over things in his head, he still couldn't believe that he might never see his son again.
At least not until he was an adult, and Max
might very well hate him by then or not remember him at all. Who knew what kinds
of thoughts Rinna was filling his head with?

As much as he hated to admit it, his parents
had been right about her. He'd just been too
blinded by her beauty, by her carefree nature,
by her pretty words of support for him and
his dream to realize none of it was real. But
by the time he had come to that realization,
it had been too late.

Noise from the bathroom reminded him that he wasn't alone in his house, that Maya's mind was probably spinning with questions regarding his abrupt departure from dinner. He was surprised by his urge to walk out of his room and confess everything to her, to see if it brought any semblance of the kind of relief he'd felt after he'd told her he'd been married before and about his rocky relationship with his parents.

But this was too personal, too raw. So he stayed in his room, avoiding her the way he had after thinking about kissing her the night before. He needed the snow to stop, to melt, so he could get her out of his house and out of his head.

THE ENTIRETY OF the next two days, Maya did her best to be invisible. She didn't speak to Gavin unless he addressed her first, but that was as rare as it had been that first day after he'd saved her. Her instincts told her that her peppy personality would not be appreciated in the aftermath of that phone call he'd received. And while she thought he might feel better if he talked out whatever was bothering him, she didn't broach the topic.

Instead, she focused on work, doing everything she could by phone to help Janie and April. Everything would be so much easier if she had a laptop and an internet connection, but she had to make the best of the situation. On the plus side, it had finally stopped snowing and the days were clear if still frigid. Even if nothing was melting, hopefully the county crews would soon be able to clear the road and she could make it back to town. Gavin would no doubt be glad to see the last of her and to reclaim his solitude.

As soon as she thought that, however, doubt pecked at her. She wasn't sure being out here alone was good for him. She knew that some people preferred it, but something deep inside her was saying it wasn't the best option for Gavin. Only the reality that they were not close friends prevented her from telling him exactly that.

Even without a computer, she was able to complete a lot of work while Gavin was out fixing a leak in the barn's roof. She'd gone outside once to make sure he hadn't fallen off, but watching him up there made her too nervous and she'd retreated back inside.

When she was satisfied with the work she'd completed, she busied herself fixing the spaghetti she never got around to making before.

There was no garlic bread or even seasoning, so they would have to make do with toasted sandwich bread to accompany the main dish.

As if he could smell dinner from outside, Gavin came into the house about five minutes before the meal was ready.

"Great timing," she said, trying to be friendly but not over-the-top chipper.

"It smells great in here," he said, sounding more like the Gavin she'd gotten to know before he'd received the mysterious phone call.

"It's almost ready."

"I'll take a quick shower unless you need some help."

"No, I've got everything covered."

With a nod, he headed into his room for fresh clothes, and a few moments later she heard the water in the shower turn on. It struck her how very domestic they seemed even though they were not a couple in any way.

As they ate dinner, Maya was glad to see that both Gavin's tenseness and the invisible barrier that had been between them since that phone call had eased. He was a bit more talkative, so she felt comfortable engaging him in more conversation.

"I'm glad you didn't fall off the barn today,"

she said, trying to make the true statement, a subject that had caused her worry, sound light and teasing. "I don't think I could have carried you to the house like you did for me. At best you would have gotten dragged through the snow."

"Snow down my collar as well as breaking my neck, sounds awesome," he said before taking a bite of bread.

The tone of his response was so unexpected that she snorted a laugh, then immediately covered her nose and mouth.

Gavin looked up from his plate. "Nice."

Then he gifted her with a smile that made her insides do somersaults. His smiles were like spotting a rare bird species. They made her feel as if the universe had allowed her to see something precious that few were ever fortunate enough to witness.

"What?" he asked, making her realize she'd likely stared at him too long without saying anything.

"You have a really nice smile."

The smile faltered and the fact that he looked flustered by her compliment was so cute that a flock of butterflies joined the somersaults. She should be embarrassed, but she wasn't. She was someone who believed in and told the truth as a rule, and what she'd said was the absolute truth.

"Um, thank you," Gavin said as he focused his attention on his plate again, spinning spaghetti onto his fork but not bringing it up to his mouth.

Realizing that he wasn't going to say anything else, she returned to eating her own dinner.

"Thank you," Gavin said again several moments later.

"You said that already."

"No. I meant for not asking."

She knew he was referring to the phone call and his reaction to it.

"You deserve your privacy, at least as much as I can give you while forced to stay here." It would have been easier to do so if she didn't have to sleep on his couch, but the house's second bedroom didn't have any furniture.

By him bringing up the topic of the phone call, she thought he might finally share who had called and why it had upset him so much. But he didn't, and she allowed the topic to drop. It wasn't her natural curiosity that made her continue to wonder about it, however. She found she was still concerned about him, about how he seemed to keep so much locked away inside himself. That wasn't healthy, but it was not her place to tell him that. If it was Sunny or Janie, sure, but not Gavin.

He was only a temporary fixture in her life. Now that the sun had replaced the snowy skies, it was only a matter of time until she was back to waking up in her own home each day. She loved Blossom, but her furry feline companion couldn't hold a conversation over the dinner table. Couldn't smile at her.

Couldn't make her feel as if her heart was ready to expand to include someone else.

CHAPTER EIGHT

HE'D BEEN WRONG about Maya. Gavin paused in his efforts to replenish the supply in one of the hay feeders and looked up at the clear blue sky. Common sense kept telling him that he was allowing himself to focus too much on the simple compliment she'd paid him, as if she'd been offering water to him after he'd crawled across a desert. But there was a part of him that really wanted to toss common sense into the nearest canyon.

The fact that she'd restrained what must have been a lot of curiosity about his behavior when Rinna had called and in the days afterward earned Maya a lot of his respect. What she'd said to him, about him deserving his privacy, had seemed one hundred percent authentic. So much so that for a moment he'd considered telling her everything. But he'd reined in that impulse, remembering that she wasn't a permanent part of his life. With the break in the weather, soon the road would be cleared and one of her friends or her mother would show up to whisk her away.

When she'd first awakened on his couch after collapsing, nearly frozen to death in his front yard, he'd wanted nothing more than his solitude back. Now there was a twinge of something uncomfortable in his chest when he thought of her leaving. It was a bit like coming out of a dark cave, experiencing sunshine like what shone overhead now, then being tossed back into the depths of the cave again.

He shook his head at that silly thought and refocused on his task. Now that the storms had moved on, the cattle had ventured out of the sheds along the edge of the tree line. Thankfully the temperature had not dropped into the danger zone for them. After all, they were hardier than humans when it came to surviving the elements.

A shiver ran through him as a gust of wind reminded him of that fact. His thoughts circled back to that day he'd seen Maya stumble then fall into the snow, and he shivered again. If he had not been where he was at that exact moment, she would have no doubt frozen to death. It was enough to make a person believe in fate or divine intervention.

As he went about replenishing the other feeders and ensuring the water supply was accessible, he really tried to focus on something other than the woman he'd come to expect to see at the end of each workday. It wasn't her cooking or cleaning that he appreciated most, though he did appreciate that she undertook those tasks even though he'd told her she didn't have to. Rather it was simply her presence.

She brought a brightness to his daily existence that he hadn't thought to ever experience again. And if he was being honest, he was attracted to her. He'd recognized she was pretty from the moment he'd placed her on his couch and worked to warm up her frigid body to save her. But as he'd gotten to know her, her kindness and laughter and way of looking at the world had made her even more beautiful.

The surprising truth was he was going to miss her when she left. He even wondered if he might find himself venturing into town more often on the off chance he might see her.

You could ask her out on a proper date.

He shut that thought down so fast he'd swear he heard the slam of the mental door. What Rinna and her family had put him through, what they'd taken from him was enough to ruin anyone on romantic relationships. What started out as great, what you could never imagine ending, did indeed end—and in a very painful way. Inviting that kind of experience into one's life again would be like escaping a wildfire only to jump into an active volcano.

No, it was for the best that once she left, he should make no effort to maintain contact, for her sake as well as his. Though he'd had preconceived notions about her based on her career choice, she'd proven herself to be a kind, respectful and fun person to be around. Fun. Yeah, he could admit that for the first time since his and Rinna's marriage had started crumbling, there had actually been some fun moments in his life following Maya's arrival. Watching movies, her streaking snowman, even her reaction when she'd realized he'd overheard her talking to her mother. He laughed a little at the memory of how big her eyes had gotten when she'd turned around and noticed him standing behind her a moment after she'd been teasing her mom about possibly dating him.

But then he remembered her mentioning

grandchildren and his heart seized up. He missed Max so much. His little-boy laughter and smiles, the way he'd crawl up into Gavin's lap so he could read him a story, how his weight had felt against Gavin's chest when he fell asleep there. It still didn't seem real that he was no longer a part of his son's life. The thought of Max growing up thinking his father had abandoned him made not only Gavin's heart ache but his very soul.

He was never giving a woman the opportunity to do that to him again. There was no way he'd survive it. As it was, he trudged through his days only because he knew Max would never want for anything. Rinna's family had enough money and influence to take care of countless children, so Max would never be hungry, never be without shelter, would go to the best schools and be able to start out his life several steps ahead. What could Gavin offer him other than a life of endless work and struggle? Certainly not a role model who'd been able to chase his dreams until he achieved them.

He shook his head, trying to clear it of the past as well as a future that could never be. Soon, Maya would be gone back to her proper place, and he could resume his life of putting one foot in front of the other as one day bled into the next.

GAVIN HAD GOTTEN used to his house smelling good when he came in after a day of work, but today the aromas were extra appealing because he smelled baked goods.

"Don't tell me you ran out of things to write and you've decided to start a bakery on the side," he said as he hung up his coat.

"No, today we're celebrating," she said as she spun toward the table with oven mitts on her hands and carrying a familiar-looking frozen package. "I hope you don't mind. I found this cobbler in the freezer, and since I didn't have anything to make a cake I baked this instead."

"Um, it's not my birthday." Not that she'd know when his birthday was considering he hadn't told her and hadn't left his driver's license out where she could easily see it.

"Nope, it's mine."

"It's... I'm sorry."

She looked at him with a slightly startled expression. "Why are you sorry? You couldn't possibly know when my birthday is."

"I'm sorry you have to spend it here, with me. I'm sure you had plans."

"I did not, in fact, have plans. I mean, I might have made some in the past few days if I was home, but I would have just as likely been working." She paused, as if remembering something. "I guess Janie was right. I am a workaholic."

"You even made your own birthday dinner. That doesn't seem fair."

"I got to stay inside this nice, warm house while you were out in the cold, so I'd say it's a good trade."

"Well, I guess my present to you will be to go remove the smell of cattle from myself before sitting down to dinner."

"Best present ever."

"Hey!"

Her laughter soaked into him as much as the heat filling his house. Wanting to evade that dangerous thought, he grabbed clean clothes and headed for the bathroom. Why, after everything he'd been through, was he allowing himself to be tempted by her? Especially after he'd reassured her and her mother that she was safe from any advances.

Still, he couldn't stop thinking about her and how cheerful she was, how she had been that way almost from the moment she'd awakened in an unfamiliar house. Maybe there were people like her in the world to offset the ones with negative attitudes about everything. He wasn't naturally a negative person, but the past couple of years had certainly chipped away big chunks of his ability to be positive.

He turned off the shower and ran his hand back over his head, sluicing water out of his hair. Though nothing could come of it, he realized how much Maya had given him something to look forward to each day. Just having someone with whom to share meals made him…happy.

When she left, was it going to feel as if something else had been ripped away from him? He pressed his hands against the wall of the shower in front of him. Why had he allowed himself to grow so used to her presence?

To be fair, he hadn't intended to. It had simply happened, little by little, escaping his notice until the knowledge that her leaving was going to create another hole in his life made itself known.

While Gavin was in the shower, Maya finished setting the meal on the table and topped it off with her hilariously bad craft project results. Granted, she'd had limited supplies, no more than pen and paper and a roll of clear tape she'd found in a drawer, but the little party hats made her smile.

She'd already received birthday calls from her parents, Sunny, Janie and even Trina, who assured her that Blossom was faring well and seemed to be perfectly fine having total reign over Maya's house.

"She has that on a normal day," she'd told Trina.

"And whose fault is that?"

"Guilty as charged."

When the water shut off in the shower, a surge of excitement went through Maya. Even though she knew it was unwise allowing herself to think of Gavin in any sort of romantic way, she couldn't seem to help it. And it wasn't simply how attractive he was, though that fact was so obvious it induced heart racing all on its own. No, it was more the way he'd taken care of her when she most needed it, how he didn't push her to leave before it was safe to do so even though he liked his privacy, and that he'd gradually warmed up to the point where they could even share laughter.

And that smile of his was like bright, warm sunshine. She got the feeling he hadn't showed it to anyone in a long time, so the fact that she'd been gifted it filled her with…how could she describe the feeling? She made her living with words, and yet she wasn't sure which ones could appropriately convey the warm, full, fluttery feeling that overtook her when Gavin smiled at her.

"Please don't tell me I have to wear that," Gavin said as he appeared a few minutes later.

Maya picked up the hat she'd made for him and held it in the palm of her hand as if it were a luxury item on display.

"It's a special, one-of-a-kind birthday hat," she said. "Not just anyone gets one of these, but I'll let you off the hook and you only have to wear it during dessert."

She placed the hat back next to his plate and took her own seat.

Gavin pulled out his chair, thanked her for making dinner as he did every time she did so, and started cutting up his pork chop.

"I'd forgotten these were in the freezer," he said.

"I had to chuckle when I saw them. They reminded me of my friend Sunny. It's a big joke that one day her dad will disown her because her family owns a cattle ranch but she's not much of a beef fan. She prefers pork."

"A brave viewpoint." In between bites, Gavin picked up his party hat and examined the little doodles she'd drawn on it.

"Pardon my amateurish artwork," she said. "My creative talents do not lie in visual art."

Gavin looked up at her with a questioning gaze, almost as if she'd said something surprising. She smiled in response.

"Not that I expect you to frame it or anything. If I had access to a computer and printer, I could have done a better job."

She took a bite of her mashed potatoes, then looked up to find him still staring at her.

"What?"

He shook his head. "Nothing." Returning his attention to the hat, he turned it slowly and examined each image. She knew the moment he got to the stick figure of him falling off the barn roof with a circle drawn around it and a line running diagonally to create the universal "don't do this" sign.

"Maybe it's not gallery-level artwork, but it's amusing," he said. "You should start your own comic strip in the paper."

"Hey, not a bad idea." She ran her hand through the air, palm forward, in the shape of a rainbow. "We'll call it the Bad Art page, and readers can submit their own work."

Gavin chuckled. "That seems like inviting disaster."

"You never know. Maybe it'll help get our subscription numbers up so the owners will stop bothering me every five seconds. Thanks, by the way, for allowing me to escape that for a while."

"Happy to serve here at Olsen's Retreat from the World."

"I like it. That's what Sunny and Dean should have called their place."

Gavin looked confused. "I thought you said they ran a ranch."

"Oh, they do. It's been in Sunny's family for ages, but when she married Dean—he's the ranch foreman and now part owner—he had lots of ideas for diversification to help provide a financial buffer against bad weather years or herd problems. And Sunny is like a geyser of business ideas. She's also a business consultant. Honestly, I don't know how they do it all and raise two little ones."

"It does sound like…a lot."

There it was again, that sound of distancing in Gavin's voice. Was he remembering his failed marriage?

"I'm sorry. I should be more careful what I say."

"Huh?"

"I didn't mean to bring up bad memories for you by talking about my friend's marriage."

He made a dismissive motion with his hand. "You didn't."

She wasn't sure she believed him, but she let the topic drop. When they'd finished the main course, Gavin surprised her by dishing up a generous helping of cherry cobbler for her.

"Too bad I don't have any ice cream on hand," he said.

"It's fine. If I ate that, I'd have to shovel your entire front yard to get rid of the calories."

Gavin snorted.

"What was that for?"

"Nothing."

"Oh no," she said. "You're not getting out of it that easily. Spill."

"Respectfully, you are nowhere near needing to lose weight."

"Yeah, because I didn't have buckets of ice cream at my disposal." Despite her making light of his comment, it had caused her skin to

tingle and grow warmer than could be attrib-
uted to the house's heating. "Now remember,
you have to wear the hat for dessert."

Gavin gave a dramatic sigh before placing
the sad little conical hat on his head.

"I'm not singing though. No one wants
to hear that, and we'd probably end up with
wolves on the front porch."

"Deal."

"NOT BAD FOR a frozen cobbler," Maya said,
drawing Gavin's attention from the stick figure rendering of Streaky the Snowman on
his hat. Without any sort of elastic or tie, the
hat had refused to stay on his head and Maya
had given her permission for its removal. He
smiled a little at the memory of how she'd
sounded almost like some fictional queen
granting her subject's request.

"I'm glad I hadn't eaten it before now so
you at least have something sweet for your
birthday. Sorry about no cake or presents."

"Don't worry about it. I'm alive to see
another birthday because of you, so I can't
think of a better present than that. And as
far as cakes go, I'll just be all pitiful when
I go into Trudy's Café next time and she'll
make something delicious for me. If I play

my cards right, I might get one from Sunny and my mom too."

"What was that you said about gaining weight?"

"Hush. I didn't ask you to make sense."

Gavin laughed then took another bite of the cobbler. As they finished off the entirety of the small dessert, he tried to think of something he could give her. But he had very little because of a combination of design and financial necessity. And the thought that he could give her a birthday kiss was all kinds of wrong. He didn't need that complication, and it went against his assertion that he posed no threat in that way.

While she might be friendly and tease him, he got the impression she was like that with everyone. She'd shown no interest in him other than as her savior and possibly as a friend.

Or had she? That night on the couch when he'd looked at her in the dim light… No, that had been all him. His attraction. His imagination. His almost mistake.

He insisted on clearing the table and doing the dishes. While doing so, he kept racking his brain for something at least remotely special to give to or do for her. He didn't think washing the dishes counted since they were his dishes in his house, after all. As he looked out the window over the sink, thankful to not see snow falling, an idea popped into his head.

After finishing the dishes, he went into his room and started digging through the boxes stored in his closet. Things he'd never unpacked after moving.

There it was. He grabbed a long box and heaved it over the other boxes, then pulled out the telescope. Even though it had been a gift from Rinna when they were dating, when she'd still liked romantic ideas such as looking at the stars under the wide-open Wyoming sky, he hadn't left it behind or gotten rid of it. He'd considered doing so but then stubbornly kept it, telling himself that while it was nothing compared to his son he wasn't going to let her rob him of one more thing.

He let out a sigh, shoving aside the telescope's origins, and carried it out to the living room.

"I don't have ice cream or birthday gifts, but how about we take advantage of the clear sky?"

"Oh, that sounds fun, even if it is freezing."

He retrieved an extra stocking cap and a hoodie for her to wear under her coat.

"Thanks."

Once they were both bundled up against the cold and Gavin had turned out the house lights, he carried the telescope outside to the end of the partial path Maya had shoveled.

"I really should finish this," she said.

"No, you really shouldn't. Just stay inside where it's warm."

"Says the man who ushered me outside at night as a present."

"We can go back in." He started to lift the telescope again, surprised by how good it felt to tease her. He'd once been that kind of person, quick to smile and prone to teasing. It angered him how much the past couple of years had changed him. Was it possible to reclaim some of the person he used to be?

But every time he wondered anything along those lines, he'd immediately feel guilty. How could he be happy and carefree when he couldn't even see his son?

"You okay?" Maya asked.

"Yeah." He had to remember how observant she was, guard against showing too much. She'd been respectful of his privacy so far, but there was always the possibility that she'd change the way Rinna had.

No, Rinna had always been self-centered and spoiled. But his infatuation had prevented him from seeing her for who she really was.

Enough of dwelling in the past. His life might never be the same again, but at least for tonight he could enjoy looking at some stars with a pretty woman. Even if nothing could come of it.

He found Polaris first, then Ursa Major, giving Maya a turn at viewing them before shifting to a new point of astronomical interest. When she was ready, he shifted the telescope to Cassiopeia.

"When I was little, I used to think this one was just a *W* and stood for Wyoming," she said. "It was about the time we were learning the states. But my dad's best friend set me straight. He taught an extra astronomy class at the high school we could get college credit for, so I took it when I was old enough. Dad's an English teacher. I don't think I ever told you anything about my family other than that Mom is overprotective and my brother is a *Star Wars* fan."

Gavin wasn't sure why she was telling

him now, but he found himself asking if her mother taught as well.

"No, not unless you count teaching people how to do home rehab or how to take their blood pressure. She's a home health nurse."

"Really? So is my aunt, Mom's sister. She lives up in Missoula." Why was he so willing to divulge personal information all of a sudden? Was the cold freezing his brain?

"Oh, that area is really pretty. I've only been there once, but I liked it."

Was the fact that Maya so easily shared information about herself what made him willing to do the same? Was breaking down metaphorical walls her superpower? That would certainly come in handy in her line of work.

But it also could pose a danger for her if she was too open with the wrong person, especially since she lived alone. At least here, with him, she was safe.

He jerked his attention away from her at that startling thought, thankful she was looking up at the sky and not at him.

After they'd located and viewed a few more celestial objects, he noticed Maya shifting from foot to foot and hugging herself.

"Cold?"

When she looked up at him, she wore an apologetic expression.

"Yeah. As nice as this is," she said, pointing at the telescope and then the sky, "I think I'm done. Another cup of hot cocoa sounds great right about now."

"Okay." Gavin only barely kept his voice from breaking at the sudden memory of the last time they'd indulged in hot cocoa. How many times had he replayed that moment in his mind, wondering what it would have been like to give in to his urge to kiss her?

He could do this. All he had to do was not sit beside her, not stand too close to her. If there was more than an arm's length between them, he'd succeed in resisting any unwise temptations.

"Great!" she said, sounding like a kid who'd been given permission to eat ice cream for breakfast.

Her joy made him huff out a single laugh. "Go on in. I'll be there in a bit."

Not only did he need to pack up the telescope, but he could use some time alone to shove all the romantic thoughts about Maya into some hidden corner of his brain where he'd forget about them and they'd dissipate for lack of attention.

But as Maya bounded up the steps and into his house, he was afraid that the attraction he felt had boarded a train that didn't stop at any stations and wasn't prone to derailment.

He sighed, his breath coming out in a visible fog. He didn't remember rational thought being something he had to part with in his divorce settlement, but it sure seemed he'd left it far behind.

CHAPTER NINE

CONSIDERING THE SITUATION, Maya thought it had turned out to be a pretty good birthday. She didn't have to cover anything for the paper, had enjoyed a good meal, gotten to do some stargazing and had heard more laughter from Gavin. She didn't examine too closely how she felt as if she'd received a burst of serotonin each time he laughed or, even more thrilling, smiled at her.

If she didn't know he had gone through what she gathered was not an amicable divorce, she might try out her rusty flirting skills and angle for a birthday kiss. Instead, she would be satisfied with sharing hot cocoa with him again.

He took a while coming back inside, and she figured he must have gone to the barn to check on his horse. She realized she had no idea if there were any other animals in the barn. She'd seen no evidence of such, and considering Gavin lived alone she doubted he had more than one horse. Despite what he had said, maybe she'd work off that cobbler the next day by finishing the path to the barn and then check out the only other building on the property. Exploring a barn wouldn't exactly be a great adventure, but it'd be something different.

When Gavin returned, she extended a warm mug toward him.

"Just put it on the table," he said. "I'll get it in a minute."

He disappeared into his room to put away the telescope, an item she'd honestly been surprised he owned. But lots of people had hobbies, and who knew? Maybe when she wasn't here he routinely pulled it out and watched the heavens.

He'd told her that he was different than he used to be, so maybe he hadn't enjoyed that particular hobby since his marriage had dissolved. She hoped he'd been able to enjoy their night of astronomy as much as she had.

Again, he took longer to return than she anticipated. Maya began to wonder if he'd fallen asleep, though she hadn't heard his door close. Curiosity almost got the better of her when she considered going to the bathroom to perhaps see more of the bedroom she'd only glimpsed once before. But she kept herself firmly in the kitchen, guessing that the bedroom was as sparsely furnished and decorated as the rest of the house.

She had no idea why, but something told her that even his bare walls were at odds with the Gavin of the past. In the wake of his divorce, anything bright or pretty probably didn't match his mood. Home decor was probably way, way down his list of concerns, if it made the list at all.

When he walked out of his room, he grabbed his mug and strode over to stand by the stove. She noticed he didn't make eye contact with her, once again seeming to put distance between them and not just the physical kind. The way he acted around her was a bit like a pendulum, swinging from quiet and distant to more open and fun, then back again. Was that part of his personality, or was she saying or doing something to cause the shifts?

Trying not to think about it too much, she carried her mug over to stand next to the stove as well. At least he didn't move away again.

"This is nice," she said. "A warm fire and hot cocoa are perfect for a night like this. Very cozy."

"Umm." Gavin's response reminded her of that first day she'd been an uninvited guest in his house, when he'd seemed like an anti-social hermit.

Maya didn't know how to respond, and that was so unlike her. But it suddenly seemed as if they had come to the end of available conversation, and that felt so odd. She almost always had something to say, or at least had a response at the ready. But now? Nothing. So she found herself staring at the stove, taking drinks of the cocoa, and feeling the awkwardness between them grow with each passing moment. How was that possible when they'd been laughing and enjoying the stars only a few minutes before?

She glanced at Gavin's profile and it struck her again how incredibly handsome hc was.

"Hey, let's take a picture," she said out of the blue, surprising herself as much as she appeared to surprise Gavin. "There are always pictures taken at birthday parties."

"I don't think two people make a party."

"Of course they do. All the best parties have two people."

What in the world was she saying? It was as if random words were attaching themselves to each other and launching from her mouth in an effort to make the situation even more awkward. She genuinely felt as if someone else had inhabited her body.

Rather than admit to the possible interpretation of what she'd just said, she acted as if everything was fine…until she remembered that she didn't have a phone anymore.

"Oh." She looked around the room as if a new cell phone might magically appear. "Never mind."

Instead of pretending his guest had not temporarily taken leave of her senses, Gavin retrieved his own phone from his room. But when she realized how close she'd have to stand to him for a photo, her pulse accelerated. She'd evidently left all her marbles out there under the snow with her bag and phone.

Gavin looked around the living area and the kitchen. "Sorry, I don't really have a good spot for a photo."

"Anywhere's fine." Maya moved closer to him, and she thought she detected his body growing more rigid. But it was too late to back out without it seeming extra weird.

She was careful, however, not to touch him. She was afraid actually making contact would allow for some supernatural transfer of her thoughts to him, and among all the current chaos in her head he might be able to detect how she was becoming more attracted to him each day.

When Gavin lifted the phone and focused the camera on them, she did her best to look her normal cheerful self, one hundred percent the fun-loving birthday girl. She deliberately focused on her image on the screen because if she looked at Gavin she would almost certainly reveal too much.

"One, two, three," Gavin said, then snapped the photo.

He did not snap a second one, prompting Maya to move away from him quickly. She barely resisted fanning herself because she felt really hot. She wasn't sure if the heat originated from him, the stove or from within her addled self. If Sunny could see her now, Maya would never hear the end of it. They would be doing crafts at the nursing home decades in the future and Sunny would still be cackling about how discombobulated Maya had gotten by simply standing close to a hot guy.

"Well, uh, thanks for a nice birthday," she said, not looking at him. "I think I'll turn in. All the festivities have made me tired."

Did her excuse to get away from him sound as fake as she thought it did? For someone who didn't like lying, she'd sure been tossing out some fibs to hide the truth of her changing feelings. If Gavin noticed, he thankfully didn't say so.

"Yeah, me too. Good night."

"Good night." She nearly dropped her face into her hands at how her voice squeaked.

This was one of those times she really wished the small bedroom across from Gavin's held something other than a few moving boxes.

As she lay stretched out on the couch a few minutes later, wide-awake, she mentally made her to-do list for the next day. It contained exactly one item.

Gather her scattered wits before Gavin realized that in her eyes he'd gone from the hermit who saved her to the handsome man she wanted to kiss.

SUNLIGHT BROUGHT SANITY. Or at least more of it than Maya had been able to muster the previous night. It helped that Gavin left the house extra early, before she'd even risen. She was going to consider the previous night a glitch in her system. Even though nothing had happened between them, the air had seemed thick with…wanting.

Wanting to know Gavin's full story. Wanting to understand what caused his mood swings. Wanting to figure out if she was really attracted to Gavin or whether the fluttery, heart-racing way she sometimes felt around him was simply a product of them being snowed in together.

And, yes, the wanting to kiss him that had sent her fleeing as far as the confines of his house would allow.

She rubbed her face vigorously with both hands. She didn't know if he would have attracted her so much if she'd met him in the normal course of her days. Doubtful since he would have probably just grunted a greeting and been on his way.

But by having to share his house, she'd had the time and limited space to get to know him better. At least as much as he'd allow.

Frustrated by her meandering thoughts, she tossed back the quilts and hurried through what had become her morning routine here—brush teeth and hair, make breakfast, eat breakfast, check in with Janie. She skipped the shower and any reporting work because she was getting out of the house for a while despite the cold. At least it was bright and sunny now, enough that the snow on top of the house was beginning to melt and drip off the icicles that had formed at the edge of the roof overnight.

She bundled up, including the hoodie and extra hat Gavin had given her to wear the night before, and headed outside for some wintry exercise. Before tackling the path, she used the shovel to knock off all the icicles she could reach so they didn't cause any damage.

Maya wouldn't say her shoveling task was fun, but it quickly had her warm enough that she didn't mind the cold so much. And it helped to clear her head. By the time she finished the path to the barn, she felt both accomplished and farther away from whatever had possessed her mind the night before, whatever had made her speak and act as if her neurons were misfiring. Her fondest wish was that it had not seemed as strange to Gavin as it had felt to her when it was happening.

She turned and looked back at the path. Parts of it had been covered in a thin layer of white from blowing snow, but it was much more passable than trudging through the fallen snow. She'd gotten warm while shoveling, but now that she was standing still the air made her shiver. She leaned the shovel against the side of the barn and hurried inside.

Since Jasper wasn't currently in residence, the barn was quiet. It was also surprisingly warm. Of course, the protection from the wind alone was a big plus. As she wandered through, she noticed things one would typically find in a barn—tools, horse tack, some hay bales, but no machinery.

During one of his more talkative evenings, Gavin had told her there was a shed down by the pasture where he kept a tractor and other equipment needed for taking care of his small herd of cattle. He'd admitted he hoped to gradually grow his operation and thus his income. From what he'd said, she gathered he was very careful with money and not prone to take on debt that wasn't absolutely necessary. It was a practical viewpoint, but like everything else about him she'd gotten the feeling there was more to the story. But she hadn't probed for more details. Letting him gradually become more comfortable with her and thus share details on his own, if he so chose, had seemed the better plan.

She paused at what was obviously Jasper's stall and considered all of her conversations with Gavin since she'd unceremoniously collapsed in front of his house. She had an innate sense of when to push for more information and when to back off, but she'd done more of the latter than typical when it came to Gavin.

It was strange how despite sensing there was so much more to his past, she'd felt protective of him instead of trying to get more information. She couldn't point to one thing that made her feel that way. It was more an accumulation of little things—how withdrawn he got at times, the occasional faraway look, what felt very much like a wall he'd built around himself, that phone call he'd received.

She spotted a wooden ladder leading up into the loft and decided to check out what she could see from the upper level. When she reached the top, she noticed miscellaneous, dust-covered detritus that she'd bet old Ansel Blackthorn had left behind and Gavin hadn't bothered to clear out.

Maya crossed to a window at the back of the barn and looked out. Unsurprising but nonetheless a bit disappointing, the view it afforded was simply more trees and snow. Oh well, at least it was a different vantage point. And to tell the truth, it was pretty. She wished she still had her phone for a lot of reasons, the ability to take photos among them.

That reminded her of the photo Gavin had

taken of them the night before. She'd been too flustered in the aftermath to ask him to email it to her. Maybe it was best that she not have that photo when she left. She doubted very much that being able to get back to her normal life included looking at Gavin's handsome face every five minutes.

When she turned away from the window, she spotted a thick cloth covering something next to the far wall. Since it wasn't covered by years of dust so that it looked gray, she assumed it must have been put there by Gavin. Curiosity drove her toward whatever lay underneath the cloth. She told herself taking a peek wasn't a big deal. It wasn't the same as snooping around his bedroom. It shouldn't be super private if it was stuck in the loft of the barn, and she was putting off going back to the house even though she could work on her article series or try to drum up some advertising for the paper. But today, she just wasn't feeling it.

Maybe because sitting in the house reminded her too much of all the little moments shared with Gavin and the temptation to assign way too much meaning to them.

She lifted away the cloth and was stunned by what she found. In this most unlikely of places was a painting with a deep blue background filled with twinkling stars and a shooting star so bright white it felt as if it might actually fly off the canvas.

When she pulled it slightly forward, the next canvas revealed a scene of dusk with a sky filled with blues, purples and a sliver of orange with a solitary dot of white to denote Venus.

In love with this artist's style and subject matter, she flipped to the next piece. The stars of Ursa Major stared back at her against an inky sky, and the painter had included a fine white line to illustrate the Great Bear around the constellation.

Maya experienced a pang in her heart. Had Gavin's divorce affected him so much that he didn't even want to hang these beauties in his home? Did they hold some sort of special meaning to him that brought up bad memories? If so, why had he kept them at all?

Though she was glad he had. She hated the idea of these paintings being thrown out in the trash.

Maya had her hand on the fourth painting, about to take a look, when she heard Gavin's voice. She quickly covered the paintings and walked over to the top of the ladder to find

Gavin staring up at her. When he glanced to the right, toward where the paintings were stored, his expression told her she'd made a mistake.

"What are you doing up there?" His voice was the harshest she'd ever heard it, enough to make her tense.

She pointed toward the window on the opposite end of the barn from the paintings.

"I came up to see what the view was like from up here."

His steely stare told her he knew, without a doubt, what she'd been looking at when he arrived. She had to navigate her way out of this like a ship exiting a rocky harbor in a storm.

"These paintings up here are really pretty. The comet one would—"

"Please come down."

Despite the look he wore, she was surprised by how abruptly he'd cut her off. But she'd been living off his kindness so she complied, wondering what she could say to make amends.

"I'm sorry. I didn't know they were something so private."

"The fact they were covered up in the barn loft should have been a clue."

Maya startled so much that it caused Jasper to sidestep. Gavin was quick to soothe the horse while not making eye contact with her. She had to press her lips together and inhale a shaky breath, then blink a couple of times against sudden and uncharacteristic tears. Gavin was obviously angry, and she had no one to blame but herself.

"I apologize." She wanted to say more, but the words refused to pass by the lump in her throat. Instead, she turned and hurried out of the barn and straight to the house.

When she stepped inside and leaned back against the door, she honestly thought she would give her next year's pay to have somewhere to escape to until she could figure how to turn back time or make things right.

GAVIN STOOD IN the same spot until he heard the door to the house open then shut. As he went about removing his saddle and tack then undertaking Jasper's after-ride care, he tried to calm down. He didn't know why he was so surprised that he'd found Maya snooping in his things. She was a reporter. He should have expected it. Now he wondered what else she might have gone through while he was away from the house.

He shook his head. No, she wasn't like that.

Or was she just really good at convincing him that she wasn't the kind of journalist who stuck her nose where it didn't belong? Was he destined to be a fool over and over again?

When Jasper was settled in his stall, Gavin knew the time had come for Maya to leave. He'd gotten used to having her around and so he hadn't checked on the status of the road, but he planned to correct that now. Bypassing the house, he walked to the end of his entrance drive to the road. He discovered that the lane going up the mountain had been plowed, which meant that the county snowplow would be coming back down the mountain in a while.

Perfect timing.

Even thinking that, he hesitated to return to the house, because he didn't know what Maya might say and how he would react. Instead, he headed back toward the barn. He grabbed the shovel Maya had left behind and started clearing enough of the snow in the driveway to allow his pickup to pass through to the road.

He half expected Maya to come outside to offer to help as a further apology, but she stayed in the house. That was probably best for both of them.

After he'd been shoveling for probably half an hour, he stopped to catch his breath and rest. In the distance he heard what he thought was the snowplow making its way back down the mountain. He glanced toward the house. Still no sign of Maya. She might very well be digging through his belongings while he was outside, sensing her last chance to do so.

You know that's not true.

Did he?

He closed his eyes and heaved a sigh. He wanted to believe he'd been right that Maya was different, that she was every bit the fun and kind person she appeared to be. Why had she found those paintings and replanted the seed of doubt in his mind?

Why had he kept the paintings? They were a painful reminder of what might have been but now would never be. He'd nearly burned them on more than one occasion, but something always stopped him. He guessed there was still enough of that once-held dream to have him shoving them into the hayloft of his barn rather than onto a burn pile.

It was fully dark by the time he reached the end of his drive and cleared it enough to be passable, including the pile of snow caused by the snowplow that had passed by earlier.

He was bone-tired and frozen despite wearing proper winter gear, and he suddenly didn't know if he had the energy to walk back to the house. But then he remembered the day Maya had arrived, how her steps had faltered and she'd collapsed, not able to move one more inch despite lifesaving warmth being within sight.

With that in mind, he trudged toward his house. When he came into view, he saw the lights filling the windows and Maya pacing the front porch. He stopped and stared. Was she worried about him, or was she waiting with another apology, hoping he'd forgive her trespass?

Could he? Maybe with time, but right now it felt as if she'd reinjured an old wound. It was time for her to go back to her world and leave him in his.

He knew the moment she noticed him, because she stopped pacing and stared straight at him, though she couldn't possibly make out more than his dark shape against the white of the snow. Having had enough of cold for the day, he continued toward the house.

"Go back inside," he said as he drew near.

To her credit she didn't argue and headed for the front door, leaving it unlatched for him. When he stepped inside, she was across the room scooping up bowls of what appeared to be vegetable soup.

"You should eat something and warm up. You've been outside for hours, and it feels like Jack Frost's posterior out there."

He heard the struggle in her voice to be amusing, but he wasn't in the mood for...well, mood lightening.

"I'll be taking you home in the morning," he said. "I don't want to chance the road being slick tonight, but the plow came by today."

"Oh, okay. Good."

Without saying anything further, he headed for the bathroom for a shower. As the water began to warm his skin and then his inner chill, he tried to let go of the anger that had gripped him when he saw Maya in the hay-loft and realized she'd seen the paintings. He knew she'd been about to say he should hang some of them in the house to cover his bare walls, but that wasn't happening. Keeping them at all was as much as he could bear.

I should have never encouraged you.

The memory of Rinna's words when he'd been declined yet another opportunity to hang his work in a gallery stung as much now as it had when she'd said them.

Your work is mediocre at best, but hot guys love to be complimented.

He sighed. What had he ever seen in her? How had she managed to fool him when she'd acted as if she loved him as much as he loved her?

He'd fallen hard and fast almost the moment he'd met her, and look where that had gotten him. As things now stood, he was really glad he hadn't given in to any of the urges to kiss Maya. But his judgment of people had to be questioned. Best to stay away from them as much as possible.

After his shower, he considered going straight to bed but his stomach felt hollow from hunger and a hot bowl of soup sounded good. He didn't plan to linger in Maya's presence, however. Beginning to sever that temporary tie was a wise move at this point.

Maya had covered his soup to keep it warm, but he resisted thanking her. That would invite conversation he didn't want.

"Gavin—"

He held up a hand. "If you're going to apologize again, don't. It's not necessary."

"I think it is because you're obviously angry and have every right to be. I'm truly sorry I let my curiosity get the better of me.

And since I'm sure you've wondered if I've dug through anything else of yours, please believe me that I haven't."

Despite his upset and his war with doubts, he did believe her. He nodded once then picked up his bowl of soup and a tablespoon.

"I would like to say one more thing and then I'll leave you alone," she said, staring into her own bowl of soup that she seemed to have not touched. When he didn't object, she continued. "I won't ask you to reveal anything to me, not about your past, the paintings, anything, but if you ever want to talk, you can contact me. I know that probably won't happen, but I have to make the offer. And this has zero to do with my job. It's me wanting to be a friend, even though I've probably ruined any chance of that."

She didn't wait for him to respond, either because she didn't expect him to or didn't want to hear a negative reply. Instead, she ate a spoonful of her soup then carried the bowl to the coffee table. He watched as she gathered the various papers she'd had spread out there, the only things other than her shoes and clothing that belonged to her. There was nothing to pack for her departure.

A pang of guilt hit him. She hadn't asked to

stay here, hadn't intended to wreck and lose everything she'd had with her. On the whole, she'd been a good houseguest. They'd almost parted on good terms.

Feeling confused by his back-and-forth feelings, he wordlessly carried his soup into his room and shut the door. He needed the barrier between them until he could have his home all to himself again. Needed the closed door to remind him not to make any more mistakes.

CHAPTER TEN

MAYA DIDN'T SLEEP a wink. She tried, but even dozing proved elusive. Her brain simply wouldn't shut down and let her rest. Instead, it kept repeating how she had ruined what had felt like an early friendship. All the thawing that Gavin had done toward her, how they'd grown able to laugh together, that was gone.

On the surface, what she'd done might not seem like a huge offense. But she'd still invaded a space that wasn't hers, and those paintings obviously embodied a story that Gavin did not want to share.

Giving up a few minutes before daylight started making an appearance, she moved quietly to the kitchen and made coffee and toast. She didn't think she could stomach anything else, but she needed the caffeine if she was to get through the day. It wasn't as if she could go straight to bed when she got home, not when she'd been away from the office for way too long.

She considered making breakfast for Gavin, but she wasn't sure he'd appreciate it anymore. If she thought there would be any passing vehicles at this hour, she would simply walk out to the road and hitch a ride to town. She'd never be able to tell her mother that or she might find a bunch of relatives dragging her back to the reservation where she would be guarded like an errant teenager prone to making bad decisions.

When Gavin emerged from his room a while later, Maya felt more awkward than she had that first day she'd awakened in a strange house with a man she didn't know. If only she hadn't crashed that day she could have saved both of them many uncomfortable and tense moments.

But she might never have met Gavin otherwise. Maybe that would have been a good thing.

"I'll be back after the sun has had time to hit the road for a while," he said before putting on his winter outerwear and stepping out the front door without breakfast or even a cup of coffee.

Maya sank onto the familiar couch and lowered her head to her arms that lay atop her knees. She hated so much that she had likely undone every positive step she'd made toward convincing Gavin that she wasn't like the type of journalists he disliked so much. She didn't even know what had caused him to look at her profession with such derision. There was so much she didn't know about him and now never would.

Her remaining time in his home crawled by with agonizing slowness, to the point where she thought she might go mad. If only she had a computer and internet access, she could occupy her time. But she was left with pacing, staring at the clock and mentally naming every resident of Jade Valley she could remember.

After about an hour of sloth-speed time passage, she decided to write Gavin a letter. There was a lot she still wanted to say, but when she was facing him and his stony expression she couldn't form the words. She wasn't sure he'd stick around to hear them anyway.

Ripping one more page from the notebook she'd been using to work, she sat at the kitchen table and stared at the blank page. Where to start?

After taking a while to consider what she wanted to say and how she should say it, she put pen to paper. When she finally finished, she folded the letter and slipped it under the loaf of bread on the counter. She didn't want him to find it until after she left. She honestly wanted to avoid seeing his reaction as he read her outpouring of regret and thankfulness.

Despite how she wanted to get the parting done and over with, it still felt as if it came too soon when Gavin returned to the house.

"The road appears to be safe now."

She didn't hesitate to stand up or put on her coat and gloves. They didn't speak as they walked to Gavin's truck, nor as he turned onto the road and headed down the mountain toward town. She'd never felt so uncomfortable in her life, so she stared out her window and tried to think of other things—seeing her cat again, how many long hours of work she had ahead of her after being gone for days, when she might be able to have her car retrieved and the damage assessed.

The silence between them was only broken when they reached town and she had to give him directions to her house. Too soon and yet not soon enough, he pulled into her driveway. Instead of immediately getting out of the truck, however, she sat for a moment with her hand on the door handle.

"Thank you for everything. And again, I'm sorry."

She didn't wait to see if he might say something in response. Whether words she didn't want to hear or silence, she'd rather not know. But as she stepped out onto her snowy driveway, she didn't hurry. The last thing she wanted to do at this point was fall, resulting in embarrassment at best and injury at worst.

After how he'd acted toward her since the day before, she was surprised he waited until she was at her door to put his truck in reverse. If she had not looked at those paintings, in this moment she would turn around and wave a goodbye. Because of that one error in judgment, she instead unlocked the door and slipped inside. She didn't even allow herself to look out the window to watch him drive away.

Her entrance woke Blossom from a nap atop the ottoman that was her favorite sleeping spot.

"Did you miss me?" Catching her unaware, Maya's voice broke at the end of her question. She pressed her lips together and blinked to keep from crying, but it didn't work.

She picked up Blossom and held her close as tears spilled.

"Why am I being this way? It's not as if we were in a relationship and broke up?"

But Blossom didn't have an answer to Maya's question, and neither did she.

AFTER PICKING UP some groceries and a pizza from Little Italy, the small carryout pizzeria, Gavin headed to his blessedly guest-free home. He would be able to kick back and relax the way he'd intended to do the night Maya had ended up on his couch nearly frozen to death.

He tried his best not to think about how dejected she'd looked as she'd walked from his truck to the front door of her little house. He told himself that he'd done nothing wrong and therefore didn't have to feel guilty.

Then why was his brain telling him that wasn't true? She was the one who'd gone snooping through his things, dredging up the past he was trying and failing to move beyond.

He hoped that the more distance he put between them, the less he would think about her. And once she was back in her normal routine, she'd likely forget about him too.

When he stepped into his quiet house, he realized that maybe distance wasn't the an-

swer to getting Maya Pine out of his thoughts.
More likely it was time because at the moment the quiet he'd wanted seemed too quiet.
He'd gotten used to Maya's bright chatter, her laughter, her—

Stop thinking about her!

He dropped the pizza box on the coffee table then took off his coat and boots. After retrieving a soda from the fridge, he kicked back in his recliner to watch TV.

As he flipped channels, he came across an old Bob Ross painting show. Of course he did. Did he burn down a village in a former life? It sure felt as if the universe delighted in poking him with sharp sticks.

He finally landed on some basketball highlights, but he found it difficult to pay attention. His thoughts kept drifting to Maya, to how she was no longer a fixture on his couch. There would be no more coming in from working all day to find her with papers spread out from one end of the coffee table to the other. No more sharing meals with her. No more unexpected funny moments like the snowman she'd built or silly birthday hats.

Having his space back was what he'd told himself he wanted, but now that he had that privacy it felt incredibly empty.

MAYA DIDN'T HAVE time to think about Gavin for the rest of the day, and yet she did. In between an interview with the head of the county road department about the state of snow removal, going to get a new driver's license, replacing other things she'd lost, and assuring her mother that she was back home safe and sound, memories of her time with Gavin assaulted her. The first time she'd heard him laugh, the way he'd fallen asleep in his chair while watching movies with her, how he'd pulled out his telescope to celebrate her birthday.

He must like astronomy a lot to have a nice telescope and paintings depicting the night sky. It seemed strange that he'd share one with her but the other drove a wedge between them.

She was so tempted to do an internet search on him, but she resisted. Her curiosity was what had ruined their budding friendship. So she focused on work, and when her thoughts strayed she dragged her attention back to work.

"Aren't you going home?"

Maya looked up at Janie's question. "Huh?"

"Home. I'll give you a ride since you don't have a car."

Maya looked toward the glass front door of the newspaper office and saw it was dark.

"I'm okay to walk."

"It's below freezing outside, and after what you went through—"

"It's okay, really. I want to finish up some things before I call it a day."

"Okay. Be careful going home. The way your luck's been lately, I feel like you might slip and crack your skull."

Maya laughed a little. "That sounds about right."

Though she did manage to get some writing and interview prep done, Maya wasn't anywhere near as productive as she would normally be. Fatigue and the inability to focus finally got the better of her. She logged off her computer and bundled up to head home.

When she opened the door, a blast of wind caused her to gasp. Though there wasn't any additional snow in the forecast, it certainly felt as if it could dump a few more inches. But the air didn't smell right for that, so this time she thought the meteorologists were actually correct. At least if a snowstorm came now, she wouldn't be stuck at a stranger's house or risk running off the road, seeing as how her car was still probably buried under snow up on the mountain. Tomorrow she'd have to check on that.

After what she hoped was a solid twelve hours of sleep.

But as she was locking the door, someone pulled into the parking lot. For a moment, she had the crazy idea that it was Gavin. Maybe he'd found her note and had come to apologize.

No, he didn't have anything to apologize for. He wasn't the one to go snooping through her personal belongings.

When she turned around, she found her best friend waving at her to get in her truck.

"What are you doing here?" Maya asked as she slid into the passenger seat.

"Girls' night!"

"Okay, I appreciate the thought but I'm way too tired for a girls' night. I could manage some takeout and a bit of chatting before I collapse in my bed though."

"You should have taken a break before coming back to work."

Maya laughed. "I've been away from the office for over a week. The last thing I needed to do was take another day off."

"Fine, takeout from Trudy's and a bit of necessary catch-up."

"What, do you need to tell me you're pregnant or something?"

"No! Whew, I think taking care of the twins, my job and helping Dean around the ranch is quite enough on my plate, thanks."

"Looks like I'm not the only workaholic around."

"Okay, I do work a lot, but I also know when to take some time off and enjoy life."

"Enjoy life." Maya snickered. "Is that what they're calling it these days?"

Sunny reached across the truck and swatted her, then pulled away from the newspaper office for the short drive to Jade Valley's little downtown area. Considering dining options were limited in a town of five hundred, it was no surprise that they'd opted for Trudy's Café.

"They should really open a place with drive-through service in this town so that tired people don't have to get out of their cars to buy dinner."

"Come on," Sunny said. "Stop being so pitiful. Who knows what interesting tidbits you might pick up while waiting for your order?"

Maya stuck her tongue out at Sunny but mentally acknowledged the truth of what she'd said. Trudy's Café and Alma's Diner, which sat directly across the street, were the hubs of gossip in Jade Valley. Trudy and Alma themselves provided some of that gossip via their longstanding feud. Maya figured her ultimate victory as a journalist would be to break the story of what had led to said feud because no one seemed to know and the feuding parties weren't telling.

She stifled a yawn as she got out of the truck and followed Sunny into the restaurant.

"Well, look who returned from the snowy wilderness," Trudy said as Sunny and Maya approached the front counter to order.

Maya laughed, unsurprised that word had gotten around about her predicament.

"I wasn't exactly roughing it in the wilds," Maya said as she grabbed a menu even though she could probably recite it. "The kindness of strangers is alive and well."

Even if that former stranger didn't think very highly of her now.

"You girls not eating here tonight?"

"No. Maya is a party pooper," Sunny said.

"I'm tired and will be lucky if I don't drop face-first into my dinner."

After Trudy took their orders and disappeared into the kitchen, Sunny turned and stared at Maya.

"So, why exactly are you so tired?"

Maya wasn't in the mood for the kind of teasing her friend was dishing out, but she also didn't want to act in a way that attracted the wrong questions.

"I didn't sleep well last night wondering if my car is salvageable and, if so, how much it's going to cost me."

"Are you sure that's all you were thinking about?"

"I'm sure I thought about something else at some point." Technically, Maya wasn't lying, because she had worried about her transportation issue. Getting around town she could do on foot or by riding with Janie, but she needed wheels to go farther afield for work.

Sunny placed her phone, screen up, on the counter in front of Maya and pointed at it.

"Is he part of the reason you couldn't sleep?"

The picture staring up at her looked like Gavin and yet it didn't. Instead of ranch attire, he wore jeans and a suit jacket paired with a pale blue dressy T-shirt beneath. He stood next to a familiar painting, the one of the falling star streaking across the night sky.

Though she didn't want to give Sunny any further fodder for thinking there was more between Maya and Gavin than there was, she picked up the phone and scanned the article that accompanied the photo.

The paintings were his.

Out of all the possibilities that had run through her head regarding why her uncovering the paintings had upset him so much, Gavin being the painter had not been one of them. The article was short, basically just one of many quick features on budding artists at an art show held in a hotel ballroom.

How had Gavin gone from aspiring artist to a rancher who hid away his work? Was it somehow tied to his divorce? Whatever the reason, it caused a tight knot in her middle.

"I take it by the look on your face that it's the right Gavin Olsen."

Maya handed the phone back to Sunny.

"Yeah, that's him. I won't even ask why you were looking him up."

"If the roles were reversed, you would have done the same thing."

"Probably, but then I also might not have had time because Dean would have found a way to get to you so you didn't have to stay in the house of someone you didn't know."

"Surely you got to know him over the course of your stay."

"Enough to say hello if I see him, but I wouldn't say we're besties."

"Of course not. That's my title."

"I was fortunate that he saved me and was kind enough to let me stay until it was possible to get back home."

Sunny was quiet for a moment while Maya examined the offerings in the pie case, wanting to take a pie to Trina as a thank-you for taking care of Blossom.

"What aren't you telling me?"

Maya feigned ignorance as she met Sunny's gaze. "What do you want to know?"

"Like how well did you get to know him? Did you all talk a lot?"

"He's not the talkative type." She had to give Sunny something or she would keep pecking away, but she didn't feel right sharing too much. "He's originally from up near Sheridan, is divorced, likes living alone and doesn't much like reporters."

"But you said you were getting along fine when I talked to you before."

"We were." No need to tell her that was no longer the case, especially since there wasn't likely to be any further contact between Maya and Gavin.

Trudy returned with their orders, and Maya

took the opportunity to exit the conversation by pointing at the pie case.

"I'd like both the chocolate meringue and the cherry pie."

"Whole or slices?"

"Whole."

"Okay, someone came home with an extra sweet tooth."

"The chocolate is for Trina for cat duty, but I fully intend to consume the cherry by myself. Call it self-pity for crashing poor Blueberry."

She really hoped her little blue hatchback could be fixed because she loved that car, the nicest vehicle she'd ever owned.

As Sunny drove them to Maya's house and they hurried inside out of the cold, Maya managed to keep the topics of conversation on anything other than Gavin. How the twins were doing, Sunny's latest business undertakings, the continued frustration of trying to keep the *Post* afloat and the owners happy.

"If anyone else were at the helm, I'm certain the paper would have shuttered long ago," Sunny said.

"Every community needs an actual news outlet to separate fact from fiction."

As they stepped inside, Sunny stopped to coo over the precious Blossom.

"Who's a beautiful girl? You are," she said to the cat.

"I'd think you get enough baby talk at home," Maya said as she dropped to the couch and tried to muster up enough energy to open her take-out container and the plastic utensils.

"Nope. I talk to the cows this way too."

Maya snorted. "Of course you do. For someone who not that long ago said she was an LA girl, you sure have rediscovered your love of ranch life. Of course, a certain good-looking rancher had a lot to do with that."

"That he did. And speaking of good-looking men…"

Maya pointed a seasoned French fry at Sunny.

"Stop. There is zero between Gavin Olsen and me. There will continue to be zero between us. Remember how I said he liked to be left alone? Yeah, that."

"Would you like there to be something?"

Maya sighed. "You've got romance on the brain."

"Hey, pickings are slim around here, so when there's a hot new guy who is also an artist—"

"He's not an artist. At least I saw no evidence of that." Which was true because while there were paintings tucked away in his barn, there had been no empty canvasses, no painting supplies, nothing to indicate he was actively still engaged in art. He'd probably tried his hand at it as a hobby but got busy with the business of making a living and set it aside.

But that didn't explain his reaction when he'd found her in the barn. That fact kept spinning in her head long after Sunny took pity on Maya for yawning so much and headed home.

The part of her that felt compelled to find answers warred with the part that didn't want to invade Gavin's privacy anymore and the substantial part that could no longer keep her eyes open. Still, as she drifted toward sleep, she thought of how Gavin was smiling in that news photo while standing next to the painting he'd created. She wondered where that smile had gone, and if there was any way of getting it back.

CHAPTER ELEVEN

GAVIN WAS GLAD to have his solitude back, but the problem with being alone was that he couldn't escape his thoughts. Despite knowing it was for the best that Maya was no longer a fixture in his house, it felt odd to step inside and not find her there.

But the end to their unexpected time as housemates was as necessary for her as it was for him. She had things to do, even if he didn't want to think about them, people who depended on her. Family and friends had worried about her while she was forced to stay with him.

He had none of those things, and it was a miracle his attitude hadn't siphoned away Maya's sunny personality. Instead, she had managed to cause his exterior to begin to thaw like the snow surrounding his house.

But had it all been part of a plan to soften him up? To get him to reveal more of his past?

Another part of his brain asked, to what

end? He wasn't someone famous. No one would care about what he'd said or done in the past. Any damage that a journalist could do to him had already been done. What he cared about most had already been taken away from him.

He crossed to the kitchen. Not feeling like cooking, he started pulling out the makings for a sandwich. When he lifted the loaf of bread, he disturbed a folded piece of paper underneath. He stared at it for a moment though he knew who'd left it there for him to find. And the fact that Maya had hidden it instead of leaving it out in the open meant she'd wanted him to find it after she left.

Gavin placed his hand on the paper, considering throwing it in the stove without reading it. What purpose would it serve?

Still, he couldn't resist opening the paper.

Gavin,
I don't really know where to start other than to say again that I'm sorry. I shouldn't have invaded your privacy the way I did. I let a weak moment of curiosity get the better of me, and I understand why that upset you after you had been so kind to me despite my in-

*trusion into your life and home. It was
not a way to pay you back for saving my
life. I don't think I'll ever be able to pay
off that debt. I know that I'll likely never
hear from you again, and that's understandable. But if you ever need anything,
you only have to ask. I owe you that. I
wish you all the best, and remember that
you deserve happiness.
Maya*

He reread the last few words—*you deserve
happiness*. They didn't make sense. He'd been
angry at her, was kicking her out of his house,
and yet she had taken the time to write that
to him. He stared at the paper, trying to un-
earth the hidden agenda. But the longer he
stared at it, the more his brain told him that
the words were genuine.

That still didn't change anything. They'd
gone their separate ways, and there was no
reason for them to interact in the future. But
even knowing that, he couldn't seem to erase
her from his thoughts.

Frustrated, he slapped together the sandwich and ate it while staring out the window at the waning daylight. He wondered
when memories of Maya would fade. After

all, they'd not had a relationship like he and Rinna had. But she was every bit as beautiful as Rinna, more so because of her personality. If Rinna had never entered his life and he'd met Maya instead, he might have asked her out. He wouldn't have had the baggage of hating her career choice. He wouldn't have so little to offer.

He sighed, wondering if he would always feel the same sense of emptiness that seemed to be a permanent part of him now. A void that for a brief time Maya had begun to make him think he could at least partially refill. Now that she was safely away from him, he finally admitted that a part of him had actually liked having her around—the part of him that remembered when he'd been more outgoing, had smiled more, had laughed. The part that Rinna and her family had damaged so much.

LIFE WAS BACK to normal. And normal meant Maya had spent the past week on the go from the time she woke up until she fell into bed at night. She and Janie covered their normal array of stories plus some spawned by the recent winter storms. She managed to wedge in necessities such as canceling the credit card she'd lost and ordering a new one, arranging for the recovery of Blueberry at the earliest available opportunity, and a quick trip out to Sunny's ranch for dinner.

It seemed Lily and Liam had grown exponentially in the short time since she'd last seen them. It made her wonder how much her aunts' grandchildren had grown since she'd been over to Wind River to visit family.

That was another thing she'd had to do, promise to visit the moment she had transportation again. Her mother had threatened to bring the whole family to Maya's house if she didn't, and she was certain not all of them would fit inside.

As she got off the paper's phone after talking with Angie about the total number of traffic accidents caused by the storms, her cell rang.

"Hey, Maya," Theo Kent said. "We can try to get your car now, but I need you to go with me to show me where to find it."

Since she didn't have any more appointments scheduled for that afternoon, she agreed to meet Theo in front of the office in five minutes. It only took about three before the tow truck sporting the faded text

Theo's Towing and Repair pulled off the road outside.

"Do you think enough of the snow has melted to get to my car?"

"Depends on where it's at, but I'm a bit of a miracle worker at towing." Theo gave her a big grin that made her laugh.

As they ascended the mountain road a few minutes later, however, she didn't feel much like laughing. She'd done her best not to think about Gavin, but it hadn't worked very well. It annoyed her, frankly, that someone she'd spent so little time with had affected her so much.

She was used to living alone as well, with only Blossom for company, and yet she'd found her house too quiet. It was as if it'd always been that way but she'd never noticed, hadn't minded. What was she supposed to do with the fact that she found herself missing someone who was glad to see the last of her?

Maya shook her head, trying to get rid of the nonsensical thoughts. She hadn't known Gavin long enough, didn't know him well enough to miss him. So why was her brain telling her that she did?

"Something wrong?" Theo asked.

"No, nothing."

But it was definitely something because her heart beat faster as they passed Gavin's driveway. Carrie Mason, the mail carrier for this route, was stopped at the end of his driveway, depositing that day's collection of mail. Maya deliberately shifted her focus to the road ahead so that she didn't miss where her car had slid into the trees. She hoped she could remember the right spot.

It didn't take long for them to approach a familiar-looking curve.

"Slow down." She looked down the slope on her right until she spotted a streak of cobalt blue against the white surroundings. A lot of the snow had melted in the valley, but at this elevation and in the shade a good bit of it remained. Still, enough had disappeared that her car was visible. "There it is."

"You sure are giving me a challenge today," Theo said as he eyed the curve ahead and how close it was to where he'd be working.

"I'll walk up above the curve and make sure anyone coming the opposite way eases around," she said.

"Thanks. That'll be safer."

With an orange flag in hand, she walked up the road a couple of minutes later as Theo maneuvered his truck into position.

"Be careful," she called back before she rounded the curve.

Theo waved and called back, "Always am!"

Maya didn't relish standing out in the cold, doubted she'd ever enjoy cold weather again after her near-death experience, but she also wanted her car back in hopefully a fixable form. So she danced from one foot to the other to keep warm, even did a few jumping jacks since there were no vehicles within sight.

She wished she could see how things were going with her car, but she needed to stay where she was to ensure Theo's safety. She didn't want anyone rounding the corner, seeing the tow truck in the middle of the road and sliding off the edge in the same spot she had.

The sound of an approaching vehicle from the other direction caught her attention, but it never appeared around the corner. Maybe it was someone who knew Theo and had stopped to see if they could help out.

A few moments later, she made use of her flag for the first time, slowing down a shiny black SUV, the driver of which she didn't recognize. Must be another owner of a vacation home, which reminded her that she should try again to get in touch with Benjamin St. Michaels. She'd honestly forgotten about the man in the flurry of work she'd been tackling since her return to the office. But she should at least call and leave a message about why she'd not been reachable by cell in case he had tried to contact her. A little part of her wanted to send him her towing and repair bill.

She began to pace to stay warm, mentally going through her to-do list. When she turned to head the other direction, her feet and brain stopped functioning. Gavin stood facing her, and she wondered why until she noticed her purse in his hands. How had he found it? Had it been somewhere in his yard the whole time, covered up with snow?

He started moving before she remembered how. In fact, she stood still until he reached her.

"I thought you'd want this back," he said.

"Oh yeah, thank you," she said as she accepted the bag from him.

"I didn't look through it, but I assumed no one else's purse would be in the woods at the end of my property."

"I didn't think you had. Looked through it, that is." She lowered her head, embarrassed all over again about how they'd parted. She had no trouble digging for information when the situation warranted it, but his private life hadn't.

"If you're about to apologize again, don't."

Her heart sank because he had to have found the note by now, and evidently it hadn't helped.

Well, at least she had her belongings back, and if things went how she hoped, Blueberry would be fixed soon. She supposed that was about all she could expect.

Gavin turned so that he stood facing the opposite side of the road. Man did he have a great profile.

"I read the note you left." He paused for a moment, and she realized she was holding her breath. "Thank you."

She didn't know if he meant for leaving it at all, for what it had said, or if he only referred to one part of what she'd written, but she didn't ask. For someone who communicated for a living, presently she was without not only appropriate words but any words at all.

Gavin turned his head at the change in sound from around the corner.

"Sounds as if he's winching your car up now." He glanced back at her for a moment before looking straight ahead again. "You were lucky you weren't really hurt. Your car slid in between a lot of trees before it finally hit one."

"All things considered, I had a lot of luck on my side that day."

He only acknowledged her words with a single nod, but he had to know that she included his carrying her into his home as part of that luck. Despite the cold air, her face warmed at the thought of him carrying her in his arms. It was a strange thought as she'd been unconscious and frozen at the time. She wondered what it would feel like if she were aware.

"Good luck with your car." With that, Gavin turned and started walking back down the road.

Maya started to lift her hand in some subconscious effort to bring him back. For what reason, she didn't quite understand. All she knew was that there was an ache in her chest as he left. It didn't matter that the ache made no sense. It was there nonetheless.

He either managed to turn around in the middle of the road or backed the whole way to his driveway to avoid driving past her. That knowledge caused a pang of sadness.

Maya was still hugging her purse to her chest long after Gavin disappeared and Theo drove around the corner with poor dented Blueberry loaded up. She hurried around to the passenger side of his truck and got in quickly.

"I take it that was the guy you were staying with," Theo said, a teasing grin on his face.

Oh no, she had to nip this in the bud before the story got out of control.

"He was kind enough to give me shelter until the road was clear and I could get back home." She looked back at her car. "I would have rather not wrecked at all than have to impose on his hospitality." She made the entire thing sound as uninteresting and decidedly unromantic as possible.

"Seemed like a decent guy." Theo nodded at her purse.

"Yeah. I lost this that day while wandering through the snow, trying to find a place to get out of the storm. He found it once some of the snow melted."

"Lucky."

Maya made a sound of agreement then focused her gaze out her window as Theo climbed up the mountain in search of a good place to turn around. If only it was as easy to turn time around so that she didn't even try to meet with St. Michaels that day. If she hadn't been trying to race a winter storm, she wouldn't have had an accident, wouldn't have almost frozen to death, wouldn't have invaded the private world Gavin had built for himself.

And she wouldn't be wondering if she might have started falling for Gavin a little without realizing it was happening.

GAVIN THOUGHT PERHAPS he'd lost his mind. Instead of simply putting Maya's purse in the tow truck as the driver had indicated he could, he'd instead taken it to Maya. After escorting her out of his home at the first available opportunity, why wasn't he continuing on the path of avoidance? Why in the world had he wanted to see her?

When he'd spotted her pacing against the cold, he'd wanted to usher her back to his truck so she could get warm. He'd had the very protective thought that he didn't want her to ever be cold again. Almost dying of hypothermia filled her lifetime quota of being cold, in his opinion.

He'd had to walk away before he said something that would invite her back into this life.

He didn't want to cave to a weak moment, to what-ifs, and make even more mistakes.

When he reached the house, he didn't go in. Instead, he sank onto the edge of the porch at the top of the steps. He stared out across his property, trying to identify exactly what he was feeling and why. Was it frustration that he'd let a few days in the presence of a pretty, cheerful woman tempt him to try living again when he knew all too well how that had turned out before? Or was it that he'd tried to convince himself that he was fine with being alone, away from any regular human interaction, but he wasn't? Would he feel this same way if any other woman had collapsed in his front yard, leading to the same progression of events?

Had he been so angry at Maya for looking at his paintings because she'd uncovered something he'd hidden away or because it was her who'd found them? Again, would he have been as upset if someone else had discovered them?

He shook his head at his inability to answer any of the questions. Ironic that when he'd met Rinna and fallen fast, he'd thought he had all the answers without asking questions. Now all he seemed to have were questions with no answers.

CHAPTER TWELVE

"WHEW, ANOTHER ISSUE put to bed," Maya said as she leaned back in her office chair after sending off the latest issue of the *Valley Post* to the printer.

"I feel like a celebratory milkshake," Janie said from her own desk.

Maya laughed. "It's about twelve degrees outside, and you want ice cream."

Janie looked at her phone. "I'll have you know it's actually fifteen degrees."

"Oh, my bad. It's a veritable heat wave." At least with the blast of arctic cold, there wasn't any snow predicted.

The front door opened, sending a gust of frigid air through the office, making Maya shiver. An attractive, well-dressed woman holding the hand of a little boy stepped inside looking not the least bit happy. Whether that was because of the weather or because the boy was fussy, or for some other reason, Maya didn't know.

"Can we help you?"

The woman fixed her gaze on Maya. "I certainly hope so. Do you know Gavin Olsen?"

Hearing Gavin's name unexpectedly sent a jolt through Maya.

"Yes."

"Thank goodness. Where is his house?"

Maya stood and rounded the end of her desk. "Can I ask what this is about?"

The woman pointed at the little boy. "I'm here to give him his son."

His son? Was this woman his ex-wife? Maya had been in the woman's presence for all of thirty seconds, and already she couldn't imagine Gavin married to her.

"Uh, he lives several miles up the mountain on the other side of the valley."

The woman sighed. "You've got to be kidding me. He said he lived in Jade Valley, so I assumed his house was somewhere in this town."

The way she said "town" made her dislike of Jade Valley evident, as if it was beneath her. Maya knew nothing about Gavin's ex, but she pegged her as a snob. What had he seen in her? Had he become estranged from his parents over this person? Maya had so very many questions.

The boy fussed even louder.

"Can you be quiet for one minute? Good grief."

Maya was horrified by how the woman talked to her son. No wonder the kid wasn't happy. Even at his young age, he could probably tell his mother saw him as a nuisance. Without thinking, Maya stepped forward as if she might somehow rescue him.

To her complete surprise, when the boy saw her he reached out his arms for her to take him. And before she could fully register how odd that was for a kid to prefer a stranger to his own mother, the mother in question had basically shoved the boy at Maya.

"Here, maybe he'll be quiet if you hold him."

On instinct she picked him up, and he promptly put his head on her shoulder. Maya was liked by her aunts' grandkids and Sunny's niece and nephew, but this little boy's reaction was completely unexpected. She couldn't have been more shocked if the CEO of the biggest company in the country had walked through the front door and told her they were building a new headquarters in Jade Valley.

Maya reached up and patted the boy gently on the back.

"Listen," the woman said as if she was used to ordering people around and having them do her bidding, "since you know him and where he lives, and Max obviously likes you, can you drop him off for me?" The woman reached into a large designer bag and pulled out a legal-size envelope, then extended it to Maya. "Here are all the legal documents giving Gavin custody."

"What? Wait." Maya felt as if she was having a truly wacky dream. She looked at Janie, who looked every bit as stunned by what was happening as Maya felt. "Call Angie."

"Who's Angie? Does Gavin have a girlfriend?"

"Angie Lee is the local sheriff. I can't be responsible for a child being dumped at my place of business."

The woman made a face as if she was incredibly offended. "I assure you everything is perfectly legal. Goodness knows my legal team costs enough to make sure of that."

"Still—"

"I have a long way to go, and the sooner I leave the sooner I get back to some semblance of civilization." With that, Gavin's ex-wife spun and headed out the door.

Maya started to move to stop her. But what was she going to do, tackle the woman? She couldn't exactly do that while holding a child who had begun to sniffle as if fully under-standing that his mother didn't want him any-more.

"Angie will be here in a minute," Janie said as she hung up the phone. "She's just down the street."

Since the boy's mother had to take the time to remove several suitcases and the car seat and place them in front of the building, Angie had time to intercept her. The woman looked as if she might be the type to report Angie to the higher-ups for questioning her, but the joke would be on her. The mayor wouldn't like her superior attitude any more than Angie would. She'd picked the wrong place to try that attitude.

While Angie carefully read through legal documents, Gavin's ex, who Maya had now ascertained was named Rinna, called a mem-ber of her expensive legal team. She evidently heard something she didn't like from them as well and gave the person an earful.

Wanting to protect the innocent child from

as much as she could, Maya carried him into the tiny kitchen and checked out what food they had on hand that would be appropriate for a kid his age. She turned back around.

"Is he allergic to any foods?"

Rinna gave her an exasperated look. "No."

Maya's jaw clenched against the not-nice comeback that begged to be set free. Instead, she walked farther into the kitchen and eyed the bowl of fruit on the counter.

"Hey, Max, do you like bananas?"

He lifted his head, and his sad eyes broke her heart. But when he nodded slowly, she smiled and peeled the banana. As she broke off small sections and handed them to him, the tense conversation continued in the other room.

"Of course he wants him," Rinna said. "I don't think he fought for custody so hard for funsies."

Maya's heart hurt for Gavin. Now she was almost certain that phone call he'd received while she was staying with him had been from Rinna. And having witnessed the woman's attitude, it was no wonder Gavin had been in a foul mood afterward. This was why he'd basically gone into seclusion. He'd lost not only his wife but also his son. And after losing that battle, the victor now didn't even want the spoils of war.

Okay, terrible to think of a child that way, but sometimes ugly custody battles seemed to view them as such.

Although Maya was usually pretty happy and easygoing, when someone hurt a person she cared about she got really mad really fast. And even though she didn't have any sort of relationship with Gavin, at least not anymore, she did care about him. So it was all she could do not to walk out of the kitchen and give Rinna a hot, flaming piece of her mind. But she reminded herself that she did not, in fact, know the whole story, and she might do more harm than good by opening her mouth right now.

Instead, she did what she could to soothe and distract Max while Angie talked to Rinna and made a succession of phone calls, no doubt to other legal types and probably Gavin. Janie stayed out front to take care of any customers who came in. Maya hated that the newspaper office was likely going to be the center of the day's gossip around town. The fact that Max was evidently the child of the man Maya had been snowbound with for several days and now that man's ex-wife

was visibly upset at Maya's place of work...
that's what you called fodder for some mon-
ster gossip sessions over the tables at Trudy's
and Alma's.

Maya felt a headache forming.

When Max finished the banana, she tossed
the peel in the trash can and gave him a drink
of water. She turned her head toward the
doorway as Janie stepped inside the kitchen.

"How's it going out there?" Even though
Maya could hear a lot of it, some wasn't
clearly audible, especially Angie's phone conversations.

"That woman is a piece of work," Janie
said, obviously referring to Rinna. "But it
seems everything is legit."

"How could she get all of this settled without even telling Gavin?" Maya was pretty
sure this hadn't been the topic of the phone
conversation that had upset him so much.

Janie lifted her hand and rubbed her thumb
and fingers together to indicate money.
Rinna certainly had the look and attitude of
the worst kind of rich people. Certain types
could buy whatever they wanted, and the
rules didn't seem to apply to them.

Again, she wondered how in the world
Gavin had ever been married to that kind of

person. Granted, she hadn't known him long nor super well, but she trusted her gut that it was not a good match. Obviously, since they'd gotten divorced.

Angie stepped into the doorway a few minutes later, rubbing her hand back over her black hair, which was pulled into a ponytail. She shook her head as if she couldn't believe what she'd just gone through. Which was saying a lot considering her job brought her into contact with all types of people.

"Is she gone?" Maya asked.

Angie nodded. "As weird as this all seems, it's legal."

"Well, she's certainly not winning Mother of the Year," Janie said, keeping her voice low so she didn't draw Max's attention to the fact he'd just been abandoned by his mom.

Thankfully, he now seemed content playing with a promotional plush bear toy given out at the fall festival a couple of years ago. Since then, Maya and Janie took turns dressing their kitchen guardian in seasonally appropriate outfits. The little guy still wore a birthday hat and a tiny T-shirt with a cake on it for Maya's birthday, which she had ended up not even spending at the office. Or at home, for that matter.

"I can't reach his dad," Angie said.

"He's probably outside working."

"Which begs the question how he's going to care for a small child alone while running a ranch."

Maya's heart lurched at the idea that child protective services might get involved.

"I'll make sure he has help."

Angie and Janie both stared at Maya, surprise on their faces.

"I didn't realize you were that close," Angie said, her expression and voice full of unasked questions, not all of them professional.

"I just think someone has been through enough, don't you?" Maya pointed at Max's back.

And so she found herself a few minutes later securing Max into his car seat in the back of Angie's sheriff's department SUV while Angie loaded the suitcases filled with Max's things. Maya noticed the luggage was not the cheap kind you bought at a discount store. Neither were the clothes that Max wore.

Thank goodness the kid wasn't old enough to be spoiled by brand names yet because Maya very much doubted that Gavin could afford them.

Glad she'd been able to finish that week's

issue of the paper before Rinna had arrived, Maya tried to think of a plan to help Gavin as Angie drove them toward his house. She didn't know if he'd welcome her help or tell her he'd figure it out on his own. He'd have to hire a babysitter, and she could already imagine how uncomfortable he'd be bringing yet another stranger into his house.

Maybe it would be different if the person was hired by him instead of being foisted upon his hospitality, someone who didn't take up residence on his couch.

One thing was for sure—he couldn't take a preschooler with him as he worked with cattle, climbed atop barn roofs and such. Maybe Max would learn how to do those tasks from his dad one day, but he was still too young now.

As Angie turned into Gavin's driveway a few minutes later, Maya took a deep breath, attempting to bring a sudden attack of the nerves under control. This was not about her and Gavin. It was about the innocent little boy beside her and what was best for him and his father.

GAVIN MOVED THE blade of the chain saw, setting it against the log again. He'd felled the tree the day before, but he'd lost daylight before he could cut it into sections and then chop it up to add to his firewood pile.

Though spring was not far away by the calendar, it would still be plenty cold at this elevation for a good while. Movement out of the corner of his eye had him turning as he let go of the throttle.

Surprised to see a sheriff's department vehicle sitting in his driveway, he set the saw down and removed his safety glasses. A dark-haired woman got out of the driver's side and headed toward him. Maya had told him the local sheriff was a woman, and he suspected this might be her. But then he wondered why she was here. Had someone else gotten lost on the mountain and she was checking with the residents to determine if the person had been seen?

But when Maya exited the vehicle, his curiosity morphed into concern. His brain worked frantically to figure out what could possibly bring both of these women to his doorstep, at least one in her official capacity. Surely... He swallowed hard at the insane thought that entered his head. What if Maya had accused him of something? Theft of some item out of her purse or, worse, that he had made unwanted advances while she was a guest in his home.

That didn't seem like something she'd do, but how well did he really know her?

"Mr. Olsen, I'm Sheriff Lee."

"Is there something I can do for you, Sheriff?"

He glanced at Maya, but she was leaning into the opposite side of the SUV. It was hard to focus on what the sheriff was saying when his mind was screaming for an answer to what Maya was doing, why she was here with a police escort. When she stepped back, he couldn't believe his eyes. He was afraid to blink, afraid that if he did Max would disappear.

"I take it from the look on your face that you know the boy."

"It's—" He had to stop speaking to clear the sizable lump that had formed in his throat, and he blinked against tears. "My son, Max."

Maya stood still, holding Max where Gavin could see him, seeming to talk to Max while pointing at Gavin. Was she identifying him as Max's father? Had his son already forgotten who he was? That he even existed?

And why was Maya here at all?

"How?" It was the only word he seemed to be able to form.

As Sheriff Lee told him about what Rinna had done, he finally pulled his gaze away from his son. Even after everything Rinna and her family had put him through, what they'd taken from him, this felt surreal. And of all the places for Rinna to stop to find out where he lived and of all the people to leave Max with, it ended up being the newspaper office and Maya. He thought he might laugh if he wasn't so incredibly stunned by the turn his afternoon had taken.

"I checked all of the paperwork, made the necessary calls, and to my surprise all the t's seemed to be crossed and the i's dotted."

Gavin couldn't keep himself from his son any longer and started walking toward Maya. Sheriff Lee didn't stop him, probably figuring that any further necessary discussion could wait. Whether it could or not, it was going to have to.

As he drew close to Maya and Max, however, his son hid his face in Maya's neck, clinging to her like a koala. Despite knowing that Max might have forgotten him, Gavin wasn't prepared for the intense pain caused by his son's reaction to him, especially when he seemed to prefer the comfort and protection of a stranger.

But he reminded himself, yet again, that he was a stranger to Max now too. If he had memories of Gavin, it might take a while for them to resurface. His body filled with anger that Rinna had not even considered this possibility. He wanted to scream at her, but he was honestly afraid to initiate any contact for fear she'd change her mind and take Max away from him again.

"I'm sorry."

Maya's soft words drew his gaze to hers. He wasn't sure if she was sorry about what Rinna had done, what had happened in the past or the fact that Max preferred to stay with her rather than go to his father, but it didn't matter. In that moment, he was just thankful she'd brought Max to him and that she was taking care with his scared son.

"Thank you."

Maya's eyes widened a bit in surprise as she rubbed Max's back to soothe him.

"Maybe you could get his stuff out of the car while I take him inside and get him some milk?"

Though Gavin wanted nothing more than to pull Max into his arms, to hold him tightly, he managed to nod. As he retrieved the luggage and large bag of toys, Sheriff Lee extricated the car seat then followed him inside.

Once everything was shoved into a corner of the living room on the other side of the couch, he offered the sheriff a soda, which she accepted.

"Are you okay?" Sheriff Lee asked.

He watched as Maya helped Max drink a glass of milk.

"I still can't fully believe he's here. I feel as if I'm going to wake up from a dream any moment."

"I gathered during my checking on the validity of everything that you and your ex-wife did not part amicably."

"You could say that." He turned his attention to the woman. "How much detail do you need to keep from taking him?"

"Mr. Olsen, I have no right to take him unless I feel he's in danger. Considering the legality of all the paperwork and the fact that Maya vouched for you, I don't see any reason to question why Max shouldn't be with his father."

Maya had vouched for him? Even after how he'd treated her following the incident with the paintings? Had he been wrong about her?

Jumped to conclusions based on past experience?

Remembering the question the sheriff had asked him, he sighed.

"I made a mistake marrying Rinna, getting involved with her at all, but I was blind to that fact for a long time. And by the time I realized it, we had Max. Let's just say that Rinna has spent her life always getting her way, no matter if she was in the right or the wrong, and when it came to custody she got her way again."

"I won't ask you for anything further," Sheriff Lee said. "The way you reacted when you saw him versus how your ex-wife treated him tells me enough to believe he is better off here with you."

"Thank you. I appreciate that."

Her radio crackled to life and she headed out to the porch to respond. That left Gavin alone with Maya, the woman he'd kicked out of his home, and his son, who was now playing with a toy train engine that Maya had evidently retrieved from the bag of toys.

Gavin simply stared at Max, marveling at how he'd grown since he last saw him, saddened by how much he'd missed. Maya looked up and caught him watching but didn't seem surprised. She motioned for him to come closer but carefully, as if he was approaching a skittish kitten.

He wanted to race to Max, but he had to hold that impulse in check. This reintroduction to his son had to be done right, even if Gavin wanted nothing more than to hold Max close so that no one could ever take him away again.

"Hey, Max," Maya said gently, as if she dealt with children every day. "Do you remember your daddy?"

Max looked up at her, but when he caught sight of Gavin again Max moved closer to Maya, sticking to her side.

When Maya met Gavin's eyes, she had an apologetic look on her face.

"It's okay," he said, though it wasn't true. He'd fantasized so many times about reuniting with Max, having his son's eyes light up and his little legs carry him toward Gavin with as much speed as he could muster. That the fantasy didn't become reality hurt, but at least Max was here. They'd take all the time Max needed.

How he was going to manage taking care of Max and his work as well, he didn't know. But he'd figure it out.

Out of Max's line of sight, Maya motioned for Gavin to sit on the floor. He did so, thinking that perhaps if he didn't tower over Max it would help the situation.

"Hi, Max," Gavin said with a smile. "I like your train."

Max didn't respond other than to keep staring at Gavin.

"Can you say thank you, Max?" Maya prompted.

Instead, Max turned and hid his face between Maya's side and the back of the couch. Maya reached up and smoothed her hand over his arm.

"Sweetie, there's nothing to be scared of. You might have forgotten him because you haven't seen him in a while, but this is your daddy and he loves you. This is his house. Isn't it nice and warm in here? What a nice place to play with your toys."

Gavin's heart swelled and his throat clogged with emotion. As he watched Maya try to bridge the gap between father and son, he knew without a doubt that she'd meant every single word in that letter she'd left for him. And he'd questioned if she'd had a hidden agenda.

The front door opened and Sheriff Lee stepped back inside then looked at Maya.

"I have to go on a call and can't take you back right now," she said.

Maya waved to indicate that it was okay.

"We're fine here. Go do your thing, and be careful."

"Nice to meet you, Mr. Olsen," the sheriff said.

"You too, and thank you."

"Just doing my duty." With that she hurried out to her SUV and left.

"I hope you don't mind me staying until I can arrange for someone to come pick me up."

"No hurry, or I can take you home." He thought about the last time he'd delivered her to her house and how cold he'd been toward her. "I'm sorry about before."

"How about we agree that we're done with the back-and-forth apologies?"

"If that's what you want."

"It is."

He nodded.

"So, how about a tour?" Maya said in a chipper voice directed at Max. Without waiting for an answer, she stood and placed Max on his feet despite how he seemed to want to stay glued to her side. She did allow him to hold her hand as she led him around the combined living area and kitchen, pointing out the chair "your daddy likes to sit in" and telling Max that he must stay away from the stove so he doesn't burn himself.

Max put out one of his hands toward the stove, but not to touch it. When he felt the heat, he jerked his attention to Maya with an amazed expression on his face.

"It's hot."

"Yes," Maya said, nodding. "It's why you should never touch it. Don't even get close. If you are playing, don't forget, okay?"

When Max nodded, Gavin's breath caught. By agreeing, did he understand that this was where he'd be staying now?

Gavin's hope continued to build as the tour continued, then as he made dinner and the three of them ate. Max still stuck close to Maya, eyeing Gavin warily, but at least he ate and didn't seem overly scared. Small steps, Gavin supposed.

After dinner, they moved to the living room and Gavin scanned through the channels until he found the channel with animated content. He'd seen it before but had always flipped past it without noting the channel number.

He felt as if luck might finally be with him because the program that was on he remembered as one of Max's favorites. Was it still? The answer to that question came quickly as Max scrambled off the couch and sat instead on the end of the coffee table nearest the TV so he could be closer to the little cartoon bears on the screen.

When Max laughed, it was the happiest sound Gavin had ever heard. He glanced at Maya, who was also smiling. She gave him a thumbs-up, but what he really wanted was to hug her, to thank her from the bottom of his heart for bringing his son back to him.

The day must have been a lot for Max because after the program was over he crawled back up onto the couch and laid his head on Maya's lap. She looked over at Gavin with that apologetic look again.

He smiled, trying to let her know it was okay. He wanted Max to be comfortable here, and if Maya helped to clear that particular path, then he was grateful to her. It didn't take long for Max to fall asleep.

"I should have taken you home before he fell asleep."

"It's fine. We can go later. He'll probably stay asleep the entire ride there and back."

She smoothed Max's hair in the way a mother would do, and the action caused a strange tugging sensation in Gavin's chest.

"Why did you come here today?" he asked.

She nodded at Max. "He was very upset earlier when Rinna came into my office. For some reason he reached out to me, and I found myself wanting to give him some comfort. It felt as if his little heart was breaking, and…" She paused and took a deep breath. "Honestly, if I hadn't been trying to soothe him, I might have said or done something I shouldn't have."

"I'm sorry."

She smiled a little. "I believe we agreed to nix the apologies."

"You're right, but I feel I owe you one. I can't believe Rinna showed up where you work. What are the odds?"

"Well, considering there aren't too many options of places to stop in Jade Valley, the odds weren't that bad. They increased by virtue of the newspaper office being one of the first buildings you encounter when coming from that direction."

"I guess that makes sense." It still felt somehow cosmic that his ex had left their son with the woman who was tempting Gavin to open up, to maybe try really living again. Good thing Rinna didn't know that.

Maya grew quiet but he could guess the question uppermost in her mind—how he and Rinna had ever ended up married. Despite all Maya had done for him, he wasn't sure he was ready to share what an utter fool he'd been. Maybe someday he could have that conversation, but it wouldn't be tonight.

CHAPTER THIRTEEN

Maya had hoped that Max would warm up to Gavin as the hours passed, but it appeared that process was going to take longer than a single day. How did she know this? Because Max refused to let go of her as they all sat in Gavin's truck outside her house.

"Max, sweetie, it's going to be okay. Your dad will take good care of you." She glanced at Gavin, who sat with his head lowered in the driver's seat. She reached up from her spot in the back and gripped his shoulder in support. This had to be hard on him, having his own son forget him and cry at the thought of being left alone with him. But he seemed prepared to give Max the time and space he needed.

While that was admirable and showed he was a good father, it was going to have to be a delicate balance. Enough time and space to allow Max to gradually settle into his new living arrangements but not so much that the adjustment period dragged on too long. The sooner Max accepted his new life, the better for everyone.

But she also didn't want to further traumatize Max or send Gavin off with a wailing child. Who knew what Max had been through prior to his arrival that afternoon? For that matter, she didn't know the extent of what Gavin had experienced either. Her heart hurt thinking about how he had lost his son, what he must have endured leading up to that.

"Gavin?"

"Yeah?" He turned his head to look at her.

"How would you feel if I stayed at your place tonight? Help through the first night and while you go out to work tomorrow, and then help you arrange child care for after that?"

"You don't have to do any of that. You've done so much already."

"But I want to if you don't object to me being there. Maybe tomorrow I can talk to him more, make him understand. Everything is new today. Maybe after he's slept there, it will feel more normal. We can have you spend more time with him tomorrow, do something fun to show you aren't a threat."

Gavin finally agreed, looking more tired

than she'd ever seen him in their short acquaintance.

"Let me feed my cat and grab a few things."
Then she turned her attention to Max, who
had quieted somewhat to sniffles. "Max, you
see that house right there?" She pointed out
the window at her home, and Max nodded.
"That's my house. I'm going to go inside for
a few minutes to get some things I need, and
then I'll be back, okay?"

Max looked as if he might get upset again,
and it was all she could do not to pull him
from his car seat and into a comforting hug.
Instead, she pointed at Gavin.

"I bet your dad can find some music on
the radio for you to listen to until I'm back.
Maybe if you're really good he'll even sing
to you."

Gavin snorted. "No one wants to hear that."

Maya laughed, partly because it was funny
and partly to show Max that Gavin was a
good person, not someone he should fear.

"Can you be a good boy for your dad until I
come back?" She resisted offering him a treat
for good behavior. That could lead to a negative cycle of a child only being well-behaved
if there was some sort of gift or sweet treat
as a reward. Even if that might be the way

Rinna had parented, even if Gavin might be tempted to do the same to win over his son, it was a bad precedent to set, especially when Max wasn't her child and she wouldn't be responsible for him long term.

There was hesitance in Max's eyes as he glanced at Gavin, but then he nodded. Hurray for small victories.

Maya hurried inside, where she first fed, watered and gave Blossom some love.

"Sorry, girl, I'm going to have to be gone overnight, but I'm sure you'll rule your queendom well while I'm gone." As if to assure Maya that she, indeed, would be fine alone, Blossom only accepted a few head scratches before she strolled away.

Hoping that Max was still okay outside, she quickly gathered some clothes, toiletries and her laptop. When she returned to the truck, she was glad to see that Max was still okay. His little feet were even bouncing along with the music coming from the radio.

"Ta-da! I'm back," she said as she climbed in beside him, though part of her wanted to sit up front with Gavin, maybe even hold his hand to help give him strength to get through this.

That's not the only reason you want to hold his hand.

In the privacy of her own mind, she could admit that. When she'd seen him earlier, watched the raw need to hold his son but the strength he displayed to give Max the time he needed to hopefully remember him, her heart had filled with a lot of different emotions. But one of those was affection. And definite attraction.

No, she couldn't think about that now. At the moment, the most important thing was helping to reestablish the father-son bond. She'd never imagined being in that type of position, but for whatever reason existed in Max's mind she was his current safety blanket. His father had saved Maya's life, and this was the way she could help to repay Gavin.

By the time they reached Gavin's house, Max was fast asleep.

"Why don't you carry him?" Maya wanted Gavin to be able to hold his son, even if the first time was when the boy wasn't aware.

"What if he wakes up?"

The question hurt her heart.

"Then you soothe him, show him that you care about him and are a safe place."

"How do you know all this? You seem like a mother."

She smiled. "Watching my own mom, aunts and cousins with their kids."

She'd never felt left out by not having children of her own, satisfied with her single life and career, but now she experienced a little twinge of…what was that? Maternal instinct? The first tick of the supposed biological clock?

Or was she just in her feels because a cute kid had been taken away from everything he knew and then thrust into a situation he didn't understand?

What she soon realized was that she'd not been prepared to see Gavin holding his son for the first time in more than a year. Though it was dark outside, she'd swear she saw the glimmer of tears in his eyes. Thankfully, Max continued to sleep, because Gavin might actually fall apart if his son woke up and became upset by being held by him.

Maya blinked several times, holding back her own unexpected tears. This was like when she saw those reunion photos of military families that had been apart a long time. They punched her in the emotions every time, and she couldn't help tearing up.

She grabbed her bags and followed Gavin

into the house. When she stepped inside, he stood still in the middle of the living room.

"What's wrong?" She kept her voice soft so she didn't disturb Max's sleep.

"I know I should put him to bed, but I don't want to let go."

Maya placed her palm against his upper arm. "Just go in and stay with him. As you must remember, I know my way around."

He smiled at that. If the man only knew what power his smile held.

As Gavin disappeared into his room, Maya turned to stare at the couch.

"Hello, old friend." She chuffed out a small laugh, then tucked her bags away next to the suitcases holding Max's belongings.

After retrieving a glass of water, she opened up her laptop and worked some more on her small-town journalism series. She'd sent out a set of interview questions to other journalists she knew across the country—former college classmates and editors of weekly papers she'd met at a conference in Las Vegas a couple of years before. She was happy with how the first article was coming together.

Typically she was able to lose herself in her work, but she kept glancing toward Gavin's bedroom. He'd left the door open, but from her angle she couldn't see him or Max. If Gavin had closed the door, she would have assumed he'd curled up in the bed with his son and fallen asleep.

Probably twenty minutes went by before Gavin emerged but left the door halfway open. He moved into the living area and instead of sitting in his usual chair, he sank onto the opposite end of the couch from where she sat.

Maya set aside her laptop.

"Don't let me interrupt your work," he said.

Maya waved off his concern. "We sent this week's issue to the printer shortly before Rinna showed up, so I'm fine. How is Max? How are *you*?"

"He's still fast asleep, but I had a hard time pulling myself away. I'm still afraid I'm going to wake up to find this was all just a very realistic dream."

"It's real."

More like surreal, but he didn't need to hear that.

"Thank you for taking care of Max, especially after how I treated you."

"You had every right to be upset and to want your home back to yourself. I overstayed my welcome."

Gavin was shaking his head even before she quite finished speaking.

"No, I overreacted." He sighed. "Full disclosure, the paintings are mine. As in I painted them."

"Full disclosure, I know. But I didn't go digging myself, just so you know. Sunny did and found an article about a painter with your name at a Denver art show at a hotel."

"Ah yeah, I remember that day. I think I spent more on lunch than I made."

"What? How is that possible? Your paintings are great."

Gavin showed her a hint of a lopsided grin. "You don't have to say that."

"I'm not just saying that to be nice or supportive. I think they're beautiful."

"Too bad that was not a widespread opinion, especially after…" He trailed off, as if he didn't know whether he wanted to continue with what he'd been about to say.

"You don't have to reveal anything more." She said the words, even believed them, despite the fact that she was so curious her brain felt as if it was itching.

"But I feel this sort of combination of I want to and I need to." He looked toward her. "If you're willing to listen."

She nodded.

He shifted his focus to his lap, appearing to stare into the past.

"I don't know where to start for everything to make sense."

"The beginning is always good."

He seemed to think about that for a few moments before nodding. "That makes sense."

Still, he didn't immediately launch into any sort of "Once upon a time there was a boy who met a girl."

"When did you start painting?" she asked, helping him with a prompt.

"First painting was in high school, in art class. To be honest, I took the class for an easy A since the teacher was known to be a breeze. But I ended up liking it, and when I had time I kept painting. My parents didn't understand, so even when I started thinking I might want to do it for a living I didn't tell them, not for a long time. It was a hobby as far as they knew, one they said I had to fund with my own money."

Gavin picked at the edge of the couch arm for a moment before continuing.

"It's how I met Rinna. I went with a friend to Denver. Even though I was an adult, I was still living with my parents and working on the ranch. They thought we were going to a rodeo, and we did go to one, but I also went to an art show I'd seen people talking about online. I'd really had no exposure to that world in person, and I wanted to see whether it seemed like a good fit or if I felt horribly out of place and it would always be nothing more than a hobby."

"And Rinna was at the show?"

He nodded. "She was the most beautiful woman I'd ever seen in real life."

"She is indeed beautiful." Physically anyway. Her personality left a lot to be desired.

"She gave me no clue what she was really like then," he said, as if he'd read Maya's thoughts. "The combination of her looks and her telling me my paintings were great turned me into an idiot, and we eventually got married. Much to both sets of parents' displeasure, I might add. Mine knew what she was like the one and only time they met her, and hers let it be known that their daughter married way beneath her."

Gavin sighed and leaned his elbow against the armrest and his head against his palm.

"It's embarrassing to admit to all this."

"Love blinds people. You're not the only one and won't be the last."

"I'm supposed to take comfort in that, I gather."

"Yep," Maya said with a smile, trying to make this conversation easier for him by lightening the mood a tad.

He did smile, so mission at least partially accomplished.

"I guess all parents of daughters probably think the men who become their sons-in-law aren't up to their standards," she said.

"That was certainly true in my case. After all, I was a rancher and mediocre painter from small-town Wyoming."

"Sheridan's not that small."

"Compared to Denver it is, and not just as far as population goes. Rinna's family is wealthy, really wealthy. Ever heard of Zachary Communications?"

Gavin looked at her right as the stunned expression must have hit her face because he nodded as if acknowledging what she was thinking.

"Yeah, that's them."

"That's why you don't like reporters?" The Zachary family owned a media empire made up of newspapers, radio and television stations, and internet communications companies under their huge corporate umbrella. If media royalty was a thing, they would be the reigning monarchs, at least west of the Mississippi River.

"Not because they own newspapers, but what they did to me using all that ability to sway opinion. And though I can't prove it, I'm certain they paid off people to get the result they wanted when Rinna and I divorced—me completely out of her and Max's lives."

Maya turned more fully toward Gavin, pulling both of her legs up onto the couch and sitting crisscross.

"Explain what you mean by that." She winced inwardly at how she sounded a bit too much like a reporter in that moment.

But as he proceeded to tell her how an art show he'd lined up at a small gallery had fallen through at the last minute, how he'd had not one but two attorneys abandon him during the divorce and custody process, how a reporter had contacted him to supposedly do a piece on his artwork but it had really been a fishing expedition for information to use against him, Maya felt her anger building. Her hands formed fists as if she could punch those responsible for hurting Gavin and Max.

"I cannot prove any of that, but I know in my gut that Rinna's family was behind all of it. They did what they could to build a case against me getting custody of Max, not even partial, saying that I couldn't provide a financially stable environment that would afford him the opportunities that they could."

"Rinna agreed to all this? From what you're saying, you did nothing to warrant that treatment from her."

"I got her pregnant."

"What? She wasn't happy about having a child?"

"You could say that."

"Then why did she fight so hard to keep Max from you?"

"I never said she did, at least not at first. Rinna is spoiled. She's used to getting what she wants, and she said having a kid would cramp her lifestyle. But then when Max was born, she saw how cute he was and she went wild buying him little outfits and toys, taking pictures and posting them on baby social media places. I told her that I didn't want Max's face and identity splashed all over the internet for anyone to see, but she waved it off as me worrying for no reason."

"She treated him like an expensive doll she could show off to all her classmates who couldn't afford one."

Gavin fixed his gaze on Maya for a few moments before saying, "Exactly."

"Until she got tired of the new toy." How could a mother have so little love for the child she'd borne?

"When I dared to point out any of Rinna's faults as a mother, however, that just made her family more determined to be rid of me. And they made sure their money and influence made that happen. Literally no one was on my side. I didn't even feel like my attorney was, though he went through the motions."

"Gavin, I'm so sorry. Sorrier than I even know how to express." Maya glanced toward the bedroom before refocusing on Gavin. "How did she manage all the legal maneuverings to grant custody to you, then? It doesn't sound as if her parents are the type to change their minds or admit they were wrong about anything."

"I don't have any idea, and I honestly don't care as long as I have full custody now. They may have paid for everything to go her way before, but she was the only one granted custody. Not them."

"So she was the only one who could legally change that."

He nodded. "I guess they didn't count on her going against them at any future point."

"That's good news, then." And yet anxiety twisted inside her. She wondered if it did for Gavin as well.

Maya opened her mouth to ask one of the questions running through her mind, but then stopped herself.

"Go ahead," Gavin said.

"I don't want to be too intrusive." She was keenly aware now of why he disliked the media, and her career hadn't changed in the past hour.

"If I don't want to answer, I won't. But you can ask."

"Why did Rinna marry you?"

If her question was rude, he didn't act as if he thought so.

"Did she ever love me, you mean? She did a good job of convincing me she did, but then there was that whole love-making-me-blind thing. I think it was a combination of physical attraction and wanting to try out rebellion against her parents."

"Rebelling against people who give you everything you want doesn't make any sense at all."

"I can't disagree, but I've come to realize I don't understand a lot about how Rinna thinks."

Maya sighed and pulled one of the quilts off the back of the couch, balled it up in her lap, and only barely resisted punching it repeatedly. If she had known any of this when Rinna showed up at the newspaper office… No, it was better she'd not known, because she would have had a difficult time holding her tongue. By not knowing, she may have saved Gavin extra heartache.

Silence stretched between them as Maya let everything he'd told her soak in. She wondered if he was regretting opening up to her. He'd said more to her during this one conversation than during the entirety of their acquaintance prior to this. It was a good thing she was on the opposite end of the couch because the urge to hug him was strong.

"So, you gave up painting?"

He nodded. "Hard to put yourself in front of a canvas when no one wants your work and when your wife tells you that your paintings aren't very good."

"Count that among the things Rinna got dead wrong. I really liked the ones I saw."

"Maya—"

"I'm being completely truthful. I know different people are attracted to different kinds of art, but I think they're beautiful."

Just like the man who created them.

CHAPTER FOURTEEN

GAVIN COULD NOT believe what he was hearing, that someone actually liked his paintings. The work he'd almost burned in his rage and brokenness. But in Maya's eyes was an honesty so fierce that it jarred every cell in his body.

"You mean that." It wasn't a question because he already knew the answer. But he was still so stunned that he had to say it out loud.

"Don't act so surprised. I mean, I've seen some art that I think is hideous auctioned for crazy amounts of money. I like yours loads better. It's simple and yet really beautiful. The telescope makes perfect sense now."

"Yeah, I've always liked watching the stars. That was a benefit of growing up on a ranch, and living here. Wide-open sky without many lights."

"It's one thing my friend Sunny said she missed a lot when she lived in LA."

"Rinna didn't have any interest in astronomy."

"Yeah, well, Rinna's an idiot, and she doesn't know good things when they're right in front of her. Your paintings, Max," Maya said, starting to tick off items with her fingers. "You."

She didn't look at him when she said the last word. Was she embarrassed?

His heart fluttered, though not the same way it had with Rinna. That had been fast and all-consuming, but he had fought his attraction to Maya from the beginning. He knew that not all women were like Rinna, but he'd used the fear of making another mistake as a personal barricade against relationships. And though Maya was a journalist, she wasn't the type who would deliberately hurt people for a story or allow herself to be forced into doing so by higher-ups.

"You're…" He wanted to tell her she was awesome, but he still hesitated to say something so revealing. "Thank you. I appreciate you saying that."

Coward.

"Just telling the truth." She uncrossed her legs and spun so that she could stretch them out beneath the coffee table. "One more question."

"Shoot."

"Rinna was the one who called you when I was here before, wasn't she?"

The mere memory of that conversation caused his jaw to clench for a moment before he answered.

"Yes. I hadn't heard from her in months, and she called to ask what storybook Max was referring to that he wanted her to read to him. He was upset and crying, and she doesn't deal well with that. She knew I used to read it to him and called to find out the name." He leaned his head against the back of the couch. "After I told her, she still refused to let me talk to Max. She said it would just make him cry more, and if her parents found out she'd never hear the end of it."

"Yeah, I really, really don't like your ex."

Gavin actually laughed at that. "You're not the only one."

When Maya yawned, he realized how late it had gotten while they were talking. He couldn't remember the last time he'd talked so much. Even when he'd been married, before things had gone bad, he'd never had such a long conversation with his wife.

"We should get some sleep."

Maya nodded. "Good idea. It's been one wild day."

After taking a quick shower, he headed to his bedroom. He noted that Maya was already stretched out on the couch asleep. Before stepping into his room, he paused a moment to look at her. He'd felt more relaxed around her tonight than he had since they'd met. She was such a kind, caring and funny person that he didn't want to keep her at a distance anymore. Her willingness to help with Max, to listen as Gavin poured out the details of his past, made him acknowledge that he liked having her in his life.

What that meant exactly, he wasn't sure. But for the first time he thought perhaps he was willing to find out.

Gavin eased into his room and slipped into bed opposite Max. Though he was exhausted, he tried to keep his eyes open a while longer so he could watch Max sleep in the dim light shed by the night-light that had been left behind by the previous owner. He didn't want Max waking up to the type of darkness he wasn't used to in his bedroom back in Denver.

Though he knew Max was right in front

of him, Gavin was afraid to go to sleep. That thought about this being a dream wouldn't leave him be, even with common sense telling him that dreams were never this long, detailed or realistic. Despite that, a part of him that had lost Max before was afraid he'd open his eyes in the morning and find that Max was no longer there. Had never been there.

No matter his fears, sleep started to claim him. As he finally surrendered, he mentally whispered a prayer that his son would still be with him when he woke again.

And that he could figure out exactly how he felt about Maya and what, if anything, he was going to do about it.

MAYA JOLTED AWAKE, much like she had the night something had hit the side of Gavin's house. But this time, there was no storm blanketing the world with white outside. It took her a few moments to discern that it was Max crying. She jumped to her feet and hurried to Gavin's door but then stopped. Max was not her son, and Gavin's room was his personal space. She couldn't continue to be the shoulder Max cried on. He had to get used to being with his dad again.

As she was about to turn around and return to the couch, the door opened and she gasped. Gavin startled too.

"I'm sorry," he said.

"Don't apologize." At the helpless look on Gavin's face, she took pity on him. "Do you want me to help?"

"Do you mind?"

"Of course not." She reached out and squeezed his upper arm, then stepped into the room when he moved out of her way.

Max sat in the middle of the bed, tears streaming down his face. Maya's heart hurt wondering how long it would take for father and son to be comfortable with each other again. Even if Rinna's parents had been the driving force between separating Gavin from Max, Rinna was ultimately at fault and was the root cause of this middle-of-the-night meltdown.

Maya didn't want her anger at the other woman to show on her face, so she approached Max with a bright smile.

"Hey, what's all this fuss about?"

Max tried to crawl into her lap as she sat on the edge of Gavin's bed, but she didn't let him. Instead, she faced him and held his hands with hers.

"Max, there is nothing to be scared of,

okay?" She pointed at Gavin. "It's been a while since you saw him, but he's your daddy. He used to read stories to you, play with you, and he loves you a lot. He just had to be away for a while, working here to make a cool place for you to stay together. Did you know he has a horse named Jasper?"

Max wiped the tears off his cheeks and stared at her for a moment, then at Gavin, then at her again.

"Really?"

"Yes, really." She glanced at Gavin and smiled. "Why don't you tell him about Jasper?"

Gavin stayed where he was at first as he began to tell his son everything he could apparently think of about Jasper. As he drifted into talking about the cows, Gavin gradually moved closer. When he sat on the edge of the bed too, Max moved closer to Maya but didn't cling or cry. That was progress, especially when Max asked a couple of questions, like if he could see the cows.

"Sure, and as you get older I can teach you to ride Jasper. Someday you can have your own horse too."

Max's eyes went wide at that, and Maya

would swear she could feel the happiness radiate off Gavin in waves.

It was nearly four in the morning by the time Max drifted back off to sleep again.

"I think that went pretty well, all things considered," Maya said softly as she stood and stretched. Her back had been aching for a while, but she'd dared not move for fear of breaking the tentative connection between Gavin and Max.

"I can't thank you enough." Gavin speaking in a soft voice sent tingles running from her scalp all the way down her arms and spine.

Yeah, time to vacate the man's bedroom even though his kid was sleeping only a couple of feet away.

"You better try to get some more sleep," she said. "Can't have you falling out of the saddle into cow patties tomorrow. Well, I guess technically today."

Good grief, was she babbling?

"Anyway, good night. Again."

Get out of the room, woman.

She obeyed her inner voice and eased out of the room, closing the door behind her. Needing some hydration, either to drink or possibly pour over her head, Maya made for the kitchen for a glass of water. Maybe she should stick her head in the freezer instead because she felt way warmer than the wood heating should cause.

When she finally did return to her familiar spot on the couch, she knew she wouldn't be sleeping anytime soon. Might as well get some work done. It wouldn't be the first time she'd worked in the wee hours when insomnia struck. Granted, this was the first time she'd done so because of a man, but there was a first time for everything.

By the time the sun rose, she was finished polishing her first article in the small-town journalism series. She was quite proud of it, if she did say so herself. Her plan was to let it sit for a while though, until she had finished at least two more articles. She didn't want there to be any lag in content once she started publishing them.

Her lack of sleep was making its presence known, and since she didn't hear any stirring from the bedroom she curled up on the couch to grab a few winks.

When she woke up again, the house was flooded with sunlight and the smell of bacon frying made her stomach growl. She rolled over and spotted Gavin in the kitchen. Her heart beat a bit faster at the sight of his broad back covered by a Henley shirt above loose track pants. It was so unlike what she usually saw him wearing, but she liked it. He looked somehow at ease in the outfit, and he perhaps deserved to be at ease more than anyone she knew.

While he was still unaware, she resisted offering to help him and allowed herself to watch him instead, the way he moved, obviously trying not to make any more noise than necessary. She smiled at his consideration and realized she was probably falling for him. She couldn't help but wonder what he would think if she admitted that out loud. Would he push her out of his life again? She wanted to think the answer to that question was no, but she wouldn't blame him if it was yes.

Before, she'd wondered if it had only been their forced proximity that had caused her to be attracted to him. But after time away from each other, time in which she thought about him every day no matter how busy she was, it had become obvious that the proximity had only been the catalyst and not the sole reason.

As if her thinking about him caused Gavin to become aware that she was awake, he half turned to look in her direction.

"Did I wake you up?"

"Maybe, but that's okay." She lifted herself to a sitting position and smoothed her sleep-mussed hair. "Need some help?"

"No, I'm good."

He looked good too. The hard angles of his face had eased, and only now did she realize why they'd been there before. He'd been carrying his loss not only in his heart but within his entire body.

She glanced at the clock and noticed it was after ten. Luckily, she'd remembered to text Janie to hold down the fort once again.

After she took a quick shower and changed, she returned to the kitchen to see Gavin had prepared what seemed like a feast complete with bacon, eggs and pancakes. He caught her eyeing the array of food.

"Max likes pancakes. I used to make them and he'd gobble up the few bites I gave him. He'd end up a sticky mess, but grinning ear to ear."

She didn't have to be super intelligent to figure out that he wanted nothing more than to see his son happy again. And she wanted it for him, for both of them.

"I hope you don't mind that I didn't wake

you up earlier," he said. "I thought you could use the rest."

She placed her hands on the back of one of the chairs at the kitchen table. "So could you."

"I slept."

"Not enough."

He smiled, causing that fluttery feeling in her chest again.

"I've lost sleep for way worse reasons."

"I suppose that's true."

She heard the sound of little feet about the same time Gavin looked beyond her and smiled.

"You hungry?" Gavin asked.

Maya turned to watch Max, to see how he would react to his father now that it was daylight and he'd slept. For several seconds, he just stared at them. Maya held in her laughter despite the fact that Max appeared as if his wee mind was buffering. Finally, he nodded.

"You still like pancakes?"

Max's eyes lit up for a moment before he said, "Nana says I can't eat them."

Even though she wasn't looking at him, Maya sensed Gavin going rigid.

"Well, it'll be our secret," he finally said, revealing none of the anger he had to be feeling.

Within a couple of minutes, they were all

seated and digging in. It wasn't long before Max was indeed sticky though he was older than the last time Gavin fed him pancakes.

Maya laughed when Max picked up a napkin and it stuck to his fingers. While Gavin freed his son from the napkin, Maya got up and went to wet a washcloth. When she returned to the table, she wiped the syrup off Max's mouth and hands.

"The pancakes are good, aren't they?" she asked him.

He grinned and nodded, then went back to eating. She smiled and patted his head. Max seemed like a different little boy than he'd been the day before, but she was still there as a buffer. She hoped he didn't melt down when he was alone with Gavin.

Maybe she could help prevent that.

She shifted her attention to Gavin, who she found looking at her as if he sensed she was about to address him. Even so, his eyes on her made her super aware of his attractiveness again. Oh, who was she kidding? She was always aware of it.

"So, um, I assume you need to do some work. Maybe when you're ready, someone could make a fun visit to the other building on the property?"

Good thing she had practice speaking in front of her cousins' kids in a way that kept them from knowing what she was talking about.

"Don't you need to go to work too?"

She pointed toward her laptop. "I came prepared this time."

"And bonus points for not passing out in the front yard."

Maya snorted a little laugh. "If you'd baked biscuits, I'd be tempted to throw one at you."

"Never waste a perfectly good biscuit."

As they cleaned up after breakfast, working together with an ease that belied how long they'd known each other or the status of their relationship, Maya couldn't help but notice how comfortable she felt. She needed to rein in those feelings before they went galloping too far ahead and right off a cliff.

"Thank you for helping out today," Gavin said, glancing over his shoulder to where Max was sitting at the table, now with a couple of toy cars instead of sticky pancakes. "I'll figure out something so that you can get back to your life. Again."

"If you don't think it's too much of me sticking my nose in your business, I think

I can help out with arranging child care for you."

When he looked at her, he wore that expression she'd seen from him before, the one that said he couldn't understand why she was saying or doing the things she was.

"That's not your responsibility. You've already done so much."

"Remember how you said that I probably had a lot of connections in town? Well, that comes in handy for more than my work."

"If you know a good babysitter, I'd appreciate a name. But—"

"But nothing." She grabbed his arms and turned him toward the front door. "Go do what you need to, and let me work my magic."

It wasn't really magic, just years of getting to know people, caring about them, being friendly. Whatever you called it, in between playing with toy cars on the floor with Max, reading him a couple of the books that were in one of his suitcases and finding the cartoon channel for him, she made a flurry of phone calls and sent a good number of texts. By the time Gavin returned midafternoon, she couldn't wait to tell him what she'd mapped out for him.

As if he had forgotten who Gavin was during the hours he'd been absent, Max abandoned his toys and crawled up onto the couch next to Maya when his dad came in. The way Gavin's face fell caused Maya's heart to ache. They couldn't go backward.

"Hey, Max," she said. "Remember when your dad told you last night that you could meet his horse, Jasper, today?"

Max's eyes lit up as he looked at her. "Yeah."

She pointed at Gavin. "Why don't you ask him if you can go do that now?"

"Are you going?"

She glanced at Gavin over the top of Max's head before answering.

"Sure, we can all go."

After Max and she bundled up against the cold, Maya led Max to the barn, following Gavin down the path she'd shoveled. When they stepped inside the barn and approached Jasper's stall, Max's eyes went wide.

"Whoa," he said in amazement, drawing chuckles from both Maya and Gavin.

"Would you like to pet him?" Gavin asked.

Max nodded, but he hesitated when Gavin lowered himself and offered his arms to give Max a lift. A glance at Jasper, however, had the desire to pet a horse winning out over any lingering fear of this man he didn't remember.

When Gavin took Max into his arms and lifted him, Maya had to bite her lower lip and look away for a moment so she wouldn't cry. The look on Gavin's face, a mixture of heartbreak dispelled and the purest happiness she'd ever witnessed, was powerful. And though it was the wrong time to have such a thought, Gavin suddenly seemed a hundred times more attractive even though she would have sworn only a minute ago that wasn't possible.

In that moment she considered she might have made a mistake by including her mother in her child care plans for Gavin.

Gavin opening the gate to Jasper's stall drew her attention. First, he showed Max how to rub Jasper's forehead and between his ears. When Max giggled, Gavin's smile could have lit up the darkest point in outer space. She moved to the edge of the stall and let Jasper sniff her hand, then rubbed his forehead as Gavin lifted Max up and placed him gently on Jasper's back, never letting go of him.

It probably wasn't the first time an animal had served as a bridge between people, but watching it play out in front of her was like witnessing a flower blooming after a rain shower following a long drought. Jasper caused Max to open up, to ask every question his young mind could form. And Gavin answered them all, not seeming to tire of them. In fact, she'd never seen him look happier. That filled her heart with joy.

To her surprise, Max didn't fuss or protest when Gavin said it was time to go back to the house for the night.

"Can I see Jasper again tomorrow?"

"Sure. He likes you."

"I like him too." Max patted Jasper's head gently, the way Gavin had showed him.

It had to be one of the most precious things Maya had ever seen.

Throughout dinner and his bath afterward, Max was a little chatterbox. She could hear him clearly through the closed bathroom door. It was amazing how much progress Gavin had made with him, considering how afraid Max had been when he arrived. The fact that he didn't ask about his mother, however, worried Maya. Would he suddenly break down at some point and cry with missing her, or was it possible for a four-year-old to understand enough to know that he was now with the parent who wanted him more? Children sometimes had better instincts about people than adults did.

While Gavin put Max to bed Maya finished washing the dishes and turned out all the lights except the night-light that Gavin kept on in the kitchen. As she headed to the couch to stretch out, tired from a full day despite the later start, she noticed Gavin had quietly come out of his room. He stood with his head lowered and a hand covering his eyes. Thinking things had taken a negative turn with Max, she stepped up to him and placed her hand on his forearm.

"What's wrong?"

In the next moment, he pulled her into his arms for a firm, warm hug.

"What is it?"

"Thank you," he said next to her ear, causing a shiver to run down her back.

For a frozen moment, she didn't know how to react. But then she remembered that if he was any one of her other friends in a similar situation she would hug him back, so that's what she did.

"I'm glad things are working out."

"Thanks to you." He pulled away but didn't let her go.

Being face-to-face while still held in his

arms made her heart thump harder and her skin feel as if it were buzzing. As he lifted a hand to her cheek, she'd swear time slowed. When he caressed her skin with his thumb, she found herself entranced, unable to look away from him.

Again moving at a pace that would allow her to protest and step away if she wanted, he looked at her lips and then began to lower his own toward them. She did not want to protest or move away. Instead, she sank into the kiss the moment his lips touched hers, feeling as if she'd been waiting for this moment half of her life.

She had the oddest thought that she felt as if she'd been floating in the ocean alone in a life raft for a very long time, so long that it had become her norm, something she didn't think about. But when Gavin had pulled her close, she'd just found land with flowers, fresh water, food and the most beautiful music she'd ever heard.

Gavin gradually ended the kiss and put a little distance between them though he didn't break contact. He still held her lower arms lightly.

"I should probably apologize," he said.

"Why?"

Her question seemed to surprise him.

"Because that's not why you came here."

She looked into his eyes for a moment before deciding to be more open and honest than she had been—not completely, just more.

"Do you hear me complaining?"

His lips tipped up slightly at the corners. "No."

She swallowed before admitting the next part. "I like you, Gavin."

"I like you too." He smiled. "Who would have thought that when I was being a jerk, huh?"

This time she was the one to lift her hand to his cheek. "You weren't a jerk. You've been hurt, and it's natural to build walls and lash out after that."

He took a deep breath then exhaled slowly. "This scares me."

"I know. But I'm not Rinna."

"Thank goodness. You more than proved that today alone." He slipped his hand down to hold hers. "You've proved it from the moment I met you, only I refused to see it at first."

"The past is the past. Live in the moment."

His smile took on a bit of a devilish look. "I think that's what I just did."

"And how is living in the moment?"

He closed the distance between them again.
"I like it. I like it a lot."

So did she.

CHAPTER FIFTEEN

IT WAS A good thing Sunny showed up at Gavin's house bright and early the next morning, because Maya needed a buffer between her and Gavin. After they'd kissed the night before, it had felt a different kind of awkward being in his house. A good, tingly awkward, but awkward nonetheless.

Gavin looked at her as he was lifting his coat from where it hung next to the front door, the uppermost question in his mind obvious: *Who is pulling into my driveway?*

"That's my friend Sunny," she said. "Sorry, I didn't think she'd be here this early. I might have arranged a series of trusted babysitters for when I can't be here because of work. Basically my best friends and family for now."

He looked stunned, but thankfully in a good way.

"I hope you don't mind. I kind of took the ball and ran with it."

"You're amazing."

The compliment surprised Maya. It did not seem like the type of thing Gavin Olsen said, but then she had a feeling the real Gavin was only now beginning to emerge. The one she'd met and gotten to know had been only an outline of who he really was and not a full-color picture.

She smiled. "You might want to save the compliment, see if you still feel that way after you meet all the friends and family members."

With that she hurried outside to help Sunny with the twins. They'd thought maybe having a couple of other kids around, albeit ones younger than Max, might help him relax more into his new environment.

"This is a nice place," Sunny said as she looked at the forest surrounding Gavin's house and barn. "So different from ours."

The Breckinridge family had started their ranch in the valley alongside the river, so the acreage was pretty flat in comparison to Gavin's property.

"His cattle are in the valley," Maya said, pointing toward the path Gavin took when he went to tend his herd.

When they stepped inside, Maya's heart jumped again at the sight of Gavin holding

Max in his arms. He looked like the ultimate protector, a man who would literally fight a grizzly to keep it away from his family.

Maya made the introductions, including telling Max the twins' names.

"Babies," he said as he looked at Gavin.

"Yes. It seems like yesterday you were that small."

Max found that funny and laughed.

"They do grow fast. I feel as if I blinked and these two went from newborns to keeping me chasing after them. I think they sometimes strategize going in opposite directions to keep me on my toes," Sunny said.

After a few minutes of chitchat to get to know each other, Gavin thanked Sunny and excused himself so he could get to work. He paused, looking at Maya for a moment longer than he probably should have. She imagined he wanted to ask if she'd be there when he returned, but he refrained in front of Sunny. Smart move.

"Janie's coming to pick me up in a while. Duty calls."

"Okay. Thanks again, for everything."

Maya's skin warmed as she wondered if their kisses were included in that "everything."

Once he was out the door, Sunny wasted no time shooting Maya a smirk. "Well, *he's* definitely more attractive than the picture I saw led me to believe, and he wasn't exactly ugly in that. And what was that look I saw between you two?"

Maya didn't feel like pretending nothing had happened, and she was dying to talk to someone other than her own overexcited brain.

"Yes, he is. And yes, we kissed last night."

Sunny squealed so loudly that all three of the kids jumped where they sat together on the floor playing with an assortment of toys ranging from cars to dolls to a punch-the-shapes thing that was filled with lights and sounds.

"Ignore the loud lady," Maya said, and motioned for the kids to go back to playing.

The loud lady pushed Maya toward the couch. "You must tell me everything."

So for the next hour or so, that's what Maya did. She left out parts that were too personal on Gavin's end, but it felt good to have someone to talk to about her unexpected feelings.

"Were you attracted to him from the start?"

"I recognized he was attractive, but I wouldn't say I was attracted at first. He was so quiet and withdrawn that it was hard to get to know anything about him."

"Understandable if he went through a bad divorce." Sunny glanced at Max. "I cannot believe what she did."

"Yeah, good thing she wasn't standing next to the river when all this went down or I would have been tempted to push her in for a good soaking."

"Probably better that the newspaper editor not get arrested for trying to drown someone."

"I would have chosen a shallow spot."

Sunny snorted.

After a moment she asked, "You really like him, don't you?"

"I do, but if you tell my mother that I'll disown you. She'll be here grilling him so much Angie will try to hire her as an investigator."

"You better not let her see the two of you together, then, or the cat is going to be way out of the bag."

That thought stayed with Maya the rest of the day as Janie came to pick her up, as she started work on the next week's issue of the paper, as she talked to her mom about what time she'd arrive at Maya's house later in the day. She was half-afraid her mom would be able to tell she'd kissed Gavin simply by listening to her voice. She managed to escape the call with her mom none the wiser. But how long would that last?

"DID YOU ENJOY playing with Lily and Liam?" Gavin asked Max as they ate dinner. Like Maya before her, Sunny had made herself at home in his kitchen and left behind a delicious lasagna and garlic bread.

Max nodded as he stuffed a bite of lasagna in his mouth, decorating the area around his lips in tomato sauce. Gavin couldn't help but laugh as he took a napkin and wiped Max's mouth. When Max grinned at him, Gavin wanted to thank Maya all over again for helping him reconnect with his son.

That thought brought back memories of how he'd thanked her the night before. He hadn't come out of his room meaning to kiss her, but he couldn't resist with her so close and his emotions so heightened. When she'd told him that she liked him—despite that incident with the paintings, despite knowing all that he'd been through and how it had changed him—he'd swear he had felt pieces of hard shell breaking and falling away from his heart. He liked her too, maybe more than liked. Even though he'd sworn never to put himself in a vulnerable position again, he realized he was already falling for her. It scared him but also filled him with an excitement he hadn't felt in a long time.

Gavin noticed Max staring at the front door, and he hoped things wouldn't backslide when he realized Maya wasn't coming back tonight. Maybe he should head that concern off before it was voiced.

"Maya will be back tomorrow, and she's bringing her mom to meet you."

If Gavin was being honest, he was nervous about meeting Maya's mother. He'd talked to the woman that one time on the phone, but facing her when she knew how many times her daughter had stayed overnight in his house was entirely different. He wondered if she would be able to tell by looking at him that he'd kissed her daughter, and more than once.

"Will she bring her cat?"

Gavin detoured away from his thoughts to answer Max's question.

"I think she'll probably leave her cat at home."

The sudden pouty bottom lip didn't bode well.

"Can we ask her?"

Gavin considered the question for a moment. "We can ask, but you can't get upset if she says no, okay?"

"Okay."

He hoped Max could keep his promise as he called Maya after dinner, trying not to think about how he'd used his son's request as an excuse to hear Maya's voice. He couldn't believe how quickly he'd gone from wanting her out of his house to never wanting her to leave.

"Hey, is everything okay?" Maya asked as soon as she answered her phone.

"Yeah. Max has a question for you."

Max stood next to Gavin, hopping up and down with his hand extended toward the phone. Gavin ruffled Max's hair, grateful to have things to laugh and smile about again.

The phone looked so big in Max's little hands as he brought it up to his ear. "Bring your kitty."

"Ask, Max. Don't tell."

"Oh," he said with a nod of understanding. "Can you bring your kitty?"

Max listened to whatever Maya said, and judging by the excited reaction he must have gotten the response he wanted. Max then proceeded to tell Maya about his day with Sunny and the twins. He was so animated in the telling that Gavin let him go on for several minutes.

"Okay, Max. Save some to tell Maya tomorrow."

Max didn't argue and after saying goodbye to Maya he handed the phone back to Gavin. This was the good-natured kid he remembered. Maybe both he and his son were recapturing who they used to be.

As Max traded conversation for playing with his toys, Gavin sank onto the couch and put the phone to his own ear.

"You still there?"

"Yeah."

"He's a bit chatty tonight."

"That's good though. It sounds as if things are going well."

As he watched Max chattering away, creating a conversation between his teddy bear and a plush dolphin, he said, "Yeah, the one-eighty has been surprising."

"Has he mentioned Rinna?"

"No. Why does that make me angry? Not at him, of course."

"Because the fact that he hasn't asked for his mother tells you that she wasn't being very motherly to him. He's in a better home now, I don't care what her family says about money and opportunities. Neither of us came from wealth, and we turned out just fine."

"Well, you did anyway."

"You did too. Listen, I want to ask you something, see what you think."

"Okay."

"I know the owner of the little art center here. What would you think about me asking if she'd like to do an exhibit for you? I know it's not a fancy gallery in Denver, but I think people would really like your paintings."

"I don't paint anymore, Maya."

"But you could."

"I have a ranch to run and a son to raise. I don't have time for it."

"Then you could just display the ones you already have."

A twinge of the old desire flickered deep inside him like an ember looking for the slightest bit of wind to flame to life, and here was Maya creating a breeze. Maybe it would be okay. Like she said, it was only a little local art center. There wouldn't be any nasty art critics, and she ran the local press so he felt certain he had no concerns there.

"You really think people would bother to go see them?"

"Can't know until you put them up, but I think so. If nothing else, *I* will go every day and appreciate them. The art center is handier than climbing into your barn loft."

Amazing that her finding those paintings had caused a rift between them, but now he found himself laughing a little at her comment.

"Well, I guess I have nothing to lose, then."

He felt very much as if he'd gained the world.

"WELL, YOU'RE CERTAINLY a good-looking young man," Maya's mom said the moment she met Gavin.

Maya hid her face in her hands, not the least bit surprised that her mother had tossed Maya's request to behave herself right out the window into the melting snow. This meeting could have gone two ways—suspicious interrogation or matchmaking mama—and it appeared her mom was going with the latter option.

"Thank you, ma'am. And I see where Maya gets her looks."

"Oh, a smooth talker too. I'm not sure how I feel about that, but since you think my daughter's pretty I guess I'll have to let it go."

"Mom!"

When Gavin laughed, Maya pointed a finger at him. "You are not helping the situation."

But man did that smile make him look better than any dessert. She was going to have to be careful not to melt right there in front of her way-too-observant mother.

Max came running into the room. He pulled up short when he saw Maya's mom but then started forward again the moment he spotted Maya. He barreled into her legs and wrapped his arms around them, acting as if he hadn't seen her in ages. She still didn't know exactly what had caused Max to latch on to her, but her heart went soft every time he showed his affection. Not in the same way as when his father showed his, of course. The latter was more as if her heart was going to beat right out of her body.

Her feelings for Gavin had felt very much like easing down bunny slopes in the beginning. But now it was as if she'd started tumbling head over heels down a black diamond trail, the world going wonky around her as she tried and failed to right herself.

"Did you bring your kitty?" Max asked, looking up at her.

"Oh, so it's not me you wanted to see but Blossom," Maya said. "I see how it is."

"If it helps, he's now more interested in Jasper than his own father." There was no hurt in Gavin's voice or expression, but rather a happiness that glowed so brightly it almost seemed he wasn't the same man as the one who'd saved her from a wintry demise.

"Max," Gavin said, drawing his son's attention. "Say hello to Maya's mother, Mrs. Pine. She's going to be staying with you while I go to work."

"Hello. Do you have kitties too?"

Maya and her mom both laughed.

"I do," she said. "Two of them, and a dog."

Max responded with a sound of awe, as if Maya's mom had told him that she lived in the middle of a zoo.

"Sorry, he seems to have a one-track mind," Gavin said.

"No need to apologize. It's perfectly natural for little ones to be fascinated by animals."

Max was indeed fascinated by Blossom, and the feeling seemed to be mutual. As soon as Maya let her out of the carrier, her little black and white fluffball curled right up in Max's lap and started to purr.

"I think it's a love match," Maya said, then

regretted it when she spotted the look on her mom's face. "Well, I have to get to work. Thanks for letting me use your car, Mom."

She'd just pulled into her parking space outside the newspaper office several minutes later when her phone dinged with a text.

You left so fast this morning you left scorch marks.

She laughed at Gavin's text and responded first with a GIF of the Road Runner cartoon character.

Her phone rang then and she stayed in the car to talk.

"What was up with the quick departure?" he asked.

"Don't tell me you didn't notice my mom was in matchmaking mode. And if you want to keep anything private, she is not the person to be around."

"Things like the fact we kissed?"

Despite the cold seeping into the car now that she'd turned off the engine, her body temperature rose a few degrees.

"Where are you right now?"

"Standing in my living room with your mom."

"What?"

Gavin laughed on the other end of the call. "Nice screech of panic."

Maya dropped her forehead against the steering wheel.

"I need to craft some excellent payback for the heart attack you gave me."

"I can think of a nice payment plan."

She lifted her head. "Seriously, who are you and what have you done with Gavin Olsen?"

"Nothing. You just found him again."

Maya thought about Gavin throughout the day at the oddest times. It was a startling feeling to be interviewing the pastor of the nondenominational church about the trip he'd taken to Jerusalem and have a memory of kissing Gavin pop into her head.

On her way back from the interview, she stopped by the art center to see Eileen Parker. As Maya had expected, the director was thrilled at the idea of having an exhibit to showcase a local artist.

"Do you need to see a sample before you say yes?"

Eileen shook her head. "I trust you, dear. If you say they're good, then they're good."

"Oh, they are."

When Eileen gave her a curious look that wasn't too dissimilar to Maya's mom's, she made the excuse that she had to get back to the office and zipped out the door.

Was she projecting some sort of bright announcement board that said she'd kissed Gavin Olsen and liked it?

By the time she returned to Gavin's at the end of the day to pick up her mother, she'd mapped out in her head how to extricate her mom before there were any too-obvious looks between her and Gavin. But that was torpedoed the moment she stepped through the front door to find her mother placing a wide array of food on the table while she shooed Gavin out of his own kitchen.

"Mrs. Pine, I appreciate this, I really do, but don't you think this is a bit much for me and Max?"

She waved off his concern. "You can have leftovers. Besides, Maya and I can stay and help you eat a bit of it tonight."

"Mom—"

"Good idea," he said before Maya could voice anything that might change her mom's mind.

Maya met his gaze, and she saw pleading there. And it wasn't because he needed help eating what looked like a feast worthy of the holidays or a family reunion. He looked as if…he'd missed her.

She wasn't sure what to do with that knowledge or her own feelings. They were all so new to her, and she didn't know how to gauge if their mutual attraction was going somewhere or was a passing infatuation, one fueled by gratitude on Gavin's side.

Somehow they made it through dinner without her mom maneuvering Maya and Gavin into a marriage proposal, but that hadn't stopped her mom from sharing embarrassing childhood stories about Maya or telling Gavin he should bring Max to one of Maya's family gatherings.

"Are you trying to overwhelm the man? Our family is a lot to handle when we're all together," Maya said.

"What? We're delightful."

Gavin laughed. "I'm sure that's true."

Maya looked at Gavin. "Don't let her strong-arm you into anything you don't want to do. You are under no obligation."

"Well, he has to meet everyone at some point," her mom said. "Might as well do it all at once."

Maya stared at her mother, quite literally open-mouthed.

"Why are you looking at me as if you're in shock? It's obvious you two like each other."

"Mother!" Maya's complexion wasn't going to be able to hide how heated her face had to be in that moment.

To Maya's surprise, Gavin started laughing. She shifted her stunned gaze to him.

"You were right when you said she was observant," he said.

"I feel as if I'm about to prove that, yes, someone can indeed die of embarrassment."

"What's to be embarrassed about?" her mom asked. "You're two nice, attractive young people. And it's about time you had a life outside of work." She pointed at Maya as if there would be any doubt who she was addressing with her last comment.

When her mom got up to retrieve a cake she'd baked, Gavin reached over and squeezed Maya's hand. The way he was looking at her, all soft and caring, made her suddenly willing to endure any embarrassment if she could have him in her life.

After dinner, her mom tried to clear the table.

"Absolutely not," Gavin said. "You made a feast fit for a king. I will do the cleanup.

You've had a long day. I hope you're staying at Maya's tonight instead of driving home."

Her mom reached over and patted Gavin on the forearm. "I am, and thank you for your concern. You're a good man." Then she ran her hand over Max's hair. "And you have a charming little boy here."

"I'll agree with the second half of that," he said.

"They're both true, so you might as well agree with all of it."

"Yes, ma'am."

When Maya started to retrieve Blossom to put her in the carrier, Max looked as if he might cry. Maya kneeled in front of him.

"What's that, Blossom?" She leaned close to Blossom's face as if the cat was speaking to her. "Oh, she says she had fun with you and looks forward to seeing you again. But it's time for her to sleep in her favorite spot on my ottoman while you have fun with your dad."

Remarkably, Max seemed to accept this as he petted Blossom's head one more time. Maya gave him a hug, and it warmed her heart how strongly he hugged her back.

Once the cat was in her carrier, Gavin

reached past Maya and lifted it, brushing Maya's hand in the process.

"I'll take this out for you."

"Oh…uh, thanks."

Great way not to be obvious about how he affects you.

After Gavin put Blossom in the back seat of the car and secured the carrier, he turned to Maya and immediately kissed her. Her body grew so warm she forgot she was standing on what was left of the previous snowfall.

Winter? What winter?

"I've been wanting to do that all night," he said when he lifted his lips from hers.

"If we're not careful, our mouths will freeze together out here."

He chuckled, his warm breath brushing her face.

Did this mean they were officially a couple now? It certainly felt that way. She didn't want to see anyone else, and she was pretty sure he felt the same. She had the funniest image pop into her head of the two of them as gray-haired grandparents telling their grandkids about how they met.

She imagined Gavin saying, "Well, you see, your grandma was so struck by my handsomeness that she passed out in my front yard."

Maya laughed at the crazy progression of her thoughts. She was getting way ahead of herself.

"What's so funny?" Gavin asked.

She shook her head. "Nothing."

After another delightful kiss, they walked hand in hand back to the house, only breaking contact right before stepping inside.

Maya hadn't even reached the end of Gavin's driveway a few minutes later before her mom started laughing, only half-heartedly trying to hide it.

"Out with it." Might as well invite her mom to say whatever was on her mind instead of waiting for it to trickle out.

"You, my dear, are in love."

"Well, I think it's a bit premature to say that."

"I don't. You know I fell in love with your dad about thirty seconds after I first saw him."

"I'm not you."

"You're part of me. It's not out of the realm of possibility you might take after me in some ways, especially with a man that handsome and caring."

Gavin was, indeed, both of those things, even if the caring part had taken a while to fully reveal itself.

"I know you pride yourself on being an independent, hardworking career woman, and that's great. But that doesn't mean you can't also have a relationship that fills the other parts of your heart."

Long after her mother had fallen asleep in Maya's bedroom, Maya lay on her own couch thinking about her mom's words. Was she in love with Gavin? Could it really happen that quickly for her?

Yes and yes.

She might be a grown woman with a well-established career, but that didn't prevent her from feeling like a teenage girl with a big ol' crush on the most handsome boy in class. Even more thrilling was that the handsome boy seemed to like her too.

CHAPTER SIXTEEN

GAVIN LOOKED AROUND at all the people filling Maya's parents' house, wondering how they had all fit inside the small home.

"Are you sure you want to do this?" Maya asked him. "We can still make a run for it."

He smiled at her, amazed again by how he'd grown used to her being there at his side.

"It's fine."

"Well, say the word at any point and we'll leave."

He reached over and quickly squeezed her hand.

"I saw that!"

Maya rolled her eyes. "I hear the geek."

Gavin looked toward the younger man approaching them, the college-age brother he'd heard a lot about.

Ethan Pine was taller than his older sister, but when he tried to ruffle her hair she put him in a headlock instead until he cried out for mercy. It was a funny and loving scene at the same time. Gavin wondered what that was like, having a sibling. Not only was he an only child, but so was Rinna. So was Max.

But maybe he won't always be.

Gavin mentally shook his head, needing to not get ahead of himself. But yes, he and Maya were a couple now though there had been no verbal "Do you want to be my girlfriend/boyfriend?" conversation. They'd simply fallen into the relationship. How natural it had felt to do so continued to surprise him, as did how happy he felt. It scared him sometimes because he'd been happy before and it had all come crashing down. He couldn't help feeling it would happen again, even though Maya wasn't like Rinna in any way.

No, he needed to stop borrowing trouble. Things were finally going well for him. He couldn't ask for anything more. He had his son back, a relationship with a woman who had chipped away at the barricade he'd built around his heart and his paintings were going to be in a solo exhibit. Sure, it wasn't a fancy, highly trafficked gallery in a big city, but even if only a handful of people saw and liked his paintings, that was enough.

Maybe he'd eventually carve out a little

time to return to painting as a hobby. Anything was better than the canvases rotting away in his barn, a hidden reminder of the horrible experiences he'd gone through.

"This is my annoying little brother," Maya said when she finally relinquished her hold on Ethan.

"That much I figured out."

"Are you sure you want to date my sister?" Gavin grinned at Maya. "Positive."

"What did you do to him?" Ethan asked Maya, as if she'd bewitched Gavin.

"Boy, do you want some more?" Maya raised her knuckles in Ethan's direction, eliciting a snicker from the young man.

Ethan lowered himself so that he was eye to eye with Max. "Hey, little man. Would you like to see some spaceships?"

"Yeah!"

"And they're off to a faraway galaxy," Maya said as they watched Ethan lead Max down the hallway.

Over the next several minutes, Gavin was introduced to a parade of relatives he hadn't already met in the rotation of babysitters Maya's family had recently sent his way. Every time he mentioned getting a permanent babysitter, Maya had informed him that her family might disown her. It did seem that her mom, aunts and cousins had adopted Max as one of their own. It was as if they'd adopted Gavin too, if he was being honest. It was a strange feeling after the strained relationships with his family and then Rinna's. Strange but wonderful.

"You must be the young man I keep hearing so much about."

Gavin shifted out of his thoughts to see a man who appeared to be in his mid-fifties.

"Dad, this is Gavin. I hope you behave better than Mom."

Mr. Pine smiled at his daughter. "Don't I always?"

The man extended his hand to Gavin, so he shook it. "Nice to meet you, sir."

"I saw some pictures of your place. Looked really nice."

"Thank you. I like it."

Sometime over the past few weeks, he'd gradually come to realize that his ranch was no longer a place to hide out from the world and the past. He was happy to discover that even in his darkest time, he'd picked well. It honestly felt more like home than any place he'd ever lived, but he thought that was in part because of the happiness that had been building there recently. Between Max gradually remembering a few things from when Gavin had lived with him before and Maya being a frequent visitor, his house had become a home.

He'd even had Maya pick her favorite of his paintings, and he'd hung it on the wall. He'd been afraid it would bring back bad memories, but the opposite ended up being true. It was as if he'd reclaimed something that had brought him joy before it had been tarnished by his life falling apart.

The sound of Max's laughter drew Gavin's attention.

"It appears Ethan has found an appreciative audience," Mr. Pine said.

"Boys and their toys," Maya said with feigned long-suffering.

A few minutes later, everyone started filling their plates from an array of food that made the feast Maya's mom had made at Gavin's house look like a snack.

"Here, you have to try the fry bread," Maya said, placing some on his already full plate. "Don't tell Mom, but Aunt Sylvie's fry bread is the best."

"Your brother will inherit everything,"

her mom called out from across the room, prompting laughter.

Gavin's heart filled to overflowing. This was what family was supposed to be like.

"Are you okay?" Maya asked him.

He nodded. "Thanks for bringing me and Max today."

"This crowd didn't leave me any choice."

"You didn't want to bring us?" A sliver of panic shot through him.

Maya looked up at him. "Of course I did." She placed her hand on his lower arm and gave him a reassuring squeeze. "Don't worry."

He knew her words and touch were meant to remind him that she was not Rinna and wouldn't hurt him the way his ex-wife had. And Maya's family was so different from Rinna's parents that it was almost as if they were from a different universe altogether.

As the meal progressed, it was not the quiet and dignified affair that he'd had to sit through at the Zachary home. It was loud and rowdy and he loved every minute of it.

"So, when are you two getting married?" Ethan asked, a mischievous grin on his face.

Before Maya could toss her brother into the

nearest deep body of water, Gavin decided to have some fun.

"I don't know," he said, then looked at Maya. "Should we do it now?"

For a brief moment, Maya looked surprised but then evidently picked up on what he was doing and played along.

"Sure, that sounds good. Won't even have to send out invitations since everyone is already here. We'll have to wait until Sunny and Dean can drive over though or she'll never forgive me."

"We can do that. Will give us time to write our vows."

"You two are no fun," Ethan said.

"And you," Maya said, pointing at her brother, "are just as annoying as you were when you were ten."

Ethan grinned ear to ear as if he'd been paid the biggest compliment ever.

MAYA DIDN'T THINK her heart could feel any fuller. She'd been a bit nervous bringing Gavin and Max to her parents' anniversary party. That they both seemed to be having a good time made her happy.

She admitted to herself that part of her wanted to contact his parents, tell them what they were missing with their son and grandson, but that wasn't her place. Even if she realized she was already in love with Gavin, that she loved Max as if he was her own child, any reconciliation would have to be initiated by Gavin or his parents. She really hoped it happened at some point though, for all of their sakes.

"Why don't you two go for a walk?" her mom said to her after the meal was over. "The weather is finally nice enough you won't freeze or blow away."

"I can help with the cleanup," Maya said.

Her mom waved off her offer. "We have plenty of hands here for that and watching little Max. Take advantage of that."

Maya glanced toward where Gavin was chatting with her great-uncle Roy. It would be nice to do something alone together, even if it was a simple walk around the paths of her childhood. They'd not had any alone time since Max had arrived, not since they'd become a couple.

She leaned over and gave her mom a kiss on the cheek. "Thanks, Mom."

When Roy got distracted by something his son Cal said, she slipped her hand into Gavin's and led him out of the house, grabbing their coats along the way. He looked back at the house when it became obvious they weren't only stepping out onto the porch.

"Don't worry about Max. He has a house-ful of my relatives to watch him and spoil him rotten."

It made her happy that after a moment's hesitation, he didn't seem worried about leaving Max in her family's care.

"Where are we going?"

"The grand tour," she said, waving her hand around dramatically.

Gavin smiled. "Sounds good."

She had another of those visions of the far future, of how she could be eighty years old with Gavin's smiles still making her heart flutter.

They passed by the school she'd graduated from, the little restaurant where she'd worked for a couple of years, the house where Mr. Eagle still lived. She told Gavin the story of when her car was stolen and placed in Mr. Eagle's yard.

"That car served me well despite its ugli-ness. It had more than three hundred thou-sand miles on it before it went to the great junkyard in the sky."

"My dad has an old truck like that he uses

around the ranch. He's had it since before I started school."

For a moment she considered whether she should take the conversational opening he'd given her. She decided to forge ahead, if carefully.

"Do your parents know you have Max now?"

He shook his head. "I've thought about calling them, but I want to enjoy my life as it is for a while longer."

The way he squeezed her hand and looked at her made it obvious that she was part of what he was enjoying. The feeling was definitely mutual.

Grinning, she veered onto a dead-end street, keeping a firm grip on Gavin's hand. At the end of the street, she led him through a stand of trees and down a slope toward a little creek. Because it was shaded, more snow still clung to the shadows.

"What are we doing here?" he asked.

"This, Mr. Olsen, is where all the kids come when they want to sneak kisses without the entire reservation seeing and spreading the news lightning fast."

Gavin lifted an eyebrow. "You brought me to a make-out spot?"

"That sounds so tawdry. Let's call it the smooching spot instead."

"Well, I guess we're obligated to help it live up to its new name."

"I think that's an excellent idea."

MAYA WALKED INTO the sheriff's department office a couple of days later, whistling.

"Someone sounds happy," Sadie, the secretary and dispatcher, said. "Gee, I wonder why."

Maya was almost certain all five hundred residents of Jade Valley knew about her and Gavin dating now. If Maya wasn't the editor of the newspaper, it would have probably already made headlines in at least one issue.

"What's not to be happy about? Life is good." She looked around. "Angie in her office? I need a quote about the wreck north of town this morning."

"No, she's in the conference room with some suits from Denver. Not sure what their business is."

Denver. Sudden concern knotted up inside Maya.

No, there could be any number of reasons for lawyers—she assumed they were lawyers—to have traveled to Jade Valley from Denver.

"I'll go wait for her."

But instead of seating herself in Angie's office, she paused outside the open door to the small conference room.

"You must agree that the child would be better off with his grandparents. They can give him a better life than he could ever get—"

"If you say 'in a place like this,' I'm afraid you're going to force me to not look too favorably upon you, Mr. Springer," Angie said.

Panic surged up in Maya like a volcano erupting. She had no doubt who "the child" or "his grandparents" were, and she couldn't let this happen. She stepped into the open doorway and made immediate eye contact with Angie. The look in her friend's eyes told her she was right.

"I'll be done here in a few minutes," Angie said.

But Maya didn't leave the room. Instead, she looked toward the two men who wore suits that looked expensive, the kind of expensive that was paid for by clients such as the Zachary family.

"This is about Max, isn't it?"

"And you are?" one of the men asked in that misogynistic way some well-off, self-confident men had. He might as well have said, "Why is this brown peasant talking to me?"

"I'm the editor of the local newspaper and a friend of Gavin Olsen's."

"Oh, you're the one Miss Zachary imposed upon to take care of the child."

"The child has a name, and she didn't impose upon me. I was glad to give comfort to Max, who'd obviously had none given to him in quite some time."

"Maya," Angie said in a warning tone.

Maya took a deep breath, trying to bring her anger under control. But she couldn't totally back down. No one had ever fought for Gavin, but she planned to. For him and for Max.

"Gavin is a great father, and Max is really happy. And, since you work with the law, you should understand what it means when a mother signs over full custody of her child and a judge approves it. You should also make sure your clients know that."

"You seem very invested in a family that isn't your own, Miss..."

Maya didn't give him the satisfaction of

offering her surname. He could make the effort to find it out himself, which he no doubt would. She should probably shut up now.

"I'm sure Mr. Olsen is a fine person, but the opportunities… Max could be given by his grandparents far outweigh what his father could."

"Not everything a child needs can be bought with money, and there's not a person on this planet who could love and care for Max more than Gavin. And Max has already been tossed around enough. He's happy, he's thriving, he has a lot of people who care about him. That's enough."

She could tell the men didn't agree, and she suddenly felt sorry for any children either of them might have. When they left a few minutes later, she was still fuming. Angie met her gaze.

"That was quite the speech you gave. If I hadn't been in uniform, I would have given you a standing ovation."

"Can they really take Max away from Gavin?" She didn't think he'd survive that.

"I want to say no, especially after what Rinna did, but people with that kind of money often get whatever they want."

Maya felt as if she might throw up.

"Why did they come see you instead of Gavin?"

"Probably because they wanted to plant the seed with local law enforcement that Gavin wasn't the right person to have custody. They wanted to play on the instinctual need to make sure children are protected. Little did they know that they were barking up the wrong tree and I don't like being manipulated or talked to as if I don't have a brain."

"Are they headed to Gavin's now?" Maya pulled her phone from her pocket, needing to warn him.

But Angie shook her head. "I doubt it. I might have stressed how people around here don't take kindly to others trespassing on their property or showing up at their front doors unannounced."

Of course, that's exactly how Maya had arrived in Gavin's life, but she wasn't going to bring that up at the moment.

"I could seriously kiss you right now," Maya said.

"I would prefer you didn't. Save those kisses for someone else."

No matter if the lawyers were heading back to Denver, she still needed to warn Gavin.

"Can you send Janie a quote about the wreck this morning? I need to go."

Thankful she'd gotten her car back a few days earlier, she hurried out to Blueberry and slid into the driver's seat. She didn't want to chance another accident so she didn't drive as fast as she wanted to on the way to Gavin's. When she arrived, it was her mom who greeted her. If Max got taken away, it would break her mom's heart too. Maya and Gavin might not be married, and Max might not be her son, but her mother already thought of him as her grandson. She'd not said so out loud, but Maya could tell.

The same way her mother could tell something was wrong the moment she saw Maya.

"What is it?"

"Maybe nothing, but maybe something." Before she could share the details, Gavin came into the house. He must have been nearby, possibly in the barn, when she arrived. Maya glanced at where Max was watching a cartoon that matched some of the toys he had. She motioned for her mom and Gavin to go toward the kitchen.

"I just came from the sheriff's office. There were a couple of lawyers there representing his grandparents," Maya said, with a nod back toward Max.

All the color drained from Gavin's face, and he gripped the back of one of the kitchen chairs so tightly that she half expected the wood to dissolve into dust. She reached out and placed her hand on his arm.

"We won't let you lose him again. You have a lot of people on your side this time," Maya said.

She told them everything she'd heard and the details of her conversation with Angie.

"If you'll excuse me," Gavin said, his tone an odd mixture of angry and distant, "I need to make a phone call."

Helplessness rushed over Maya as she watched Gavin walk toward his bedroom. When he closed the door, Maya sank onto one of the chairs. Her mom patted her hand.

"Don't worry. Like you said, he has a lot of people in his corner now."

Maya would do whatever she could to prevent Max being ripped away from Gavin again, for both of their sakes, but she couldn't deny a significant amount of worry. Would the entire state of Wyoming be enough to triumph over people with the kind of money, power and influence the Zacharys had if they truly decided to fight? She wondered if they cared about Max at all, or if they simply couldn't stand the thought of someone with their blood living the kind of life they considered inferior to their own.

Max abandoned the TV and walked over to the kitchen. He moved close to Maya, putting his hands on her leg.

"Was Daddy sleepy?"

Maya ran her hand gently over Max's hair. "No, sweetie. He had to make a phone call and didn't want to bother your cartoon watching."

"It's done."

"Do you want a snack?" Maya's mom asked Max.

Thankfully, Max was at the age where snacks were a good way to draw his attention away from other things. Maya wished it were that simple for her. Instead, she resisted the urge to pace, not wanting Max to pick up on the fact that something was wrong. He deserved to live in blissful ignorance of the disagreements between his relatives.

It seemed to take forever, but Gavin finally emerged from his room. Maya again had to restrain her instinctual response to jump up and hurry to his side, instead waiting for him to come to her. He sank onto the chair at the end of the table, looking as if he'd aged a decade since she'd arrived.

"What happened?" she asked gently.

He glanced toward where her mom and Max were fixing a tray of snacks, half of them healthy and half of them of the cookie variety.

"I talked to Rinna. She said her parents were furious with what she did, told her she still hadn't grown up. I can't disagree with that last part. In many ways, she's like a spoiled child."

"She still had the legal right to do what she did." A sudden horrible thought occurred to Maya. "They wouldn't go so far as to have her declared incompetent or something, get the ruling overturned?"

Gavin didn't immediately answer.

"I don't think so," he finally said. "They'd think that would reflect poorly on them."

Thank goodness for small favors, she supposed.

OVER THE NEXT few days, Gavin only did the work that was absolutely necessary for the safe running of the ranch. He couldn't stand to be parted from Max for too long, irrationally afraid that someone from Rinna's family would come snatch him away while Gavin wasn't at the house.

He'd consulted an attorney, a local one Maya had recommended. It seemed even a town as small as Jade Valley managed to have a couple of lawyers, one of whom specialized in family law. It had been Mr. Bancroft's advice to do everything he could to prove that Max had a stable, safe home environment. To that end, Gavin had installed a variety of safety measures including a gate around the stove, childproofing the lower cabinets, getting new bedroom furniture and fixing up the extra bedroom for Max. He also hired a regular babysitter instead of depending on the kindness of Maya and her family and friends.

Max had at first fretted that he didn't get to see his variety of adopted relatives, but after a couple of days his friendly nature won out and he and Mrs. Grimes were getting along. Gavin's attorney had approved of the new child-care situation, saying it looked better to have consistency and to be bringing a middle-aged, married woman into his home to care for Max instead of his girlfriend.

Gavin had been offended at first at the implication about Maya, but Mr. Bancroft had told him in no uncertain terms that if he wanted to ensure he kept Max he had to think like the other side. He had to eliminate any situation that could be used against him.

That thought had bored deep into his mind to the point that he'd distanced himself a bit from Maya. When she offered to come out to the ranch to help him with preparing for the art exhibit—the farthest thing from his mind at the moment—or just to see him and Max, more than once he'd declined. He hated the idea that he might be hurting her, but the voice in his head kept saying that the Zacharys might insinuate inappropriate things were going on under the same roof where Max was living. He couldn't take that chance. But he needed to find a way to tell Maya that in a way that wouldn't hurt her feelings. Did that way even exist? She'd done so much for him that he felt horrible even thinking about pushing her away, plus he'd miss her like crazy.

He was trying to stay positive, but it was difficult to silence the voice that told him he should have known he was too happy. That, at best, he would only get to keep one part of his life that brought him happiness. He couldn't have his son, his creative outlet and the woman he loved.

Gavin reined in Jasper on his way back toward the barn and looked up at the blue sky. Spring was around the corner even if the air was still crisp and cold.

And, yes, he could admit, if only to himself, that sometime in the past weeks he'd fallen in love again. It wasn't the fast-to-flame, banish-all-rational-thought kind he'd experienced in the early days with Rinna, but this felt more solid, more real, deeper. And here he was afraid he'd have to let it go, at least until he was certain it wouldn't contribute to having to suffer through another custody battle.

He closed his eyes, took a deep breath of the clean mountain air. It must not have dispelled enough of his agitation though because Jasper fidgeted, so Gavin urged the horse forward.

When he arrived back at the house, he noticed Maya's little blue car in the driveway and his heart sank. He really didn't want to have the necessary conversation, but he also wanted to be completely honest with her. And the sooner the better.

She'd taken over for Mrs. Grimes with Max, who was thankfully taking a nap when Gavin stepped inside the house. Maya's bright smile almost caused him to reconsider what he'd come to say.

His mood must have been visible on his face because Maya's smile faded away.

"What's wrong? Have you heard something?"

He walked straight to Maya and pulled her into his arms. His heart urged him to tell her he loved her, but that wouldn't be fair considering what he was about to ask of her.

Maya was the first to pull away.

"Tell me." She was a smart, observant woman, so it was no surprise that she knew he had something to say.

"I need to ask something of you that I don't want to ask."

"I think at this point you know you can ask me anything. I'll help however I can."

Needing to break contact to get through this, Gavin took a couple of steps back so that Maya's hands fell away from him. The momentary flash of panic and confusion in Maya's eyes almost derailed him.

"When I talked to my attorney, he said I needed to do everything I could to make sure it appeared to anyone looking that Max was living in a safe, happy, and...wholesome environment."

Maya nodded. "That's all true. We all understood why you hired Mrs. Grimes."

She didn't really. Well, only part of the reason.

"Yes, having a married older woman as his caretaker looks good to anyone who might question the moral environment."

Maya tilted her head ever so slightly, and he could almost see the gears turning to figure out what he was really saying. He couldn't stand this dragging out, so he plunged ahead.

"For now, I think we should hit pause on our relationship."

He watched as the confusion gave way to a hurt he hated to see. But then Maya, being the person she was, nodded.

"Because we're not married, you're concerned the Zacharys might turn our relationship into something it's not to convince a judge to give them custody."

Gavin seriously wanted to cry, but he forced himself to reply. "Yes. I know it's not fair—"

"Stop." Maya took his hands in hers. "I understand. I don't have to like it, I might even think it's going a bit overboard, but after what you've been through I do understand."

"Why are you so awesome?"

Maya released him and framed her face with her hands, as if she was a pretty flower in a pot, and smiled.

"Just born that way."

He wanted to kiss her so much, but that would only make things harder.

Her smile changed to one of sympathy, but she didn't touch him again. Instead, she grabbed her coat from the couch.

"I should get going."

She didn't say to let her know if he needed anything as she usually did before leaving, and that perhaps hurt more than anything. Not that she hadn't offered to help him— she'd already given him so much—but that she wasn't hesitating in fully pulling away.

CHAPTER SEVENTEEN

MAYA SAT ACROSS from Sunny at Alma's stuffing crinkle-cut French fries into her mouth. She preferred going to Trudy's, especially since she adored the older woman, but Trudy knew that as the editor of the paper Maya had to spread her business around. Also, Alma's fries were better, not that she would ever tell Trudy that.

She looked up to find Sunny staring at her. "What?"

"You don't have to consume those at the speed of light."

"I'm hungry. And busy. Lots of work to do."

Granted, she was way ahead on material for future issues of the paper and had made a lot of progress on the follow-up articles about small-town journalism. She was probably going to run the first one the following week if something hugely newsworthy didn't require the space.

"Okay, I've lived in Jade Valley for a big chunk of my life, and I know there isn't enough news to keep you as busy as you've been the past week," Sunny said. "You are working to forget your pain."

"Pain? If you're talking about the situation with Gavin, I told you I understand where he's coming from."

"You can understand and still be hurt."

Sunny's direct hit on how Maya was feeling erased her appetite, and she dropped the fry she was holding into the ketchup on her plate.

The truth was she missed Gavin and Max a lot. And while she really did understand why Gavin was distancing himself, she couldn't deny that a little part of her was angry at him for it too. She kept reminding herself that they'd made no promises to each other, hadn't even said the three simple but important words that would take their relationship to the next level.

She wasn't certain Gavin would ever be able to say those words again. She didn't doubt he cared about her, but that didn't mean he'd ever be able to commit to a long-term relationship. In a not-so-little corner of her heart, she was afraid that this time apart would become permanent, that away from her he'd remember why he'd chosen to be alone before. That the happiness of having his son back would be enough.

"You love him, don't you?"

"Yes." No sense denying it when Sunny knew her so well.

"And you haven't told him."

"It seemed too soon to take that step."

"I don't believe in timelines when it comes to confessing one's feelings, at least not anymore."

Maya knew that her friend was probably thinking about the mother she'd lost, the brother and sister-in-law who'd died too soon, leaving Sunny to raise their children.

"We're not guaranteed tomorrow," Sunny said, confirming Maya's guess.

"I know, but there's a lot more to consider here than if it was just Gavin and me and none of the other factors involved."

"That's true, but I don't want you to sacrifice your happiness either."

"It's temporary—we're just putting things on pause." At least she hoped so.

Feeling a little sorry for herself, she ordered a big slice of banana cake. Caving to the allure of dessert, Sunny ordered a slice of strawberry pie. While they waited for the infusion of calories and sugar to arrive, Maya's phone buzzed. She sighed when she saw the text was from Mr. Clarke, the owner of the paper.

"Oh joy. I wonder what he could be pestering me about today." No doubt it was of the same "Get the circulation numbers up" or "Sell more ads" variety.

But when she clicked on the message and started reading, her heart sank.

"What's wrong?"

Instead of answering, Maya kept reading. When she got to the last vital piece of information, not only did she lose her appetite for dessert she also thought she might be sick.

"Maya?" Sunny's voice was full of concern.

"The paper's been sold…" She looked up and met Sunny's gaze. "To Zachary Communications."

It took Sunny a moment to connect the dots.

"As in Rinna's family?"

Maya nodded.

"This does not feel like a coincidence."

The nauseated feeling in Maya's stomach intensified. "No, it doesn't."

Did her encounter with Rinna lead to this? Or was it those lawyers for the Zachary family she'd unloaded on? She pressed her hand to her stomach.

Please don't let this hurt Gavin and his custody of Max in any way.

"I need to go call and find out more," Maya said. "You take my cake, give it to Dean or your dad."

Though it was a short walk back to the newspaper office, she didn't wait to place the call to her boss. Well, former boss, it seemed. But he wasn't available or was simply avoiding her call.

Janie was on the phone, her own lunch in front of her, when Maya stepped inside the office. Maya wished she knew more before she had to break the news. When Janie got off the call, she looked up at Maya.

"Um, why are you staring at me like that? Do I have pasta sauce on my face or something?"

Instead of answering, Maya pulled up the message on her phone and handed it to Janie. She watched Janie read it and imagined the changes in her expressions mirrored what Maya had gone through a few minutes before.

"Did you know this was going to happen?"

Maya shook her head. "Not even a clue. I mean, they were pressuring me to get circulation and ad revenue up, but they've always done that."

"What does this mean?" Janie knew as well as Maya did that media consolidation often didn't bode well for journalistic freedom or even unbiased reporting. Or job retention.

Maya thought about how Gavin had looked at her when he found out she was a reporter and how he had gradually come to realize that she was honest and fair in her reporting.

She knew she couldn't abandon her beliefs and integrity simply to keep her job.

"I don't know, but I intend to find out."

While working on the layout for the next issue of the paper, Maya kept trying to reach her former boss. Evidently he wanted to be rid of her, because he finally sent a text that pointed her toward a contact at Zachary Communications. Maya wanted to reach through the phone and strangle the man.

Instead, she took a couple of deep breaths and called the number he'd given her. After being transferred to three different people, she was told that she would be receiving an official letter from the company shortly.

It seemed no one was willing to talk to

her on the phone. Her thoughts went back to that day in the sheriff's department conference room. Had those suits gone back and told their bosses that she was difficult to deal with? That she wasn't the type to simply nod and comply?

A bad feeling settled in her middle, and late in the afternoon she found out why. The universe had been preparing her for a sucker punch.

When a registered letter arrived from the legal department at Zachary Communications, she and Janie looked at each other as if doom lay inside the envelope.

"This can't be good, can it?" Janie asked.

Maya didn't answer. Instead she ripped open the envelope, thinking that, based on the timing of its arrival, whatever message was inside had been in the works before the sale of the paper had been finalized. Would it be the same types of demands about circulation and ad revenue that she'd been working to address for a while? Or was she being replaced by someone from Zachary?

This letter is to inform you that Zachary Communications has taken ownership of the Valley Post newspaper operation, building, and all equipment, files, and property previously owned by Clarke Communications. Let this letter also serve as notice that the operation of said newspaper is to cease immediately. All personal belongings must be removed and any keys to the building left with local law enforcement by the end of the business day on March 15.

The next day.

For a few moments, Maya stared at the letter, rereading it, stunned. Then the significance of the day hit her. Her own, personal Ides of March.

GAVIN OPENED HIS mailbox to retrieve his mail, but the week's issue of the *Valley Post* he'd been expecting wasn't there. After he and Maya had started dating, he'd subscribed so he could read her articles.

How he missed her. He'd lost count of how many times he'd almost called or texted her, especially since he'd heard nothing more from Rinna's family. Of course, that made him nervous that they were planning to weaponize some other part of his life to get what they wanted.

When he returned to the house, Mrs. Grimes left for the day. He spent the evening feeding and playing with Max, then getting him into bed. He ended up reading him three stories before Max started drifting off. Even after Max fell asleep, Gavin couldn't pull himself away for several minutes. He sat and watched his son sleep.

He could not lose him again, and not just for his own sake. Based on how Rinna and her family acted, and a few things Max had said, he'd become convinced Max was better off with him. He firmly believed that most objective observers would think the same. Even if the Zacharys did love Max, Gavin thought they also didn't want to lose out to someone they considered lesser than them. What a toxic mindset to have. How could anyone be happy with those kinds of thoughts? Maybe they weren't. He hadn't been around them enough to know if they ever looked genuinely happy.

Finally leaving Max to rest, he left the room and retrieved the laptop that until recently had lived in a box in his closet. When he'd finally let Maya and other people into his life again, he'd started to reconnect with the world—setting up internet service, talking a bit more with people when he had to go into town, subscribing to the paper. Each day it had felt as if he was discarding another layer of his solitude. Even now, he'd not totally backslid.

No, you just pushed away one of the two most important people in your life.

Had he made a mistake? Would it actually look better for him to be in a committed relationship?

He shook his head, not wanting to think that way. Maya was not a vehicle to help him secure custody of his son. She had her own space in Gavin's heart. And despite her saying that she understood his actions, he couldn't help but worry that he'd let his fear of losing Max lead him to losing Maya instead.

Trying not to worry, he logged on and searched for the *Post*'s website. When the site loaded, however, he didn't see articles or an image of the front page of the latest issue. Instead, there was a "Notice to Our Readers" message.

Thank you to those who have faithfully read the Valley Post, whether you were a newer subscriber or your family has been getting your local news from us for decades. The most recent issue of the paper was its last. We are sorry for not giving you notice, but this sudden change came as a surprise to staff as well.

Gavin stared at the screen, not quite believing what he was reading. He knew Maya's boss was always pestering her, but she'd never indicated that the paper closing down was a possibility. He couldn't imagine how she was feeling.

He picked up his phone. He was done with pushing people away, especially the ones who cared about him. He'd done nothing wrong regarding Max, and he had to believe that if his son's custody ended up in court again he'd be able to prove he was the right parent to raise Max.

And if she would have him, would forgive him for letting his fear get in the way, he wanted Maya to be there beside him.

His concern grew when he couldn't reach her by calling or texting. Though it went against her personality, he imagined her sitting at home alone with her phone off, wondering how she was going to make a living in a town without many job opportunities.

His heart lurched at the thought that to keep pursuing her career, she would likely have to leave.

He wanted to hop in his truck and race to her house, but he couldn't. Max was asleep. And no matter how Gavin felt about Maya, his son would always come first. As much as it pained him to not be there for her, she was an adult capable of taking care of herself. Max was a child who could not.

Still, he had a difficult time quieting his mind and heart enough to sleep. And even after falling asleep, he didn't stay that way for long. His worry for Maya invaded his dreams. His rest was so fitful that he gave up and rose even earlier than normal. As soon as Mrs. Grimes arrived to watch Max, he informed her that he had to go to town and only barely kept himself from running to his truck.

When he reached Maya's house, her car wasn't there. Even so, he knocked a few times. Next he drove to the newspaper office in case she was there cleaning out her desk or something, but that was a bust as well.

Sitting outside the darkened building, he tried calling her again. When he still didn't reach her, he called Sunny.

"Are you searching for Maya?" she answered instead of saying hello.

"Yes, she's not answering calls or texts, and she's not at home. I know right now I don't have the right to be upset about any of that, but I heard about the paper and I'm worried about her."

"I'm glad to hear that."

"Huh?"

"It means I was right, that you feel about her the same way she feels about you."

The same way she feels about you.

"What did she say?"

"You need to hear that from her, not me. She's at her parents' house."

Thankful he knew the way and that he trusted Mrs. Grimes to take care of Max while he was gone, he headed immediately to the Wind River Reservation. All the way there, he had the hopefully irrational fear that she wouldn't be there either, that she would have disappeared to start her life anew somewhere else far away. So when he made the turn onto her parents' street and saw Blueberry sitting in their driveway, he breathed a huge sigh of relief.

She stepped out onto the porch before he

could even cross the distance between his truck and the front door.

"Gavin, what are you doing here? Is something wrong?"

He bounded up the steps and pulled her into his arms, planting a kiss atop her head.

"Gavin?" she said against his chest.

"I'm sorry," he said, his throat thick with emotion. "For everything."

Maya pulled away enough to look up at him but not completely out of his arms.

"I guess you heard about the paper."

"Yeah. I can't believe they shut it down."

Maya did slip out of his arms then and sat on the edge of the porch, her feet on the middle step. She patted the porch next to her, and he sat too. Alarm bells were tolling in his head, but he didn't say anything. Instead, he waited while it seemed she was collecting her thoughts or figuring out how to say whatever she needed to.

"They actually sold out and the new owners immediately shut us down."

"What? That doesn't make sense. Why would someone buy a business only to close it?"

She turned her head to look at him. "It was Zachary Communications."

Maya might as well have punched him in the sternum. It took all of two seconds for him to figure out why they'd done it. It was to punish her for siding with him. White-hot anger rushed up in him like the water in one of Yellowstone's geysers, but in the next moment Maya placed her hand on his arm.

"Don't say or do anything. You keeping Max is more important."

Gavin took her hands in his. "Yes, Max is important, but so are you. I shouldn't have pushed you away. That wasn't fair."

"I underst—"

"Don't. I know you understand, that's the kind of person you are, but you shouldn't have to. They shouldn't be able to instill that kind of fear in me, and I refuse to let them do it anymore. Everything I've done shows I'm the more stable parent. I've done nothing to indicate Max would be better elsewhere, and that includes being with you. If anything, it should be beneficial because you're kind, well-respected—"

"Jobless."

"You weren't until they made it that way, which I am more than willing to point out to a judge if they dare to make your employment status a point in their favor." He looked out toward the small house across the street, at the multicolored whirligig blowing in the breeze. Listened to the wind chimes as he tried to calm himself at least a fraction.

He tried to think of what the best next step would be to ensure that everything turned out the way it should. Well, first things first.

Gavin shifted his gaze back to Maya, let his gaze roam the hair tucked behind her ear, her pretty dark eyes, the lips he'd kissed. She was a huge, important part of the new happiness in his life, and he'd missed her terribly since he'd pushed her away.

"Can you forgive me?"

She didn't even hesitate before giving him an understanding smile. It was amazing how well she could read him.

"There's nothing to forgive. I won't lie and say it didn't hurt, but life and feelings are rarely as black-and-white as lots of people like to think they are. We do the best we can in the moment and deal with the consequences, good or bad or somewhere in between, after the fact."

He framed her face with his hands and kissed her, not caring in the least who saw.

After the kiss, they remained sitting next

to each other, hand in hand. He never wanted to let her go again.

"What are you going to do now?" he asked.

"I don't know yet. It's difficult to get a job in journalism now, especially in rural areas. I'll probably try freelancing."

"Why not start your own news site? Be your own boss. Sure, it wouldn't be the same as the paper, but I bet a lot of the locals would subscribe for a small amount. And you could publish things you never could before." He hesitated a moment, considering the wisdom of what he wanted to say next. But he'd determined he was through with living in fear of what might happen and under the shadow of the past. "I think you should publish the first article in the series you were writing, but include what just happened, the reality of the control the big media companies have over honest journalists trying to cover local news."

"Gavin, I don't want to do anything to endanger your custody of Max."

"That's what people like the Zacharys bank on, that everyone will cower and bend to their will because they're rich and powerful. But by selling the paper, they also freed you to say whatever you want. So say it. Contact every other editor you know to see if they'll run the piece too. At the same time, I'll prepare to hit back legally regarding custody. Sunny told me earlier that she knows a big-time attorney in LA who has done some high-profile custody cases and who owes her a favor. If it becomes necessary, she said he would absolutely help out my current attorney and wouldn't even flinch taking on the Zacharys."

"I sometimes think Sunny knows half of LA and half of those owe her a favor. She told me she wanted to send one of your paintings to a gallery owner friend of hers once your exhibit here is done."

"She's a good friend."

"She is indeed."

Maya waved as a couple of older ladies walked by.

"You two sure are a good-looking couple," one of them called out.

"Thanks! I think so too," Maya said, then surprised Gavin by stealing a quick kiss, much to the delight of their audience.

Much to his delight too.

CHAPTER EIGHTEEN

MAYA WATCHED AS Gavin talked with one Jade Valley resident after another. At first he'd seemed anxious and looked as if he might bolt at any moment, afraid that he'd be hurt again because of his creative passion. He'd looked a mixture of relieved and nervous when the first couple of people had entered, then increasingly stunned as more and more people filled the art center.

He'd seemed genuinely surprised that attendees were praising his work. At one point, he'd even glanced across the room at her as if to ask if she'd put them all up to it. Marveling at her ability to tell what he was thinking, she'd shaken her head and smiled at him.

After that, he'd relaxed more. She loved seeing his conversations becoming more animated as he chatted about a mixture of art and ranching. Maya realized that both jobs had strong ties to the natural world—earth and sky. And watching him like this was akin to witnessing the first buds of spring, a re-birth.

Her heart so full she wanted to stride across the gallery and tell him she loved him, she instead turned and passed through the doorway on the opposite side that led to a room that had been converted to a little hands-on art space for children. There she found Max with Sunny and the twins making what she thought were small animals out of modeling compound. Three other children, siblings from another ranching family, were painting brightly colored pictures at another child-size table.

"How's it going out there?" Sunny asked.

Maya sat on one of the miniature chairs. "Pretty well. He's loosened up and is chatting more now."

Sunny smiled. "So, when are you two going to admit how you feel about each other?"

"We have."

Sunny's eyes widened.

"Not how you're thinking. We haven't literally said those words yet, but…" She glanced at Max, who seemed to be pouring all of the concentration in his little body into creating an orange-and-green creature of some sort.

"I know why you're both hesitating, but if you love someone you should tell them."

Behind Sunny's words was the always-present loss of the three people she'd loved and who'd been taken too soon. A shot of fear arrowed through Maya's middle. The thought of losing Gavin the way Sunny had lost her mom, brother and sister-in-law caused a pain in her heart that had her pressing her palm against her chest. Ranching wasn't a profession without dangers. Disease and car accidents claimed lives every day, the lives of people who had family and friends who wished they could have one more day to tell them how much they meant to them.

Sunny reached over and placed her hand on Maya's shoulder.

"Don't wait to live life to the fullest. Don't hold back words that need to be said for a better time."

When the last of the guests had left the gallery and Dean had taken the twins out to secure them in their car seats, Sunny accompanied Maya and Max to where Gavin was talking with Eileen Parker, who was thrilled with how well the exhibit opening had gone.

When Gavin spotted them, he smiled at

Maya in a way that filled her with joy. She was going to tell him tonight.

Sunny pointed at the painting behind him, one of those with a midnight blue background filled with little points of white light, the ones making up the Pleiades constellation the brightest.

"This is the one my friend in LA wants you to send him. I'll text you all the information tomorrow." Sunny gave Maya a meaningful look before she also headed for the exit.

Maya reached out and entwined her fingers with Gavin's.

"How do you feel?"

Gavin caressed Max's head with his free hand and scanned the gallery around them, seeming to soak in the fact that his paintings were, indeed, hanging on the walls of a gallery and that people liked them.

"Happy." He turned to face her. "Thanks to you."

He was lifting his hand to her face, causing her heart to start thumping harder, when the front door opened behind her. Gavin glanced in that direction, and the happiness drained from his face.

She quickly turned around to see Kevin

Bancroft, Gavin's attorney, standing there. The man wasted no time approaching them.

"What's wrong?" Gavin asked at the same time his hand gripped hers a bit more tightly. She squeezed back to give him strength, to let him know again that she was there for him.

Kevin glanced at Max, who was leaning against Gavin's leg, obviously tired.

"The Zacharys would like to have a meeting. Their lead attorney suggested in the afternoon two days from now at the company headquarters."

No, they couldn't have the home court advantage.

"They can come here." She hadn't meant to say it out loud, but her anger at Max's grandparents overrode her understanding that this was Gavin's decision, not hers.

"Maya's right. Let them bear the expense of the travel." He glanced down at Max, who was thankfully unaware of the content of the conversation. "His home is here, and I'm not taking him back to a place that I believe holds bad memories."

Poor Max had experienced a few nightmares after he arrived, but according to Gavin they had thankfully become less frequent.

Kevin nodded. "I'll make it happen."

"Thank you."

After they were alone again, Eileen having gone into the kids' room to clean up, Maya faced Gavin.

"Are you okay?" She hated that his wonderful evening, the recapturing of this part of his life, had been tarnished again by Rinna's parents.

"I will be when this is over."

MAYA SAT IN the waiting room of Kevin Bancroft's law office, Max on her lap. He'd finally fallen asleep after initial upset at seeing his grandparents. Max had clung to Gavin and then Maya, saying he didn't want to go. It would be the grossest of understatements to say it had been difficult to refrain from expressing her opinion when she saw the annoyance on the Zacharys' faces at their grandson's reaction.

She looked down at Max and was glad to see his face was free from worry now. How she wished she could say the same for her own. Gavin had been in the conference room with Kevin, the Zacharys and their attorney for more than an hour, this after Kevin had met with Max to ask him how he liked living with his dad and carefully inquired about his mother and grandparents. Maya did not believe any of them had ever abused Max, but she didn't think they'd given him much in the way of warmth and affection either. Even if they did actually care for him, they hadn't done a good job of showing it.

Maya had wondered, still did, about the wisdom of her being there, especially since during the two-week delay for the Zacharys to arrive in Jade Valley her article had been published and had gained more attention than she'd ever imagined.

Small media outlets across the country— at least ones not owned by Zachary Communications—had shared it with their readers. She'd been extra careful to stick to only the facts, not tainting the article with personal feelings or the vindictive reasoning behind the Zacharys' actions. The truth was giant media companies were a bit like kings who moved the pieces across the chessboard however they liked and sometimes swiped them off the board entirely. That was not unique to Zachary Communications, and she'd added some other journalists' stories of it happening to them to show that.

Gavin had asked that she be there though.

One, because she'd done nothing wrong and had, in fact, been wronged. Two, it would be good for Max.

Though Gavin hadn't said it, she'd gathered that having her there would help him too. Despite not being so legally or even in name, she couldn't deny that they felt like a family. And the residents of Jade Valley had rallied around them, sending droves of letters in support of Gavin keeping custody for Kevin to have at his disposal. She'd seen tears in Gavin's eyes when Kevin had told him about the letters.

When the door down the short hallway opened, it startled her from her thoughts. Max grunted in his sleep, so she caressed his head to help ease him.

Mr. and Mrs. Zachary were the first to appear and they gave her only the briefest of looks before settling their gazes on Max. Unconsciously, Maya hugged him a little tighter. But then she saw something she hadn't earlier, a hint of sadness. While she was still processing her surprise, Max's grandparents turned and walked out the front door without a word.

Maya sat staring at the closed door. Did their departure mean what she thought it meant?

A few moments later, their attorney followed them out, not even sparing her a glance.

When Gavin finally came into view, all of her questions must have been written in bold, all-caps print across her face because he smiled.

"It's over." He looked at his son in her arms. "He's not going anywhere. They agreed to not contest my full custody again as long as they can have supervised visits at least twice a year."

Instant tears pooled in her eyes. She looked up at the ceiling and blinked so they wouldn't fall.

"I love you, Maya."

Gavin's admission in the middle of a law office waiting area surprised her but also didn't. When had anything between them been conventional?

So she smiled and said, "About time you said that out loud. I wasn't sure how much longer I could hold it in."

Gavin looked as if he'd been poleaxed, which caused her to laugh.

"If you love me, doesn't it make sense that I love you too?" she asked.

He stared at her for a heartbeat before he smiled again. "I guess it does."

GAVIN COULDN'T TRUTHFULLY say he was more nervous than he'd ever been in his life, but that did not negate the fact that he was so nervous his stomach was twisting itself into knots.

In the two weeks since Rinna's parents had assured him that they would not seek custody of Max, he'd been busy on his secret project when Maya wasn't around. Today, it was finally ready. He was ready.

He heard her car pulling up outside a moment before Max hollered, "Maya!" while looking out the window.

The fact that his son loved Maya had helped Gavin to make his decision. He'd been impressed by how Max had been able to keep the secret Gavin was about to reveal. Of course, his son only knew half the story.

As Maya came inside, gave him a quick peck, then sat down next to Max to hear about his day, Gavin thought he might expire from the need to spill his surprises. But he'd waited this long, so he could wait a while longer. It wasn't until Max had been tucked into bed for the night that Gavin was finally able to take hold of Maya's hands and begin the big reveal.

"I have something to show you."

"Oh yeah? Wait, did you finish the new painting you've been working on?"

"I did." He'd told her she couldn't see it in progress because he didn't like for anyone to see his paintings until they were finished. That was only partly true.

He led her through the kitchen, to the closed door of the small room off the laundry room. He'd fibbed and told her he'd been using it to paint. Again, only partly true.

"Go in," he said, motioning toward the door.

"Well, this is all very mysterious." When she opened the door, it revealed not a former storage room turned artist's studio but rather a freshly painted, furnished and decorated office. "I don't underst—"

Her words faltered the moment she saw the nameplate on the desk.

Maya Pine, Editor-in-Chief.

"Gavin?"

He stepped up behind her and pointed over her shoulder at the desk.

"It's not fancy, and it's not as big as what you had before, but it's a start."

She had begun to pick up some freelance work, but it wasn't yet enough to pay all her bills. But if she accepted the second surprise, she wouldn't have to worry about rent anymore.

"I… I can't believe you made an office for me." She slowly moved toward the desk, ran her fingertips across the smooth surface, then looked up and saw the painting on the opposite wall, the colorful spiral of the Milky Way galaxy. "Oh, Gavin. It's beautiful!"

"Not as beautiful as you."

She laughed a little. "I don't think I can compare to a celestial wonder."

"You can in my eyes."

"Thank you, for everything."

"There's one more surprise. Open the top, right-hand drawer."

"Don't tell me you went crazy with office supplies too." She opened the drawer and simply stared at the one thing it contained.

Gavin's heart beat a furious tattoo in his chest as he waited for her reaction.

"Yes."

Her single-word response surprised him.

"I haven't asked anything."

She lifted her gaze to his.

"Unless engagement rings mean something else I don't know about, then you did ask the question." The teasing lilt in her voice was one of the many things he'd grown to love about her. He decided to tease her back.

"You don't know that an engagement ring is what's inside the box."

She lifted a brow. "Am I wrong?"

He shook his head slowly.

"Then come over here and ask me properly."

He complied, rounding the desk and opening the box. He met her gaze.

"Thank you for coming into my life. I love you, and if you'll have me I want to spend the rest of my life with you. Will you marry me?"

She looked up at him with obvious love in her eyes. "Are you sure?"

He knew what she was asking, whether he was truly ready to let go of all the doubts and pain from the past and believe in a forever kind of love again.

"Yes, completely."

"Then my answer remains the same. Yes, I will marry you. Now, I think these types of things are usually sealed with a kiss."

He slipped the ring on her finger, grinned then pulled her close. "Happy to oblige."

Maya might have entered his life on a rush of frigid winter, but as he kissed her he felt nothing but soul-filling warmth. She'd given him a second chance at sharing his creativity with the world, a second chance at believing there were good people and kindness in the world, a second chance at raising his son.

A second chance at love.

* * * * *

Get 4 FREE REWARDS!

We'll send you 2 FREE Books <u>plus</u> **2 FREE Mystery Gifts.**

FREE
Value Over
$20

Both the **Love Inspired**® and **Love Inspired**® Suspense series feature compelling novels filled with inspirational romance, faith, forgiveness, and hope.

YES! Please send me 2 FREE novels from the Love Inspired or Love Inspired Suspense series and my 2 FREE gifts (gifts are worth about $10 retail). After receiving them, if I don't wish to receive any more books, I can return the shipping statement marked "cancel." If I don't cancel, I will receive 6 brand-new Love Inspired Larger-Print books or Love Inspired Suspense Larger-Print books every month and be billed just $5.99 each in the U.S. or $6.24 each in Canada. That is a savings of at least 17% off the cover price. It's quite a bargain! Shipping and handling is just 50¢ per book in the U.S. and $1.25 per book in Canada.* I understand that accepting the 2 free books and gifts places me under no obligation to buy anything. I can always return a shipment and cancel at any time. The free books and gifts are mine to keep no matter what I decide.

Choose one: ☐ **Love Inspired**   ☐ **Love Inspired Suspense**
                  Larger-Print   **Larger-Print**
                  (122/322 IDN GNWC)   (107/307 IDN GNWN)

Name (please print)

Address   Apt. #

City   State/Province   Zip/Postal Code

Email: Please check this box ☐ if you would like to receive newsletters and promotional emails from Harlequin Enterprises ULC and its affiliates. You can unsubscribe anytime.

> **Mail to the Harlequin Reader Service:**
> **IN U.S.A.:** P.O. Box 1341, Buffalo, NY 14240-8531
> **IN CANADA:** P.O. Box 603, Fort Erie, Ontario L2A 5X3

Want to try 2 free books from another series! Call 1-800-873-8635 or visit www.ReaderService.com.

*Terms and prices subject to change without notice. Prices do not include sales taxes, which will be charged (if applicable) based on your state or country of residence. Canadian residents will be charged applicable taxes. Offer not valid in Quebec. This offer is limited to one order per household. Books received may not be as shown. Not valid for current subscribers to the Love Inspired or Love Inspired Suspense series. All orders subject to approval. Credit or debit balances in a customer's account(s) may be offset by any other outstanding balance owed by or to the customer. Please allow 4 to 6 weeks for delivery. Offer available while quantities last.

Your Privacy—Your information is being collected by Harlequin Enterprises ULC, operating as Harlequin Reader Service. For a complete summary of the information we collect, how we use this information and to whom it is disclosed, please visit our privacy notice located at corporate.harlequin.com/privacy-notice. From time to time we may also exchange your personal information with reputable third parties. If you wish to opt out of this sharing of your personal information, please visit readerservice.com/consumerschoice or call 1-800-873-8635. Notice to California Residents—Under California law, you have specific rights to control and access your data. For more information on these rights and how to exercise them, visit corporate.harlequin.com/california-privacy.

LIRLIS22

Get 4 FREE REWARDS!

We'll send you 2 FREE Books plus 2 FREE Mystery Gifts.

FREE Value Over **$20**

Both the **Harlequin® Special Edition** and **Harlequin® Heartwarming™** series feature compelling novels filled with stories of love and strength where the bonds of friendship, family and community unite.

YES! Please send me 2 FREE novels from the Harlequin Special Edition or Harlequin Heartwarming series and my 2 FREE gifts (gifts are worth about $10 retail). After receiving them, if I don't wish to receive any more books, I can return the shipping statement marked "cancel." If I don't cancel, I will receive 6 brand-new Harlequin Special Edition books every month and be billed just $4.99 each in the U.S or $5.74 each in Canada, a savings of at least 17% off the cover price or 4 brand-new Harlequin Heartwarming Larger-Print books every month and be billed just $5.74 each in the U.S. or $6.24 each in Canada, a savings of at least 21% off the cover price. It's quite a bargain! Shipping and handling is just 50¢ per book in the U.S. and $1.25 per book in Canada.* I understand that accepting the 2 free books and gifts places me under no obligation to buy anything. I can always return a shipment and cancel at any time. The free books and gifts are mine to keep no matter what I decide.

Choose one: ☐ **Harlequin Special Edition** ☐ **Harlequin Heartwarming**
(235/335 HDN GNMP) **Larger-Print**
(161/361 HDN GNPZ)

Name (please print)

Address   Apt. #

City   State/Province   Zip/Postal Code

Email: Please check this box ☐ if you would like to receive newsletters and promotional emails from Harlequin Enterprises ULC and its affiliates. You can unsubscribe anytime.

Mail to the **Harlequin Reader Service:**
IN U.S.A.: P.O. Box 1341, Buffalo, NY 14240-8531
IN CANADA: P.O. Box 603, Fort Erie, Ontario L2A 5X3

Want to try 2 free books from another series! Call 1-800-873-8635 or visit www.ReaderService.com.

---

*Terms and prices subject to change without notice. Prices do not include sales taxes, which will be charged (if applicable) based on your state or country of residence. Canadian residents will be charged applicable taxes. Offer not valid in Quebec. This offer is limited to one order per household. Books received may not be as shown. Not valid for current subscribers to the Harlequin Special Edition or Harlequin Heartwarming series. All orders subject to approval. Credit or debit balances in a customer's account(s) may be offset by any other outstanding balance owed by or to the customer. Please allow 4 to 6 weeks for delivery. Offer available while quantities last.

Your Privacy—Your information is being collected by Harlequin Enterprises ULC, operating as Harlequin Reader Service. For a complete summary of the information we collect, how we use this information and to whom it is disclosed, please visit our privacy notice located at corporate.harlequin.com/privacy-notice. From time to time we may also exchange your personal information with reputable third parties. If you wish to opt out of this sharing of your personal information, please visit readerservice.com/consumerschoice or call 1-800-873-8635. **Notice to California Residents**—Under California law, you have specific rights to control and access your data. For more information on these rights and how to exercise them, visit corporate.harlequin.com/california-privacy.

HSEHW22

Get 4 FREE REWARDS!

We'll send you 2 FREE Books plus 2 FREE Mystery Gifts.

FREE
Value Over
$20

Both the **Romance** and **Suspense** collections feature compelling novels written by many of today's bestselling authors.

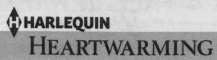
#423 THE COWBOY SEAL'S CHALLENGE
Big Sky Navy Heroes • by Julianna Morris

Navy SEAL Jordan Maxwell returns to Montana ready to take over the family ranch. Proving himself to his grandfather is one thing—proving himself to single mom and ranch manager Paige Bannerman is another story.

#424 HEALING THE RANCHER
The Mountain Monroes • by Melinda Curtis

City girl Kendall Monroe needs to cowboy it up to win a much-needed work contract. Rancher and single dad Finn McAfee is willing to teach her lessons of the land. But will lessons of the heart prevail?

#425 A FAMILY FOR KEEPS
by Janice Sims

Sebastian Contreras and Marley Syminette were inseparable growing up in their small fishing town. The tides of friendship changed to love, but neither could admit their true feelings—until a surprising offer changes everything...

#426 HIS HOMETOWN REDEMPTION
by LeAnne Bristow

Caden Murphy can't start over without making amends for the biggest mistake of his life. But Stacy Tedford doesn't need an apology—she needs help at her family's cabin rentals! Can this temporary handyman find a permanent home?

Visit
ReaderService.com
Today!

**As a valued member of the
Harlequin Reader Service,
you'll find these benefits and more at
ReaderService.com:**

- Try 2 free books from any series
- Access risk-free special offers
- View your account history & manage payments
- Browse the latest Bonus Bucks catalog

Don't miss out!

If you want to stay up-to-date on the latest at the Harlequin Reader Service and enjoy more content, make sure you've signed up for our monthly News & Notes email newsletter. Sign up online at ReaderService.com or by calling Customer Service at 1-800-873-8635.